CLAPHAM HIGH WAY

OLIVER MERLIN

Cover design by Allen Betchley ©2015

Author photograph by James Betts, http://jamesbetts.com/

ISBN: 978-1-4834-3176-5 (sc)
ISBN: 978-1-4834-3177-2 (hc)
ISBN: 978-1-4834-3175-8 (e)

Lulu Publishing Services rev. date: 07/30/2015

For Spedd, for life.

Thanks to Matt, Flex, The Spurge and H.A.

There were signs early on that the center would not hold.
The Night of the Gun, David Carr

.

Soon the stormy clouds will pass over me
And the fear I hold inside will be no longer.
Loving You More, Brian Transeau

If you squinted hard enough, it felt like you'd been transported to Ibiza. Honest.
London's Lost Nightclubs, Kentishtowner.co.uk.
Stephen Emms, Tom Kihl

For more information about the book and the author and a full track listing of all songs featured in the book please go to https://www.facebook.com/ClaphamHighWay

CONTENTS

RENAISSANCE

The four of us are trancing furiously side to side and up and down in chaotic unison. We are in our usual spot at the front right next to the DJ booth, Renaissance is ours, glorious momentous joy, huge crescendos are ripping through our skulls, chemicals show us the way into our brains, to the soaring piano breaks to the crystalline waterfalls, to the heavens. Laser beams criss-cross in front of our eyes. Our nervous systems re-interpret their shapes as beautiful heavenly bodies outlined in green and it all looks like astronomy. Above my head several recognisable star formations appear on the ceiling of the nightclub. I see Orion and the Big Dipper, Luke is dancing like the Little Bear and Pleiades is spraying beatific 'W's across the crowd with his arms. Ursa Minor is looking *fine* in her little black dress. A large sea-horse swims across the ceiling as Max's flailing arms are a blur in front of my eyes.

The same group of people go to Renaissance every month, a miscreant bunch of misfits, all relatively successful young professionals whom if you saw in a suit during the week you would never be able to guess at their nocturnal weekend activities. We work in the City; IT; marketing; PR; consulting and recruitment we're the white collar, the oh-so-dangerous Middle-Classes, nothing special all a bit run of the mill but all something that you might need half a brain for, all right maybe not fucking Recruitment. And whatever, we almost never talk about the other parts of our lives when we are at Renaissance, its unimportant and purely functional. What we do is not very original but seems to entertain us nonetheless, we all get high, mashed, *mullered*, fucked, dance the whole night away, laugh, drink, take drugs, make

1

friends and then eventually head back to mine for a an after-party. We shouldn't mix drink and drugs but we do, we shouldn't smoke, but we do. There'll be casualties I'm sure, but that's in the future, not for now, for now we're flying high, on cool Britannia waves.

It's the last Saturday of January 1999. The first month of the last year of this Millennium and we are part of it. It's half past one in the morning and Nigel Dawson is behind the decks. I look over to his hands, a blur, as he twiddles, tweaks and spins. The two white labels give us snippets and hints of songs we love and recognise interspersed with new and unheard-of beats. Is that *Three Drives* or *Gouryella*? Or BTs *Loving you More*? I can definitely hear a hint of Madonna in there though. What-on-earth?! Its mixed-in, in the background, which one though? *Ray of Light*? And it's some mad Dave Seaman remix or maybe it's Sasha? It doesn't really matter. I don't fucking care, it's not the Ritzy where you want to sing along to all the words. For starters there aren't that many songs with words in. House music isn't about "*Ooh I love you baby, I'm so happy,*" or "*Ooh my baby's left me, I'm so sad.*" It's all about the *feeling* the tune gives you and that comes through the throbbing bass lines; the chord changes; the beats. It's about the skill of the DJ, the way they mix the tunes, it's about the atmosphere they build up working the crowd. Tonight, Saturday January 31st 1999, the first Renaissance night of the year, it's Nigel Dawson building us up, levelling us out, laying us down gently only for the crescendo to kick in once more and the whole crazy process to re-ignite.

Max is looking at me. "You're looking caned! You should eat more," Max shouts in my ear.

"I should *eat* more?"

"What?! No. I said, Nalin & Kane, *Beachball*. That track, its Beachball, by Nalin & Kane".

He smacks me on the back, grins and whirls his arms around again like a human windmill.

Renaissance takes place on the last Saturday of every month at a nightclub called The Cross in Kings Cross. The area is run down and the venue is hidden off of York Way, which is at the back of the goods yard a few hundred metres behind the station. Lying low and obscured from view from the road, the nightclub hides as if it is slightly embarrassed by its shabby location. Or maybe its self-consciousness comes from a complicit acknowledgement of the activities hosted inside? Only as you turn off the road and descend the slope of the cobbled yard do you become aware of a nightclub anywhere in the vicinity. The bass throbs through the cobblestones gently at first then more insistent as you get nearer, carrying the rumbling threat of some rapidly approaching avalanche. Each deep note seems to reach out of the ground with hundreds of little invisible hands pulling you in, touching and clutching at the soles of your shoes. Then you see the light; a small but exotic-looking halo of colour, usually purple and orange and green merging like some rainbow on acid rising up through the combination of dry ice, steam and the cold night air. A couple of palm trees line the entrance to the club giving us our own piece of the Mediterranean even in the putrefied depths of an as yet un-regentrified patch of North London.

Exalted and sweating Max and I retreat from the dance floor to the relative quiet of the bar to take a breather. Breathing fast, beads of sweat gather on his forehead and in his thinning blond mop. It's cooler in here than in the main room and the sweat evaporating from my body produces a pleasing chill as it leaves my skin. The changes in temperature are deliberate on the club's part and are designed to bring you up on your drugs. Looking back through the arch I can see swirling lights and heaving bodies, glistening limbs and heads thrown back in ecstasy on the dance floor.

Renaissance is a night that believes in giving you a luxurious setting in which to do your clubbing. They believe in making the night an event. Not that there are any freak shows or circus novelties. Not for Renaissance the live sex shows or the fire-eaters on stage or stilt-walking bar staff. The formula is simple: a music policy that brooks no argument: nothing but the best house music of the day; décor that suggests glamour yet gives luxury and comfort; and unassuming and polite, skilled and knowledgeable bar staff. The club is a simple series of exposed-brick railway arches which might look industrial and uninviting but are transformed on Renaissance nights with heavy purple and scarlet velvet drapes and plush comfy sofas bedecked with huge billowy cushions and throws. Glitter-encrusted angels hang suspended from the ceiling as if flying through heavens of dry ice. Then there's the glamorous dress code, not strictly enforced but universally adhered to: make an effort or don't bother leaving home.

"Mate, I think I might find her in here tonight," says Max leaning in confidentially, his round friendly face genuinely optimistic. He obsesses with finding his soul mate even on nights when he's so wasted he can't even find his own pint. "It feels different tonight. *I* feel different, really confident. I've been using that Black & White you gave me on my hair, looks good doesn't it?"

"Not tonight mate," I reply, looking around. Who knows, maybe he will, you never know. "It's not really the place for pulling is it?"

"Why not? All these beautiful people, all loved up," he beams at me. I smile, he's high.

I stare back at him and grab him by one shoulder. There is so much I want to say but I can't quite find the words. I stare at him, my best mate. I'm mute.

"When's it going to happen then?" he implores, "It's got to happen soon".

I sigh, "One day, just when you least expect it, just when it's inconvenient. That's always how it happens," say I, twenty-eight and still single, like I'm some sort of authority on the subject. Max and I had been friends for four years and I had never known him to be in a long term relationship (or a short one for that matter). He was always too interested in work, or technology or music to have enough time to worry about girls. He was always hanging out in the DJ booth annoying the DJs asking about the music; which mixer they were using, what was the BPM? rather than dancing out on the dancefloor, where I would be talking inanely to girls wondering where my wing man was. Then I'd see his furry bonce and flail my arms around trying to get his attention. He thought I was dancing, I was always flailing.

At that point Shannon makes her entrance and spots us from the bar. She is looking gorgeous.

"Aaaaaahhhhhhaaaaa! There you are! My Renaissance Men, my darlings, my super heroes."

She hugs us, we hug her, we all hug, she kisses lipstick all over us. With our faces now a blotchy-vermillion we sit her down in between us and start stroking a thigh each. I feel like I may explode with happiness.

"Are *you* her?" Max asks her, wide-eyed and hopeful.

"She *is* the one, definitely. She is the babe of all babes," and I lean in to kiss her cheek. She puts her finger to my lips then touches hers. It's a Renaissance Saturday and Shannon looks stunning as usual, her make-up flawless, her high cheekbones accentuated with a subtle blush, her pale bright blue eyes shockingly beautiful, like two pristine ice cool arctic lakes I really want to swim in. She is a striking woman in a very handsome Nordic way, tall and toned, a sharp golden blonde bob haircut, improbably large white teeth and an oceans-wide smile.

She's high, her pupils are huge and wide and she smiles as she looks at us. "So, you naughty, naughty boys. How are you feeling?"

"Naughty!" we reply in stereo grinning from one ear to another.

"Will you take us into the toilets and spank us?" Max asks her, his pupils now completely dilated and watery. I look and see him in soft focus. I guess he must be the same. I feel so happy.

"Of course my darling, anything you want baby, anything at all."

"Anything?" I ask.

"As I said, *any*-thing," she winks and squeezes my thigh. I touch her bare arm. Her blonde hairs catch the light beams. She smiles at me and raises her right eyebrow. I meet her stare and then I lean in because I think she is going to kiss me, but she jumps up and says hello to someone else.

For Shannon this is *progress*. A year ago, she was coming out of hospital. A combination of an alcoholic ex-boyfriend, still jealous after nearly ten years of her having left him for London and Richard Gardiner, 'bumped into' her in Norwich and broke her nose and her right arm; that and her own drugging excesses had put her there, but she was making a brilliant comeback. Shannon is basically a delinquent country bird from Norfolk, our very own Bernard Matthews job. She's the sort of girl you imagine misspending her youth hanging around corners on council estates with the listless local boys. She got into drugs and boys early and had tried just about every one there was, travelled the world apparently, though I got the feeling some of that may have just been in her head. She might have had a daughter when she was seventeen but she was always a bit vague on that too when pressed for details. She moved from Norwich to London as soon as she could afford to and her natural effervescence got her a receptionist job at an IT software sales company in which she excelled. She stayed with the same company, Digitech, and now just five years later is regularly their number one sales consultant in EMEA winning annual prizes. Shannon is gorgeous, knockout, adorable, utterly adorable. She's all together until you get to know her a bit better. Then you find out that she is a little bit unsure and more than a little bit insecure. Her last boyfriend before Richard, the violent one, killed himself unintentionally after an overdose. Shannon had left him behind in Norwich for the bright lights in London. He was a small-town boy and wanted to stay there all his life, close to what he was comfortable with. When it became obvious that Shannon was intent on getting a job in London and moving down there, he became aggressive and violent towards her and then violent towards himself. Shannon told us about the times he would threaten her and the beatings he gave her, twice putting her in hospital. This only strengthened her resolve, though, and she got that job with Digitech. And when that happened the ex decided that self-harm would be the best way to get Shannon to change her mind. He started off with cuts to his arms, chest and face. This tore Shannon apart, but she knew what he was trying to do and she stayed firm. So when that didn't do the trick, he moved onto threats of hanging himself and slitting his wrists. The night Shannon left, she had a big party. He didn't come, couldn't face it the thought of her leaving and they found him at home, in the morning, on his own covered in puke; bottle of JD by his bed; empty Valium bottle by his body.

And then you find out that her Mum, Linda, is wheelchair-bound after her husband ran her over in the supermarket car park, her two brothers died in the first Gulf War in 1991, and you realise what a fucked-up life she's had. Her father's been put away in a home after losing it and running over her Mum in the car. It happened eighteen years ago when Linda was thirty-five. Shannon was in the back seat of the car when her Dad, in a blind rage about Linda having bought the 'wrong type of chips', ran her over in the car park of the out-of-town Asda. Shannon remembers that her Mum was smiling until the moment of impact. The expression on her face not turning to horror and anguish until well after the bumper of the grotty but sturdy old Volvo estate had started to bend and buckle her legs like some horrible

Stretch Armstrong. All the eggs in the shopping bags broke. Shannon says she remembers the yellow of the yokes, running into the pools of blood and turning orangey swirls like a bad tie-dye experiment on the car-park tarmac. She had jumped out of the car to race to her mum's side while her Dad sat in the driver's seat coughing and muttering to himself about the wrong chips, as he lit another Embassy. Shannon was twelve.

So Linda is wheelchair bound, but one of the sunniest people you could ever hope to meet. She dismisses her disability as an accident, even though the man is still locked up to this day – the verdict of attempted murder seemed harsh to all but ensured that he had not yet been out – well – he was now in a mental institute, rather than prison, but still nobody goes to visit. They had discovered crazed scribblings in neat stacks of notebooks he kept under the bed full of phrases like "I'll kill her. Useless bitch can't even keep a family together. Can't run a household. I'll kill her." These were repeated over and over in different scrawls like he was experimenting seeing which one he liked best. They proved intent, planning and pre-mediation. So Linda comes to London to see her daughter who is her only remaining child. She'd had the boys one after the other in her early-twenties. "Popped them out quickly so I could get on with my life," she would often say to me when she'd had a couple of gin and tonics. "Bloody pain they were. Shannon was a bit of a mistake. When she came along a bit later, it was totally unexpected. And now she's the only one I've got left."

So considering all of this, it is remarkable how upbeat Linda always is. And that too makes you understand Shannon a little bit more. So she's been through a fair bit our Gang Mother. She looks after us, but really she needs looking after herself.

At that point Luke, my younger brother, returns from the toilets where he has been powdering his nose with Dan his new beau. They are accompanied by Flex, our dealer-cum-best friend from Croydon, a superstar who has the added bonus of being the size of Mr Incredible, so he is actually incredibly useful in crowded club situations in clearing a way to the bar for example, or clearing a big enough spot on the dance floor for all of us. Simply wind Flex up and ask him to do his famous-Flex dance and thirty seconds later you have a small clearing big enough for eight people to dance in.

Luke is tall, beautiful and slim as a rake. At around six foot he has fine features and a perfect square jaw and with his fair freckled skin he could be a model. He sports the obligatory gay French crop and tightly fitting white ribbed vest (though he has the body for it, the bastard - I can't blame him). He also has the acid tongue to go with his campness.

Shannon turns to Luke and gives him a kiss on the cheek. "Such a shame!" she says running her fingers along his jaw line.

"For *you* maybe," he sighs theatrically and turns away in mock disgust. He goes through the archway and onto the dance floor directing Flex to the desired spot and followed closely by Dan.

"I love you guys. You've been such good friends to me, especially you Alex. Remember how I was when we met? This time last year. So nervous, so scared."

"I know, that's understandable, what you went through, we look out for you and you've looked after us in your own way."

"I feel so lucky to have met you."

"Do you remember how we met? On the bed, outside."

"Ha yeah, course. It was brill. How could I forget? You were stroking my leg."

"I thought it was beautiful. The most beautiful leg I had ever seen."

"Richard got jealous."

"I didn't know you had a boyfriend. I just saw this, this expanse of naked leg," I touch it again and I feel a shock. "I just saw you."

"I know, I looked down thinking, that feels nice, who is that and I saw your smiling face."

"Then I saw Dick, scowling at me."

"Alex…he wasn't…"

"Hey, Shannon, have you got any pills on you, at all babe? We've done all ours already," Max asks.

I'm not entirely convinced we need any more.

"Of course, my darlings, of course. Don't I always? Just give me a minute. They're tucked away at the minute," she smiles at me and winks as she points at the front of her trousers. "You can't be too careful in here. Back in Norwich, I know all of the boys and it wasn't an issue, but down here…I'll go to the loo and I'll be back in a sec, boys."

"Perfect. It's like having a second Mum," says Max after Shannon has disappeared.

"You mother sorts out pills for you?!"

"You know what I mean!"

"Numpty!"

"Shannon is our Gang Mother. *Where would you all be without me?* She says it all the time. She loves looking after us all. *You'd* be lost without her."

We return to people watching and looking out for minor celebs. Kate Moss often comes to Renaissance.

"Is that Kate Moss?"

"Shut up, Numpty."

"Stop calling me Numpty."

"I'm not."

"You are."

"You're high."

"You are."

"Shut up."

"We both are then."

"She's been a while."

"She has."

"Something's gone wrong, surely? Maybe she hasn't got any more pills. Or lost them?"

"If I know Shannon, she'll have been in every cubicle: disturbing the snogging queens and nervous first timers surreptitiously racking up a line in the toilets whilst listening for bouncers."

"Yeah and buying up all the good ones en route."

After a few more minutes people-watching at the bar, we spot Shannon barging through the crowd, easing people apart expertly, using her smile and her eyes to get boys to make way and her touch to manoeuvre girls aside.

"I'm really sorry, boys. Slight problem: I have lost the pills."

"All of them?" I ask.

"Yup," she says.

"Fuck. How many did you have?" asks Max askance.

"Twenty-five," she says her bright eyes suddenly dull and trained on the floor.

"Oh fuck, Shannon. That's really shit. I'm sorry, babe." I say.

"What are you sorry for? It's my own stupid fault." She flicks the ash of her cigarette.

"What about Richard? Won't he have any?" Max asks.

"No, Rich never brings pills in," replies Shannon.

"Not his own anyway," I hiss under my breath.

"I heard that!" Shannon kicks me on the right shin.

"Ouch. What now then?" I ask.

"I'll find Star and she'll score you some more."

"Star?" I ask. "Who's *Star*."

"She's this artist's daughter; one of the Brit Art lot apparently; I met her last month. We were dancing together. She's only seventeen, but she's gorgeous. *So* switched on, really mature for her age. They've just started letting her in and of course she has access to all of the best gear, doesn't she, from her Dad, probably. She gave me a couple of Double-Doves last time and they were dynamite. I don't want to take the piss with her coz I've only just met her but this is an emergency. Stay there and I'll go and find her."

And with that she's off through the crowd. Resourceful Shannon, the Gang Mother: every good gang's got one.

We watch her weave and dodge and occasionally buffet her way through the crowded club. She wasn't afraid to barge through people when needed; she'd been clubbing long enough to know that it was necessary every now and again. I follow her bobbing head and I see her calling out to someone. I follow her eye-line as she shouts out "Star!" I grab Max because now Shannon is now enveloping a stunningly beautiful, if lanky and slightly estatey-looking girl in one of her bear hugs. She's tall and has beautiful dark olive skin. Her parentage must be Mediterranean or Indian and English mixed. She's gangly, her arms are twig-thin and her body has not filled out yet; that and her teenage stoop disclose her youth. She looks like a cross between Naomi Campbell and Kate Moss; but more lithe, and more 'street' too. I can see that she's wearing trainers, Nike Air 90s – not bad; her white-clad feet standing out through the crowd. Eventually Shannon releases her. Shannon is on tiptoe to talk into Star's ear and then she's pointing across at us.

"Fucking Hell! Is that, that Star girl?" Max asks.

"Yup," I say, getting higher and higher, I hope that nobody asks me anything more difficult than my name soon.

"Christ," he says. "They get younger and younger."

"Beautiful…" I say, although by now I think everyone is.

Star smiles across at us whilst nodding at Shannon and raises one of those long slender arms. Through the dry ice and lights, she looks like some sort of alien being, just landed on earth signalling other worldly greetings.

Max and I stand there just dumbstruck, in awe and maybe possibly in love with the street-urchin beauty that is Star. I am day-dreaming of the Close Encounters of the Third Kind. I am daydreaming when Shannon appears by my side, taking my VLS from my hand, she takes a long slug and then gasps: "Sorted! That was Star! She's going to see her brother who should be able to sort us out. Beautiful isn't she?"

"What? Sorry about that! I was miles away, light years. Excellent news about the pills!" I blurt.

Shannon looks at me, smiles, arches a questioning eyebrow at me and takes my drink again, still eyeing me curiously. "Are you sure you *need* any more? You're not going to fizzle out on me are you? I've got plans for *you* later."

In walks Richard Gardiner, Shannon's boyfriend. I feel this spike go through me and I look at Shannon. Then I look again at Dick and wonder, *why?* Nobody likes him and he doesn't care. He's like the Millwall Football Club of our clubbing community. Well actually it's not that he doesn't *care*, it's more that he doesn't *notice*, which is slightly different. You see there are some fundamental differences between him and us. He doesn't take Es, only Charlie and doesn't really get into it like the rest of us. Thinks he's above it.

"Here's the man now! Gardiner, *Dick!* How are you?" I go to greet Richard Gardiner, looking very flash tonight, in his blue shiny Ted Baker shirt, narrow-cut black Hugo Boss trousers and alligator-skin Oliver Sweeney moccasins, oh and the slightly too-large hooped ear-ring: very faux-gay chic.

"Yeah good thanks. You know, been lucky."

"Right, to the bar with you Dick. Are you pilling tonight?" I ask knowing as ever the answer will be 'no'.

"Nah, nah Mate. I thought I'd give it a miss tonight," answers Gardiner defensively.

"A MISS?! Quite frankly mate, that's crap, in fact, I do have to ask you a very basic and important question: if you are not planning to take any drugs here tonight, then WHAT THE FUCK ARE YOU DOING HERE?" I shout.

"Fuck you!" Gardiner retorts.

"There's a forfeit for that you know?" says Max trying to wind Gardiner up even further.

"Oh yeah? What's that? Because I'm *really* scared," says Gardiner.

"You have to buy a bottle of champagne from the bar," Max tells him.

"I was going to do that anyway," retorts Gardiner.

"Oooooohhhhhh! Big spender!" everybody chimes in.

"Mug. Falls for it every time," Max whispers in my ear.

"What a wanker!" I say, perhaps not as quietly as I had thought.

"Who's a wanker?" someone says in my right ear, an insistent hand on my shoulder pulling me away from Max. "You're Alex right? You want some pills, then, do ya boss?" It's a female voice, affecting a street patter and young.

"Yes. Right on both counts," I answer.

"Right, don't turn 'roun' den. I'm going to put my 'and in your pocket and put ten pills in there. That enough for you?"

"Yep. That'd be great. Thanks."

"Then you put your hands behind your back with a fiddy, and we're done. Then we can say hello. OK?"

"Cool. That'd be nice," I say.

"'Nice'? You a 'nice' boy den?" She's asking me but I'm not thinking that much about answering because a snake-like little hand has snaked it's way round my waist and insinuated itself into my right trouser pocket. I feel the pills drop to the bottom of my pocket. Then the hand rubs my thigh and then is gone. If I did such things, I would swear I was about to swoon. I turn around and look up, and up. "Fuck me, you're tall."

"Or maybe *you*'s short? Eh?" She replies, as quick as a spark.

"Quite probably. Although I have researched this and I am above average height. Five foot eight is the average height for the British male, and I am five feet nine. And that would be above average. So I think it's you that's tall. Very tall. You *are* quite beautiful though."

"Thank you. And *you*, are observant."

"Woah! A little bit sure of oneself aren't we?"

"I was talking about da height comment."

"Oh OK. I thought...I mean...How old are you?"

"What the fuck has dat got to do wid anyting? Why is it people like you always got to aks me dat?" She sucks her teeth at me.

And so it's back to the street lingo. Obviously hit a raw nerve there.

"Can I get you a drink?"

"I get mine free here," she looks away.

Thankfully Shannon comes over to save me. "I see you two have met." She smiles at us both. "Sorted?"

"Oh yeah, deal done," I say. "Thanks!" I say to both of them smiling awkwardly. Shannon gets up on tiptoe and kisses Star on the lips. "Thanks Gorgeous."

"I, er, better go and ration these out to the boys then," I stutter.

"Run along then, Shortie," Star smiles at me, and winks. I think The Precocious One may have forgiven me.

Dry ice fills our throats; powder our nostrils; pills are popped and the coloured lights dance us a merry, bright and beautiful jig once more into the night and the following morning. Beautiful people dance in front of us, and all around us people are happy, smiling and we sort of know where we're going because we've been here before, but then again, every journey *is* different. Each night is precious. Each night is unique and will never be again. These are nights of our lives. They are almost too good to be true. And even now I can see that they may be transient and ephemeral so I am taking in the faces of my gang and total strangers alike. I am taking mental photographs. My internal jukebox is recording all the sounds that pound through those powerful speakers. Registering the emotions, I wonder will I ever feel them again.

Shannon goes to the bar to help Richard with the drinks whilst the rest of us invade the main room where Nigel Dawson has just thrown on *Silence* by Delerium, one of my favourite tunes. I am looking at Shannon and want to pull her on to the dance floor with me but Star drags me into the centre of the sweating crowd, she moves in front of me in perfect time with the music, her dark skin glistening, a sheen of sweat catching the dancing lights. I'm mesmerised. I drop another pill. I mouth a thank you to her and she slides a long slender finger over my cheek and places it over my lips. Max is dancing next to me, his eyebrows are questioningly raised but then he shuts his eyes. He's coming up again. Luke and Dan pull beautiful moves from their toned bodies and dance like they've known each other for years and years. They hug and stroke. I feel a pang of jealousy wash over me, I want it gone and my heart aches for someone like that, to feel about someone like that. Flex whoops and flails his arms incessantly. The sheer fucking joy in his body makes me smile, at everyone. The crowd heaves together again. The temperature noticeably rises. The lights swell from cool distant blue to hot bright reds and oranges. The crowd screams in collective delight as a huge billowing cloud of dry ice is pumped out of the massive industrial pipe above the dance floor and falls about our shoulders. The temperature drops and everybody shivers in ecstasy, skin gooses up. I look up and see a sea of joining hands clapping and punching the air, making shapes and carving wormholes in the shape of our spirits in the dry ice and the smoke and the lights that make our very modern art.

Max opens his eyes and gives me a beaming toothy smile. He sticks both thumbs up. I lean over to give him a huge hug and we bounce like mad hatters. Dr. Seuss and The Grinch; The Cat in the Hat; the Green Eggs, the Ham - we're having the fucking lot. I have a mad idea of something I want to do for Max, something that he'd never do. Nigel Dawson is his favourite DJ and Max is the biggest house music geek I've ever known so I start stamping my feet in time to the 4x4 beat that's throbbing throughout every sinew of all of our bodies. Dripping with sweat, my neck taut and veins bulging, I stop dancing, stand stock-still on the spot and raise my eyes to the heavens and I shout slowly at the top of my voice:

"NI-GEL ! NI-GEL ! NI-GEL !"

The second time I do it, Flex notices and joins in lending his considerable volume to my chant. At the third time of asking they're all on board. After a while, everyone on the dance floor is chanting the name of the DJ, NI-GEL. Now we're louder than the fucking music. Nigel Dawson brings the record he's playing to a stop. He takes off his headphones, stops to light a cigarette, and climbs up onto the table where his decks are. He has to crouch because of the low arches of the club, which are dripping condensation, but he manages a bow nonetheless. Everyone cheers and he jumps back down and we're off again. Max grabs my face with both hands and plants a slimy sweaty kiss on my cheek. He *is* ecstasy. Nigel starts up the decks again to the familiar strains of *Perfect Motion* by Sunscreem. And we're away once more on another cycle of the night's unique journey.

* * *

I've been going clubbing for about eight or nine years. In 1990, when I was seventeen, I went to this little sweat-box just off Tottenham Court Road called the Milk Bar with a couple of school mates. We didn't know what we were doing. I did my first pill there. I remember that Trevor

Fung was playing and he fucked up a couple of mixes, or rather his records jumped on him and the crowd laughed because he insisted on playing this record that kept jumping, fuck knows if I can remember what it was, but it was still a brilliant night. I remember the collective spirit, the happiness and the never-ending smiles. Pills were much more expensive back then (it wasn't unusual to pay £15 in a club) and my mates could only spare me a half, but that was all I needed. What I remember most, was from the moment I had the half in my sweaty palm, all sorts of people kept coming up to me offering me their water; asking if I was ok; was I "having a good night?" People hugging me; patting me on the back. "I heard you're taking your first one tonight. That right?"

"Err, yeah. It is," I would reply, not exactly sure what else to say, and as yet not feeling anything out of the ordinary.

"Fucking wicked one mate! Enjoy." And then they would give me the thumbs-up or the peace sign.

And then it hit me.

At first I thought I was getting pins and needles in both my feet simultaneously, so I got up, slightly irritated and feeling just a little bit anxious. I tried shaking both feet, but the feeling only got more intense. The same thing then started at the very ends of my fingers and rapidly spread along them, along my hands and up my arms to my armpits. I remember shivering and savouring the sensation. All the hairs on my arms stood up and I felt giddy with excitement. I had never felt anything like it ever before. I looked down, *m-i-l-e-s* down to where my right foot was tapping firmly and perfectly in time to the throbbing bass-line that was by now ripping through my body. It felt as though I had had a huge amplifier and speakers installed inside my rib cage, somewhere just behind my heart. My whole torso was throbbing. I remember grabbing at a rail at the top of the stairs as I felt a massive wave of nausea hit me; I was sure I needed to be physically sick but it passed within a second and was replaced with a warm feeling in my chest. I let go as I started moving as one with the rest of the crowd. I felt euphoric. Everyone that I could see was smiling at me and moving in perfect motion with me. They were all shimmering in front of me as if I was seeing them through a soft mist of tiny silvery droplets of pure stardust. Every light I looked at refracted and sent a million tracers off in all directions and in all colours. And the music. Christ! The music. I no longer heard the song, I heard the individual sounds. The notes. I *was* the bass. Every time I moved one of my feet I was hitting a perfect note. I *was* the music. That night was the best night of my life. I don't know if I will ever feel any more ecstatic than I did that night.

And then when I went to Uni in Birmingham I was a regular at Miss Moneypennys on a Saturday at The Steering Wheel – where Jim 'Shaft' Ryan played and the girls were beautiful and the boys were so cool; Crunch on a Friday – where all the young kids of the Midlands would come to get totally mashed out of their skins. And Wobble – so called because the upstairs dance-floor was suspended on huge chains and well, wobbled. Jon of the Pleased Wimmin, LuvDup, The Lovely Helen, and of course Phil Gifford all played us out of our little minds. I remember grinding my teeth so hard in that venue – called *well*, The Venue – that I thought my teeth would surely crack and give way. The first thing I always did when I woke up was check my teeth for damage. Then we used to go to Trade afterwards where Tony de Vit rocked it until well into Sunday. Before he died. And then maybe onto Sundissential at The Pulse, for those who still had a pulse by Sunday afternoon.

And then when I graduated and came back to London, I started going to Renaissance at The Cross and I've been going regularly since 1995. The last Saturday of every month I would beg Max to come, and every month Max would decline. Max had never taken ecstasy before and was scared to try it. He studied Physics and Chemistry at Cambridge and understood exactly what E did to you on a physical, psychological and emotional level. He actually looked down on the people who did it. He loved the music and would spend hours playing the records on his decks in his bedroom. But he didn't understand the need to take drugs to enjoy it. But I never gave up hope of changing his mind. I kept haranguing him, and every fourth Monday would regale him with tales of the Renaissance Saturday night before. Of beautiful creatures I had seen and met; new friendships made; hilarious tall stories; amazing physical feelings; the rush; the adventures; the euphoria; the Ecstasy. Every month Max would listen, feign disinterest, promising to come 'next month'. It was always 'mañana' with him. He always managed to find a credible excuse at the end of every month: illness; parental visit; work. I didn't want to force Max into it, I just wanted to make him curious. Max finally agreed to go in August 1998 after the two of us had been on holiday together with some of the regular Renaissance crowd. Over that week in Ibiza, the draw became too much for Max to resist. He took his first pill watching a sunset at the Café del Mar and he was hooked.

* * *

At 4am Max is on the look out for love again. Looking, seeking, and searching. He's recovered his poise enough to be able to approach strangers without talking utter gibberish. "There she is," he grabs me and points to a tall blonde in the middle of the dance floor; clearly out of her mind on E but absolutely stunning in a vacant kind of way.

"Go for it my son!" And I shove him towards her.

And he does too. Luke, Dan, Flex and I stand by and watch in amazement as he fearlessly studs up to her and ventures: "Hello. How are you? What a great night, eh?" She nods in agreement, shuts her eyes, smiles and throws her arms around his neck in a loose noose.

Ten minutes later, which is the average time we give Max with women, he's still dancing in the middle of the packed dance-floor with her; both dripping with sweat and glistening and shimmering in the chasing laser-beams and strobe lights. He stands behind her and holds her hands in the air, stroking her arms up and down. We can't believe it and so we have to go to the bar to drown our sorrows or celebrate for him. It doesn't really matter which because by now we can't tell the difference. "Three TVRs please!" I manage.

"I can't believe it!" says Luke, "Good for *him*. It's about time. I was starting to think you heterosexuals had given sex up."

"I'm not sure. Keep an eye on him. He's pretty fucked," I say.

We don't see him again for another hour or so but something in me just makes me feel that Max might *not* have actually pulled the blonde girl; that her mates might have turned up and dragged her away; and that actually he is still in here somewhere on his own. I am totally high as a kite myself now. It *is* five in the morning, but stumbling over the cobbles on the terrace and through the archways, I decide to go looking for him. I'm smiling and chattering away to myself. "So I'm just going to stroke this leg…It's beautiful. What a beaut! Up and up and up. Up up and away in my beautiful, my beautiful …leg."

I find Max alone: standing with one foot up against the wall in the back corridor leading out to the courtyard.

"Hey Max. How's it going with that tall, leggy lovely?"

"She thought I was someone else," he replies, staring disconsolately into his glass.

"Fuck it! Let's go shall we? Reckon we've had our share."

I coax him back inside and we slowly gather our joyous rabble together, although this activity takes some time with all of us in a bit of a state. In fact it's akin to herding cats, whilst pushing water uphill, being a fish on a bicycle, with only one leg, on acid. No sooner do we think we're ready to go than we realise someone has wandered off to get another drink, go to the toilet (a really futile exercise), say goodbye to some new life-long friend, have one last dance or to get their coat.

At approaching 7am, we finally come out into the nascent day. A heavy, gunmetal grey sky hangs over us. However, far from weighing us down, it provides a shelter from our responsibilities. A tent, a Wendy-house of protection that affords us, for another few hours at least, cover from the inevitable hangover that will come down just as surely as wretched Monday morning will be upon us in less than 24 hours. We weave our way through the flyers and taxi-touts; carefully stepping over the glammed-up waifs slouching lying strewn on the cobbles, the lustrous silver slivers of last night now workaday-greys in the struggling sickly winter morning light. Those of us in high heels mind the pot-holes in the cobbles and finally we're all slumped round the picnic table outside the café; sitting on benches and on each other; some of us ready-brek glowing, others feeling the chill. There's never rhyme or reason to internal body thermostats.

Up above us, it looks like it might snow.

Somebody organised is ordering the teas. "Coke for me please, Shazza," I shout, just in time. I hate drinking tea as soon as we get out of a club. I can't understand people who do; I needn't have worried: Shannon remembers.

"*You* want to get home for a nice-cold, ice-cold Stella, don't you darlin'?"

"Aaaaaahhhh! You read my mind. That would be heaven." I light a cigarette and toss the packet on the table for general consumption. "Oh Alex, you star!!" "Wicked." "Nice one!" I'm always the only one who thinks to go and stock up on fags at 5.30am whilst the second cloakroom (the one selling fags) is still open.

"Nice one Alex. Can I have one?" Star asks. She looks properly fucked now and not as brash as before. We may become friends I think. It passes through my mind that seventeen is a very young age to be getting into such a mess with total strangers. I'm sure I didn't do such things at such a tender age. But then again, maybe I did. I can't really remember. And besides, we're not strangers anymore. Clubbing like this gives you a boil-in-the-bag family, ready to go.

"Yep. Everyone help themselves. And I've got loads more back at mine. And moreover, chaps and chapessessesses, loads of Stella. And, some other alcohol - vodka. And probably some more pills and Charlie too."

Smiles all round. Star has attracted another admirer. This time it's a pale sweat-soaked boy. He is wearing a massive Liam Gallagher-type parker which is falling off of his left shoulder. His hair is lank. He approaches us and offers us a bite of his huge, sloppy and dripping burger.

"Urrgh! I'd rather eat broken glass," sneers Star. She fake gags in our direction.

"Ahl-right then luv." The Gallagher Mancunian drooler slopes off non-plussed, but still gurning inanely at her. Sweating and grinning from ear to ear, steam rises from his whitey-pink shoulders, neck and ginger head, making him look like some sort of apparition. He disappears into the early morning mist.

"How can people eat *now*?!" Asks Luke who never seems to eat these days, "I won't be able to eat all day."

"And how can anyone *ever* eat *that*?!" Star adds.

"What time is it?" Max asks nobody in particular, "I can't be sure but I think it's getting pretty cloudy."

"It looks like it might snow."

"I didn't know Oasis came to Renaissance? Thought they were into guitars and all that rubbish?" asks Flex.

Everyone looks at Flex, and then at the sky.

"That was one of them Brit Pop bands wasn't it? Lee Gallagher... an...and what's that other one? Blurred with Damien Albran."

"That's right."

"Were you eating peaches at one point in there tonight? I could have sworn you were..." says Luke to Dan.

"No but I was dancing with Peaches. Bob Geldof's daughter," he replies

"That's not Bob Geldof's daughter," says Max, "Has anyone got the time? It's Paula Yates' child."

"Well who do you think he had it with?"

"Paula Yates is not a he. It's a woman. *Paula*. She."

"She..."

"Paula Yates."

"Yeah? And?"

"Fifi Trixibel."

"Do you use Microsoft Project for that?" I ask.

Everyone looks at me like I'm mad, which I perceive to be a little unfair.

We talk cod-shit and boulders until people get cold and I start moaning about not having a Stella in my hand.

"It's all you, you, you!" says Luke, the silly bitch. Dan laughs and kisses him.

No-one's been stupid enough to drive to the club tonight, which is rare, so we split into four cabs and meet again back at mine in Clapham Common.

We always make our way back there. I've got a good place for after-parties with very understanding/deaf neighbours. I always try to make sure to have supplies of everything you need for those elongated sessions and to try to keep everyone happy: more drugs, some booze, comfy clothes and comfy sofas. My mission is to get everyone back to mine so I don't have to go home alone. My ultimate paranoia is of the lonely comedown, and I make every effort to provide everything that anyone might ever need. Everyone takes more drugs, or just relaxes and chills out.

Luke jumps in the shower, and I provide lounging clothes and jump around making tea or alcoholic beverages, just trying to make everyone feel as at home as possible and to try to make them stay as long as possible. I don't like to be alone, it makes me feel unloved.

Shannon and Star help me with the catering, sorting out drinks for people and getting people their drug of choice out; racking up lines on one of the many mirrors lying around my flat; dishing out pills; rolling spliffs.

Shannon the drug queen now has an able assistant. The decks are switched on and I put on a few mellower tunes. It's ten in the morning and the mood is becoming subdued – starkly in contrast with that of the evening before which was a true winner of a Saturday night out at the big-R. Everyone eventually gathers together in a hushed circle in the middle of the living-room floor, holding each other. The blinds are pulled down, darkening the room again. There seems to be a collective feeling of fragility. Of course, the drugs induce it. The comedown is inevitable. We sit around looking at each other, holding hands, talking less than usual. I try to get people going with various exhortations of "Dance you fuckers!" or "More booze?!!! Who wants some more drugs?!!!" But, eventually I give up as the take-up is slack and so I sit down too. I slump down next to my brother Luke, who is collapsed on the old red sofa. He is half-lying on Dan.

Eleven am. We've got the Sunday morning papers in. Max is trying to decipher the Sunday Times. I don't know how he can do that. I can hardly see. The news is terrible apparently.

"Clinton's started bombing Iraq," explains Max. "War mongering bastard."

"He'd better take his knob out of that intern first," quips Luke.

"He's going to be impeached for that sordid little episode."

"Gunmen open fire on Shia Muslims worshiping in a mosque in Islamabad, Pakistan, killing 16 and injuring 25. A 6.1 Richter scale earthquake hits western Colombia, killing at least 1,000."

"Are you deliberately trying to depress us Max?" I ask.

It's all over the front page and in fragile states of mind it's the last thing we need to see I suggest.

Flex grabs the paper off Max.

"OK how about this one? 'In one of the largest drug busts in American history, the United States Coast Guard intercepts a ship with over 9,500 pounds (4.3 tons) of cocaine aboard, headed for Houston, Texas.' Damn shame that. What a waste, could they divert over to Clapham, London please?"

Max puts the paper away and it's clear that he's coming down hard.

"What's wrong with us?" he asks. "I mean, look at us all. We're young, successful, make more money than most, we're nice boys, not bad looking," he says to me so that the others can't hear.

"Don't start with this now, mate. You're not in the right frame of mind and I really don't want to have this conversation right now."

"But why am I always coming home alone?" Max asks.

"Mate, drop it."

"No. Come on. Why?!"

"Oh fucking hell. Look, you don't go to a club like Renaissance and pull. It's not a fucking Ritzy you know."

"Other people do."

"No they don't. No one does."

"Yes they do. I see them." Max says.

"Well, do you want to be like other people?"

"No, I'm just fed up being alone."

"You've got me, and all of us," I gesture to the rest of the gang.

"I'm trying to be serious. You have always got to make everything I say into a joke."

"I'm not. I'm being serious too. You *have* got me," I say.

"That's not what I meant and you know it.."

"You can't force it. You could go out and pull every night of the week. Where would that get you?"

"I wouldn't feel so lonely. *You've* got Rachel"

"What? I have *not* got Rachel, and that's for sure! She has a boyfriend. And nothing's happened."

"She still with that posh chod?"

"Firstly, that's rich coming from you, and yes, unfortunately she is."

"You need to make sure he's out of the picture, pronto."

"I'm not in charge. I can't make her ditch him."

"Well have you said how you feel? Have you shown any commitment?"

"Erm…"

"She's not just going to fall into your lap mate. Especially if she's already got another fella. For once in your life, you may actually have to work at something Mr. Greene."

"Hmmn."

"Well that's if you really want it. Like I want it. And it doesn't happen for me."

"It will happen, mate - naturally. You can't force it. It has to be the right person. You just need the right person. Don't change just because you haven't found her."

"Hmmmn. It's hard…" And his eyes roll back in his head; his head lolls against the wall and he nods off. Thank fuck.

The gang leaves in dribs and drabs between midday and one. It's a grey day in Clapham and depressing. I watch my friends and family leave and although I'm waving at them through the window, inside I'm dying, drowning in the tears I'm crying. The day will pass for all of us in an irritating and sketchy haze that has no sense of time, rhyme or reason. I will ignore my emotions though. Numb them out. I will blank out my aching heart. I've learned the hard way that it is downright dangerous for one's state of mind *not* to perform this ritual suppression of emotion. If you don't, you're just leaving yourself open to your innermost demons. Prey to your own subconscious, and mostly that's a bloody uncomfortable experience for me.

At around 5.30pm Sunday I'm still dozing but my phone starts ringing.

"Hello?"

"Mate," says my mate.

"Mate. Oh I thought it was someone else."

"No, I am not someone else!"

"… You OK?" I ask.

"Yeah. No. You? Did she call? Or come over?"

"I don't know. I've been asleep."

"Oh…you should call her."

"Yeah, maybe. You manage to sleep?" I ask.

"Ish."

"Much?"

"No. Hour…two tops."

"What you been doing?"

"Don't know."

"Get some more sleep. Call me later."

"Can't."

"Fine. I'll come over."

"To do what?"

"Nothing. Yeah?"

"Yeah all right."

I put the phone down and check for messages. Nothing.

I get a taxi over to Max's.

"Well that was a fucking good night, wasn't it?" I ask.

We're sat in his front room in his flat in Southwark. Max is skinning up, watching the footie. Chelsea are playing Spurs. We always beat Rottenham. So that's good. At least there's some positive news.

"Yeah."

"You all right?" I ask because I know he's not.

"Yeah. Just starting to think about work. Monday. I always have to around this time," he shrugs with a sigh.

"I wonder how many other people do it." I say.

"What, lead this terrible double life you mean?" Max shrugs. He's finished constructing his spliff and he starts the search for a functioning lighter.

"Oh. OK. Lighter. Here you are." I pass him the lighter that was lying on the table right in front of him.

"What is going on with that Rachel then?" He sighs as he sparks up, and takes a deep first drag.

"Nothing's happened and I don't think it's going to."

"You make me laugh. I *know* you like her."

"Hmm, don't know. She is definitely *not* into all this. She hates drugs and clubbing."

"So? So do most people. *We* are the abnormal ones. You need another freak. Like you, like *us!* Like Shannon!"

"Come off it. I couldn't. Maybe you haven't noticed, but she seems to be rather attached to Dick Gardiner."

"Oh, sod him. Go for it!"

"Mate, they've been together for ages. She's a good mate. Nothing else."

"Whatever, I've seen how your eyes go all gooey when you talk to her."

"Shut up, Numpty."

"Fuck off with all this numpty shit!"

And so Max and I and approximately two million other lost souls who had partied all weekend; not slept at all Saturday night; and slept sketchily for only some of Sunday night, cover the scars, suppress the feelings and memories of the weekend and attempt to re-integrate ourselves into the 'normal' world and all its machinations on Monday morning. Secrets stashed safe for another week, knowing deep down there is probably no future in it.

MONDAY

feel vague and low, like I've had a lobotomy. I have no idea what that feels like but my head doesn't feel like it belongs to me. It's like I have swapped it with a vegetable, a cabbage perhaps or maybe a turnip, at any rate something deep and dark underground that only becomes remotely useful to man when boiled, hard, for hours.

I have diarrhoea. And both nostrils are painful, very painful. They take it in turns running down my top lip, leaking clear bitter snot into my mouth. I am nearly through this packet of Kleenex. My stomach churns constantly with endless acid.

It's Monday morning and I am at work. I work at Fortworth Consulting, the largest management consultancy in the world. I don't know how or why I got here, and I don't mean just today, I mean in general. So far, somehow, I've been here three and a half years, which is a *lot* longer than I planned to be, but you know how these things go. You go somewhere, you get comfortable and it gets difficult to leave. You earn a lot of money. You start to live the lifestyle. You get attached to certain things. The five-course meals on the firm's expense account at pretentious restaurants with unpronounceable names; the warehouse apartment with exposed brick walls, exposed timber floors, exposed everythings; the unnecessary gadgets; the ridiculously expensive clothes; the Platinum cards; the Champneys memberships and the spiralling debts.

I remember my tutor at university sitting me down and letting me know in no uncertain terms, that he didn't think that Fortworth's would be the right place for me. God, why didn't I listen to him? Something about a round, or was it jagged, peg in a square hole.

I've got no real interest for the work I'm doing, none at all. I have this vague notion that one day I would like to paint, (as in art, not decorating), but I never seem to find the time.

Today, I managed to get here because I had some coke left over from the weekend, so I did a sharpening line this morning to help me along my way. I had another after lunch to get me through the afternoon. But that was a long-time ago. Three o'clock. And now I'm nearly there, although running on empty. Nearly made it through Monday again which unfortunately is the sum of my ambitions today.

The grey desks, the grey décor and the grey people suit my grey mood and my grey skin.

"Greene. Here are the documents from all the sub-projects. You'll need to merge them in order to produce the Programme Status Report by end-of-play today."

With that my line manager dumps a large pile of documents on my desk and walks off. I glance at my watch. Quarter to five.

"Go fuck yourself!" I mutter under my breath.

My line manager stops and turns around as if he thinks he's heard what I said. I look up and give him my best *fuck you* smile. It's practiced. I can see that he's standing there thinking, 'Did he just say what I thought he said?'

Of course I did you wanker. I *did*. I told you to *go and fuck yourself.* He stares at me. I stare back and smile. He looks puzzled and I don't know why. *There can be no doubt about it. I told you to 'go fuck yourself.' Where's the confusion?* Eventually, expressionless, he turns again and walks off.

Pretty soon after I got the job I found out that I could do it using approximately 60% of my brain. I therefore made the calculated decision that I could afford to blow the other 40% out every weekend. The weekends are *my* time. My time to be free, to be myself. Mondays are the payback though; the pain for the weekend's gain. And that's my life. It's a sort of living, but that's all, and it's not to be aspired to. I find Monday re-integration really difficult. Mondays are hard. They are about re-joining the other part of my double life. The part I hate. I hate my job with a passion on Mondays. I hate everything and everyone on

Mondays. I hate life. I lose my vocabulary and my short-term memory on Mondays. Walking towards Clapham Common tube on the way to work on a Monday morning, I pass the drunks and tramps and seriously contemplate life as a homeless artist. 'No responsibilities!' I think fancifully. 'No mortgage; no job to get up for; no job to hate'. Less aggro in my life, therefore I'd be a nicer person. 'Good logic' I somehow manage to reason. Although, as the chemical comedown generally lasts until Tuesday or Wednesday, nothing that I think or say until at least Thursday is worth listening to. I walk past Dave the Drunk and my ridiculous self-pity is tempered only by the knowledge that by the end of the week, these feelings will have dissipated into mere ambivalence and apathy. Then the weekend will approach again. Plans will need to be hatched; drugs will need to be arranged. The mind wanders, the heart flutters and the feelings of last Saturday night are revisited and reignited; the glittering memories of promises given and secrets shared under a twinkling sparkling twilight are remembered and rejuvenated and just-out-of-reach they are turned into breathless hopes and unspoken desires in anticipation of the coming weekend.

I've known Max for a while; a common love of house music brought us together when we started work at Fortworth on the same day. Amongst the corporate wankers who populated our 'start group' we were drawn together. On the first weekend away on the residency training course, in Oxford, we found ourselves out at the local club, when all the straight-heads and beer boys had gone home. We couldn't find any drugs, but for a glorious five minutes, we danced like we were off our tits in the middle of the dance floor grinning at each other to Freefall's *Skydive*. I knew I had a friend for life. A gent and a genius; I love the man. Max has tufty, thinning blond hair that is receding from a friendly and ruddy round face. In short he looks, because he *is* very public school and is a bit taller than me, maybe five eleven, maybe six foot, and a lot brighter. He works in the City for a large American investment bank now and makes a lot of money from the City and is making a lot of money for that large American investment bank. He's not unhappy there, but not ecstatic though he's earning and learning. It's a kind of living. But it's not to be aspired to either. Not in my book anyway.

Max's Dad left home when he was fourteen; a very impressionable and fragile fourteen. He went to school in Hammersmith, West London. He tried to be one of the black kids at school. Sickly, he could easily have been bullied but, as he was incredibly bright, the kids from the estates got him to do their homework in exchange for membership of the gangs. He even got to participate in their ritual terrorisation of the rest of the playground, when a dozen of them would link arms and march menacingly around the playground chanting "Move ya! Move ya!" The only white kid in the line, Max felt special. He belonged. He was one of the gang, which was all that he ever wanted.

On Mondays Max sits at his trading desk at Parks, Miller and Schwab where he buys and sells currency derivatives and options based on some very convoluted, complicated mathematical equations. This he likes. Maths and esoterical equations turn his brain on. What he doesn't like are the tossers he works for and the way that they try to impose the tossy way they think and work on *him*. Max ensconces himself at his terminal; tries not to talk to people; watches the markets, planning his positions, doing the maths and chortles to himself painfully through a chewed-up mouth and thick head. "Tuesday should be better," he writes to me in emails.

I go back to Fortworth Consulting, to managers who I swear at under my breath and endless acid in my stomach. "Tuesday *has* to be better," I reply back to Max.

It's only time, after all, to be passed. It will pass.

I bought some decks about two years ago without any intention of learning how to use them. Max had had a set for years and he used to play endless records to me that I recognised but couldn't name. Max *could* of course. He could tell you the title, artist if there was one - sometimes there was no artist and those seemed to be his favourite, date of release, BPM, that's beats per minute to any normal individual and even then still irrelevant to most and which remix it was, who was the remixer, who was the producer and sometimes even which studio it had been recorded at. It was as if he'd been let into a privileged secret society. 'Artist Unknown' he would say, always 'Artist Unknown' as if that was the name of the artist. They always had plain white labels and took pride of place in his collection; more mysterious, more 'in-the-know' and maybe even a touch illegal.

I ended up buying a set of decks to get people back to mine. It was all part of the plan to get people back to mine after the club. I figured that I needed to provide the perfect post-clubbing environment for that to happen, and a set of Technics 1210s were definitely part of that kit. And of course it had to be 1210s, the only decks. Some DJs will disagree, some will opt for Vestax a good set, maybe even technically better than Technics; some for Gemini, generally cheaper; but for all round class and longevity I chose the *Technics 1210s*. I wanted the standard-bearers; the industry yardstick. I just liked the sound of saying. "Yeah, I've got some 1210s. Come back to mine. The more the merrier." And I always wanted people to come back. I wanted to be the one who had the great parties. I wanted to be the one where they said, "Let's all go back to Alex's". I wanted to be the one where they said "Fuck me, do you remember that night back at Alex's, after Renaissance? Mental!" I wanted to be The Great Gatsby.

I wanted to never be alone on the morning after. The comedowns hit me really hard and the feelings of loneliness and despair are too frightening a prospect to contemplate tackling alone. I would often find myself crying at nature programmes on a Sunday night. That bloody Attenborough again, making me cry. *Antelopes being savaged by crocodiles whilst crossing the Zambezee. They are just trying to cross the river for fuckssake. Or three lionesses ganging up on and taking down a small elephant. And as the creature would scream in agony, so would my heart.* Just watching the news I would well up on some far-away tragedy; or if there was a film on, I would start sobbing away on my own at the most cringe worthy moments. I mean, I once found myself in floods of tears at the part in The Gladiator, when a slave says to Russell Crowe: "I will see you again, but not yet." Thing is though, all these tragic episodes didn't lead me to the conclusion that the best thing to do would be to lay off the drugs. Oh no. Obviously all I had to do was to gather some similarly serotoninally-challenged mates around me and everything would be all right, just fine and dandy, hunky-dory. Any serious examination of my drug problem could be swept under the carpet for another week. So that's why I went out and bought decks seemingly on a whim. It was a Saturday afternoon around 4.30pm and there was a Renaissance on in the evening. And although the prospect of the stupendous joy of the evening ahead filled me with giddy delight, the threat of a lonely and gut-wrenchingly depressing Sunday also loomed large just beyond the horizon. Something needed to be done. I got out the yellow pages for London South and looked under Hi-fi and Electronics Retailers. I found *Clapham High Way* – quality hi-fi and DJ equipment. It was on Lavender Hill and open until 5.30pm on a Saturday and had the all-important 'Technics' logo in their ad panel. I gave them a call, the man on the other end confirmed the availability of two Technics 1210s, a box of assorted house music vinyl, a Numark mixer, 2 Stanton needles, a pair of Sennheiser headphones and other odds and sods. He gave me a price. I called a taxi and I was there by 5.10pm and home again by 5.45pm. So now I had these decks that I would never spin a single tune on myself. Although that is not, strictly speaking, true. I do enjoy putting one on and fading it out and then putting a different one on. But proper mixing seems beyond me. Max tries to teach me, or tried to teach me – he's given up now. I can't count, apparently. Truth is, I never wanted to be able to mix, that was never important. I just wanted people to come back to mine afterwards so I wouldn't have to face the comedown alone.

RACHEL

The night I first met Rachel she told me that she was trying for babies with Rupert. I was also three- quarters of an hour late for a team dinner with work and wasn't wearing any underpants.

I joined the Project she was working on at a major Bank with propitious timing. The manager on the project was going on maternity leave. The silly mare having become pregnant just before her promotion meant that she wouldn't get it, which sums up the cuntiness of the HR department at Fortworth's perfectly.

Therefore the entire project team (which numbered thirty) was being taken out to dinner by one of the Partners to wish a fond farewell to Jane, the heavily pregnant and popular middle-manager.

I was greeted onto the Project Team and seated next to a beautiful if slightly drunk woman. I was glad of the pristine white orchids on the table of the restaurant as they masked her awful perfume. Ironically, the first thing she remarked upon when I took my seat next to her was my aftershave.

"Hi. I'm Rachel Jameson," she said presenting her hand.

"I'm Alex Greene. Pleased to meet you, Rachel." I sat down.

"Wow. You smell great! Do you mind if I ask you what aftershave that is?" she beamed at me. She had a sprinkling of deep brown freckles that ran over the bridge of her nose which crinkled up as she smiled. She had a beautiful smile.

"Not at all," I replied. "It's D&G, just the normal one."

"Ooh!" And she smiled at me and raised her glass and eyed mine on the table. I raised my glass obediently. I liked Rachel and I instantly recognised something inviting yet unfamiliar in her eyes. Something that made me want to go in.

"Why are you so late? I was beginning to think that I wasn't going to have anyone sat next to me on this side. And have you seen who is on the other side of me?" She leaned in and whispered this last sentence to me so that the fat man next to her wouldn't hear.

"Err, I had a bit of trouble finding the place," I sniffed.

"I thought I was going to be left talking to Old Bore Billingham," she hissed. The Old Bore she referred to was the Project Partner, a very senior Partner within the firm who had a reputation for boring you to death through his endless shop-talk. That was if you survived his halitosis for longer than five minutes. It was Old Bore who had requisitioned me onto the project. No doubt he had asked the HR department for any drug-addled chancers they had left lying around and he had got me.

The real reason for my tardiness was that I had been at the pub with Flex, Luke and Max. Luke had just landed his first major project at work and was out wanting to celebrate/blow his commission on some quality ching. We had met in the 101 Bar on Tottenham Court Road for a few warmer-upper beers. We had cracked open a gramme, done a few lines and gone on from there. Between the three of us we had built up a decent head of steam when I remembered the Project team dinner at Hakasan, a formerly cool and underground pan-Asian restaurant in the West End, now a subterranean prole-hole over taken by corporate team bonding dinners like ours, hen nights and stag dos and birthday parties.

But I had to go. I hadn't even started on the project, so I couldn't miss the first event. I was expected. Tomorrow would be my first day and I had to make a good impression. Well, any sort of impression at all would do at the moment actually. Things were being mentioned to me in Performance Reviews about raising my profile around the firm if I wanted to get promoted. It was all I could do to persuade Luke, Flex and Max that I really did have to go to this bloody meal. Several attempts at escape proved futile and premature. And Luke in particular laid on the guilt trip big time. "Come on Alex," he shouted over the din of the noisy West End racket. "It's my first major commission. We have to celebrate! We always celebrate things together!" And so I stayed for another pint, another shot; to combat the drunkenness, another line. So by the time

I absolutely had to leave the bar I had had seven different drinks and several decent-sized lines of coke. I was wired.

Flex dragged me to the bar. I ordered four pints. I hear a snatch of conversation behind me.

"Yeah... that's him!"

"No!"

"Yeah it is! It's Luke Greene."

"Is it? It's never!"

"Yes! Him! He's gay! I'll tell ya. He is!"

"No, is it?"

"Yeah it is! Look he's with that bloke, there. He was in our year at school in Wimbledon. Always knew he was fuckin poof."

"Err, do you mind? Do you know that's a good mate of mine?" I hear Flex asking.

"What?"

"You fucking heard!"

"Yeah? What? That fuckin poof Luke Greene? And, whachugonnadobou'it?"

I'd heard enough. I turned and hit whoever wasn't Flex. Which was the two blokes. I hit one. Flex grabbed the other and wrestled him to the floor. My punch made the blokes nose bleed but he hit me back in the stomach, at which I doubled over but I used the opportunity to gather my breath and punched straight up into the air above me. I connected with the bloke's face who thought he'd come in to finish me off. He got a kick in, but my punch knocked him flying. Then I went to help Flex. I needn't have bothered. He was sat on the other bloke, slapping him about the face saying, "Don't mess with the bull young man, you'll get the horns!" (I have told him he's watched *The Breakfast Club* too many times). The bouncers slung us all out. The two twats apologised. We had to bang on the window to get Luke and Max to notice us and come out.

In the icy winter air outside, and having finally secured my escape and having left Flex, Luke, Dan and Max threatening to go onto 333 in Old Street for a 'Maseeev One!, I decided to surreptitiously ease the pressure on my inflated bowels: an embarrassing mistake. The problem was that this stuff was having a funny effect on my stomach, which coke sometimes does. In fact for me most amphetamines tend to make me want to go to the loo within about five minutes of taking them. The coke was giving me awful wind and I couldn't just very well let one off in the middle of crowded bar, so I had decided to wait until the short walk I would have to make across Charing Cross Road and up Tottenham Court Road from the bar to the restaurant.

The other problem of course was that amphetamines suppress your hunger so all in all it was not the ideal preparation for a five-course meal with a new Project Team upon whom I was supposed to make a good impression.

I managed to sneak a couple out of farts fairly innocuously, although the second did cause an elderly bag lady to stop and sniff the air and decide to cross the road. *What on earth was she doing out this late?* The third one, which I thought would slip noiselessly out of my body ripped out with an extraordinary raspberry that had, it seemed, most of the people in the W1 postcode sniggering and looking in my direction. By the time I made it up Tottenham Court Road to Hanway Street I was letting out a sizeable eruption of air with every step that I took. Disaster struck as the bouncer let me through the unnecessary rope (who were they kidding?) and ushered me down the polished concrete stairs. I don't know whether it was the jiggling down the stairs or the nervousness at the prospect of having to negotiate the evening ahead whilst in this condition and surrounded by boring corporate wankers who would want to talk to me about skills matrices, performance appraisals and system requirements, but something made me shit my pants. I farted uncontrollably (but mercifully silently) just as the glamorous and unfeasibly tall and slim door-whore opened the glass double door to invite me in. "Good evening sir. You must be with the Fortworth group. They're already seated. My colleague Mitsuki will show you to the table." A warm leakage travelled down from in between my buttocks and down the top of each of my inner thighs. "Err, I'll just use the bathroom first if I may." And I tottered Bambi-like, to try to minimise the spread of the leakage, to the gents at the end of the dark marble and glass corridor. Being a Thursday night and therefore relatively busy, there was a Toilet Room Attendant in attendance. I cursed him as soon as I saw him which was a little unfair as it wasn't his fault that I had a penchant for ingesting diuretic substances and it's also a shit job (if you'll pardon the pun), which probably paid a pittance, so I shouldn't have held his presence there against him. Still, it did mean that I would have to rectify the situation with whatever was available to me in the cubicles. I wasn't about to ask a total stranger to let me perform a bidet routine in front of him whilst he disposed of my soiled underwear. I greeted him as breezily as I could and headed for the end cubicle. Once inside I took my shoes off and gingerly slid my trousers down. Luckily the seepage hadn't escaped any lower than the bottom of my boxers or indeed through the material. The seat of my trousers appeared on inspection to be mercifully non-soiled. I must have breathed an audible sigh of relief or uttered an excited expletive because the Washroom Services Executive (I assumed it was him) coughed outside my door and asked me in broken English if everything was ok. I managed an 'uh-uh' as I slid my boxers off as quickly as possible. Resigned to ditching them, I set about looking for a hiding place for them. I was sure the Toilet Services Executive would be in here straight after me to ascertain the causes of my strange noises. He had looked like a responsible and investigative kind of Restroom Officer, the worst kind.

The cistern had a heavy-looking marble lid, but I suspected a fake. So after a cursory pull dislodged it, I decided to lift it completely. It actually turned out to be a cheap and light-weight piece of plastic. So in they went with a pleasing splosh. They gathered water and sank to the bottom of the tank. Now to clean myself up. I cursed myself for having chucked the boxers in the cistern. There was no other thing for it but to use the toilet water. After checking for floaters, pubes and other general detritus I decided the water was clean enough for me. I took a big wadge of toilet paper, wetted it and commenced dabbing at the strangely coloured yellow and greeny slime that I had followed through with.

Upon re-dressing, I snaffled another line as I flushed the toilet and then headed out to brave the night ahead.

I stuck my stomach out and pushed my chin down in to my neck giving myself several chins. In my best public school / Fortworth's partner voice I mocked Old Bore Billingham: "Young Miss Jameson, what do you, errr, errr, I, I, I, *you*, think of the new customer billing system that the firm has installed at United Utilities? Do you have an opinion on what lessons can be applied from that project to the bank's customer services work?"

Rachel was in stitches and Old Bore glowererd over in our direction. I smiled back at him. "Evening, Mr. Billingham." He looked away.

"Alex, you're so funny!" She leant into me as she said this and a strand of her caramel-coloured hair brushed my cheek.

"So Jane O'Driscoll's knocked up then is she?" I asked.

"Yes, might be twins apparently," Rachel whispered back conspiratorially, still close.

"Fuck."

"Yes, Alex. That's generally how it happens."

So she was witty as well as cute. What would I do about the perfume though?

Rachel's cheekbones are high and her eyes, large and milk-chocolate brown and smiled at me. I felt alive. I felt the evening hold some promise and I was as high as a fucking kite.

"I'm trying at the moment too."

"What? Just you, on your own? You won't get very far like that dear. Didn't they do biology at your school? It takes a bird *and* a bee you know."

She was in stitches again. Good God, a woman who found my inane coke-fuelled natter hilarious, wonders will never cease.

"No silly. We. Me and Rupert. Oh, Rupert and I."

"Rupert?" I cut in. "Rupert?" I repeat, "Nobody's called *Rupert*!"

"Yes. Rupert."

"What as in the Bear?"

"Do you know any others? Smart-Alex?!"

"Well there's that gay actor Rupert Everett. And he's a bit of a posh toff too?"

"Rupert is *not* gay. He is well educated, well spoken. And I'll grant you that Rupert is a posh-sounding name, but he's not *that* posh."

"Oh, yeah, right."

"He's not," she screeches in protest, grabbing my shoulder.

I was enjoying this even though I had to admit to being disappointed to discover the existence of a boyfriend.

"Right, let's play a little game shall we? I'll ask you a few questions about Rupert and if I get them right, we get to try to make babies, rather than you and Mr. Paddington Bear."

"Alex, are you on drugs?! I don't know where to start correcting on your last sentence. But let's get a couple of things sorted out. First of all, I do love Rupert, so no amount of flirting from you is going to change that. And secondly his name is Rupert, as in the bear with the yellow checked trousers. Paddington was a different one. You loser," and as she said this she made an L-shaped sign with her thumb and her forefinger on her forehead. I didn't really care, I *was* on drugs as a matter of fact. I took a long slug on my glass of champagne, downed it and started on Rachel's. She grabbed it out of my grasp. I didn't know if her question was serious, but was pretty sure I oughtn't to confess to her that I was as high as a kite just yet. "So has he got a pair then?" I asked.

"Pair of what?" she asked, playing the game at least.

"Yellow checked trousers of course."

"No!"

"OK. But I'll bet he has a double-barrelled surname."

Rachel looked away; picked up a dim-sim and fingered it.

"Does he? Come on Rachel, it's only a bit of fun. What's his surname?"

"Aren't you hungry?" she asked with a cocked head and raised eyebrow.

"Surname?"

"You'll laugh."

"We're already laughing. It's all a laugh. Come on."

"Bingham-Smyth," she says it all slowly and added emphasis where it is demanded and somewhere in my beating heart I imagine she is on my side. Needless to say I burst out cackling like the proverbial hyena. Rachel put her bottom lip firmly out, which is cute. I had to recover the situation.

"That's not too bad. It could have been something like Cholmondely-Warner, or, or.." my mind working over-time to think of the worst possible combination. "Du Chesney-Parnell, or Grimshaw-Pukesbottom."

"Lame Alex, lame. The last one was lame."

"I'm just trying to get you to put away that beautiful sulky bottom lip."

"Alex, are you flirting with me or patronising me?"

"Errm, I…"

"Because neither is allowed. More champers." It wasn't a question, and she reached straight across Old Bore to where the nearest bottle was and grabbed it. And suddenly I was in danger of falling in love.

* * *

The following morning was not a good day to start on a new project. I didn't get much sleep - fault of the amphetamines. And when I woke up it was to a sawing, throbbing head - fault of the alcohol.

Then there was the tube strike which made the tubes even more crowded hot and sweaty than usual, and made me late. I considered not going in, calling in sick on my first day. But that was before Rachel texted me, which changed everything.

Morning new boy. 1st day at ur nu skool. U must be very excited. Come and find me when U get in and Ill show U around. R x

The promise of being shown round; the tone was definitely familiar, flirtatious even, and the kiss? I couldn't remember having exchanged numbers. I scrolled down my phonebook though and there she was. **Rachel Jameson**. She must have put that in I thought, because otherwise it would have been under something stupendously witty like **AceTits**, or **Champers Bird**, or **Bad Smell**, **Great Knockers**, although that might have been too long, as Nokia only allow fourteen characters for a contact. I was counting the characters in B-a-d S-m-e-l-l-G-r-e-a-t-K-n-o-c-k-e-r-s when I realised I was at 90 Chancery Lane; an unprepossessing grey-glass-metal edifice that would be my workplace for the foreseeable future. Bleary-eyed and hung over, I made my way to the 5th Floor where I was due to meet Old Bore for an Orientation Briefing. Mercifully it seemed Old Bore had had an even larger night than myself and wasn't in yet! Result. I spotted Ms Jameson at a desk near the window looking even more beautiful than she had last night, better in natural daylight. She looked up and waved, then cocked a finger in my direction. I told Billingham's officious PA that I knew Rachel Jameson and that I would learn the ropes from her.

"Hey, 'morning," I croaked.

"Good afternoon, Mr. Greene. I thought you were going to stand me up again like you almost did last night. What's your excuse this time? Couldn't find the place again?"

She was sharp, Rachel, and I loved her for it. Only trouble was I couldn't put two words together to fence with her.

"What's the matter? Not had our caffeine injection this morning?" she asked mocking me with her best sad face again which she did with aplomb. More like cocaine injection I thought. "Do I need to apologise for anything last night?" I ask.

"Err, no. You were taking the mickey out of Billingham quite a bit. I think he heard you a couple of times, aside from that and trying to grope me a few times, no."

"I didn't?!"

"No I made that bit up. Did you get home ok?"

"Yeah. Taxi wasn't it? You?"

"Yep fine. It's a bit of a nightmare all the way out to Richmond. Some cabbies won't go that far out west."

"Yeah. What did you do when you got in? Did you try for babies?"

"Fat chance. Rupert was asleep when I got in. We actually haven't been that good about trying recently."

I smiled and smelt the coffee.

THE 60%

On the 8th of March 1999 it's my Mum's 58th birthday. It's at least seven days since the last Renaissance so I'm no longer on a comedown. However, it's precisely twenty-two days until the next Renaissance.

We're at her favourite restaurant La Loggia in Wimbledon, where my parents live, though tonight when I see her it looks like she hardly knows where she is. Outside its pouring with rain and water runs down the floor-to-ceiling windows we're sat at. Dad walks in and gives his keys and his coat to the Maitre d'. Mum looks a little happier if still a little distant. We order some prosecco, nibbles, and then veal, sea-bass and salmon. Then Luke takes the wine list from me,

"We need to get through this. Let's get a few bottles of white wine in!" I nod and Luke orders three bottles of Chablis.

"Alex, so, how is work? Forth-worth." my father asks, staring at me intently.

"It's okay, I guess," I reach for the bread, something.

"Just okay? You're working at the best management consultancy in the world. We invested so much in your education for 'It's okay'? Are you making progress in the firm?"

"I'm not sure. I think so."

"You don't know? You should be more proactive. Find out. What happened at the promotion round?"

"I just carried on." I look at Luke for help, eyebrow raised. He simply buries his head in a glass of fizz and blows bubbles of exasperation for me.

Mum raises her glass and waits for someone to propose a toast. I decide to take up the challenge. "To, the Millennium, the end of an era and the beginning of another. Happy Birthday Mother!" And we crash glasses together. My Mum smiles, raises her glass again and sits back down looking around.

Luke fills up Mums glass and wishes her Happy Birthday again. The waiter brings our food and knows where each dish belongs which I like. After serving us he refills all of our glasses.

Mum picks at her sea-bass and raises her glass after every mouthful. I look across at Luke and he winks back at me.

"Okay, well you must keep us abreast of how you're doing. Sounds on track though."

"On track for what?"

"Well, partnership of course, isn't that the *plan*?" my Dad raises his eyebrows and then smiles.

I look down at this piece of veal which I feel guilty about ordering and which to be honest would double quite handily as a sole of my shoe. I cough and excuse myself. I wish I'd brought some fucking ching.

In the cold Spring air outside I feel refreshed and I pull out my phone to text Rachel.

How you doin? Hope I haven't interrupted. Having a ball at me Mums bday dinner. What you up to? We should go to Renaissance together...

I realise as soon as I send it that I am drunk and that I possibly didn't mean that, too late now. The response is instantaneous: **He he you are funny. It's not out of the question I suppose. Hope you are having a nice time with your Mum x**

I am considering my reply when I am shocked back to the present by Luke banging on the window of the restaurant. I run inside in time to catch my Mum who has fainted. A waiter is standing over her. My father is looking around, his hand rubbing his forehead. My father announces that he is going to bring the car round and walks straight out of the restaurant. I cradle Mum's head in my hand and talk to her telling her to wake up. She opens her eyes and smiles vacantly.

My Dad is pressing his horn outside. The Maitre d' approaches and I realise we haven't paid. Luke looks at me and shrugs. I take out my company Amex and hand it to the Maitre d'.

The waiters watch me and Luke carry our Mum outside and into the passenger seat of my Dad's Volvo.

* * *

On Monday at 9:15am Rachel walks in and smiles at me as she heads towards my desk. In one movement she swoops by and mouths a 'Morning' and drops a bag from Pret-A-Manger on my desk. I don't even have time to thank her and she's gone. I look inside and glimpse a cappuccino, an orange juice and a ham and cheese croissant. I turn and follow her hips down the corridor with my eyes. She's wearing a black trouser suit and her thighs and bum swim smoothly under the fabric. She doesn't look back.

At 12:31 Rachel walks up to my desk. "Alex, it's lunch time. Do you want to go to the canteen?"

"Sure." I look up. Rachel's freckled smiling face is beaming down at me.

"Shall we?" and she offers one hand.

I push back from my desk, pick up my wallet and put out my arm. She places her hand in the crook of my elbow and we head for the canteen.

"So, good weekend then? Happy Birthday to Mrs. Greene."

"Well, yes. I suppose. You could describe it as that."

"Oh?"

"It's a little forced, family occasions I mean, since Luke came out. They haven't taken it very well. And, and I suppose I am losing patience with them both."

"It's different darling. Not every generation is the same. You're more forward thinking, but it must be difficult for them."

She orders a tuna salad and I ask for smoked salmon and then the lasagne.

"How was *your* weekend?"

"Oh, ok, good. Watched Rupert playing rugger on Saturday, then you texted, then we had a few drinks in the clubhouse and then on Sunday we went for a roast at Rupert's parents'"

"Oh, nice."

"I did like your text."

"You did? What do you think?"

"As I said, maybe," as she put a mouthful of salad in her mouth and wrapped her lips round her fork smiling before sliding it out, putting it down and looking at me.

In the evening, around 9pm, Dad phones. He had Mum taken to St George's, Weybridge.

"Can you come home at all? She is drinking again." He doesn't know why. I could tell him why.

"It's a bit difficult Dad."

"Why?"

"I'm supposed to be going out tonight."

"Alex, your Mum needs you."

"What would I tell Luke? He's my brother."

"He doesn't need to know."

"Dad, I live with him."

"So?"

"Luke is my brother and I am proud of him. Until Mum and you get your heads round it I'm not sure how we can move on."

"We're still your parents."

"Yes, yes you are."

"Well why can't you just do as I ask? And respect us and come home?"

"It doesn't work like that Dad. I'm sorry."

"Bloody hell, Alex. Why are you always so stubborn?"

And then he puts the phone down.

I put my phone on the window sill and look out across the Common, a clear and warm night. Joggers are out already. I open the window and breathe in freshly cut grass. I feel like going out for a walk and bumping into Rachel on the Common.

My phone is rattling on the window sill.

Home <<calling>>

I don't feel ready, so I ignore the call and let it ring off. He leaves a message. When I listen to it on Tuesday morning whilst having breakfast in the Canteen at work, sitting across the table from Rachel, it's just a re-run of all the previous and usual complaints of a lack of respect, a lack of understanding and how stubborn I am. I sigh and pour some more ketchup on to my bacon.

"What is it?" asks Rachel, "Parents?"

"Yep. Me, stubborn? Fucking 'ignorant'?"

"Oh Alex. Maybe you should go home for a bit."

"I dunno. It might just make it worse. I feel so angry at them. I don't feel ready."

"How's your Mum now?"

"I think she's going mental," I say, "She *IS* mental, she keeps calling it a *phase*."

TO GET ADDICTED

"What is Renaissance like then?" Rachel asks me on Thursday morning.

"It's mad, beautiful, fantastic, energetic, hot, sweaty and fun."

"Sounds full-on."

"Well it can be what you want it to be."

"Is everyone on drugs there?"

"Not *every*one," I reply.

"Do *you* take drugs when you're there?" she asks.

"Sometimes," I lie.

"Why?"

"They just make it even better."

"So without the drugs it wouldn't be as good?"

"Not quite, but it would still be good. The drugs take me somewhere else. Somewhere where all I feel is good."

"I *am* tempted. To come at least, not take drugs. I don't think I would ever do that."

"Look, at least just try it once. You don't have to take any drugs, if you don't want to. Don't do anything, just come and see what I'm talking about. Bring Rupert even!"

* * *

And so at 9pm on Saturday night there she is, Rachel, amongst all of these strangers. And we *were* strange, to be fair. We're getting ready at mine; glammed-up boys with glitter in their hair; gorgeous young girls making each other up, wandering around the house semi-clad.

"Shannon, can I ask you where you got that top? It's gorgeous," Rachel asks.

"You can, indeed. It's from these friends of Alex's who import stuff directly from the wholesalers in Italy. You have to go to this shop of theirs in Denmark Street. What about you? Where did you get those hipsters from? They're nice. You look fabulous in them."

"Oh, err, well they're TopShop actually."

"Oh. Oh right. Well, cool."

"You *all* look so gorgeous."

"So do you, darling. So do you. Star, don't you think Rebecca looks good?!"

"Hey? Oh yeah, man, totally wicked, she looks wicked."

"It's Rachel…I'm…Rach…"

"See, you look great. Do you want any of these?" She holds out her palm, in which were about half a dozen little pink pills. "Or any ching? Star's been a star and got us this great stuff in at the moment. It's rocket fuel! Isn't it, Gorgeous?" And she kisses Star.

"Have you two met?" Shannon asks Rachel.

"No. I don't think we have."

"Oh, God! How rude of me! Star this is…" she looks at Rachel blankly, "I am so sorry! Is it…?"

"Yes, it's Rachel."

"Sorry darling. Really sorry. Rachel. Of course. Of course it is! This is Star. Star this is Rachel! Rachel, Star."

"A'ight," says Star.

Rachel stands on tip-toe and still can't reach Star's cheek. Star swoops expertly down and pecks her lightly on the cheek.

"So do you want any gear then?" Shannon asks again. "Star gets great gear in from her Dad and brother. Her Uncle runs Renaissance – doesn't he babe?"

"Yup."

Rachel glances at me, shakes her head and looks over at me again with eyebrows raised. I wink back at her.

"Oh, right. Oh ok, well, cool, well, no worries then I suppose." Shannon looks across at me with eyebrows raised. I shrug.

"Well, if you change your mind, just come and see me or Star, right darling?" she says touching Rachel on the wrist and running her hand up to her elbow. Star says yup again and then swoops in for another kiss.

Everyone's sipping on something: Stella, always Stella, for the boys, the only lager to ever grace my fridge, and only ever the 33cl imported bottles. For the girls it's vodka & anything: tonic; red bull; lime & soda; orange. There's only me who isn't drinking. As far as I'm concerned, the night never starts until it starts, and that means at Renaissance.

After the usual eternity of endless parades of nearly-nude women trying on different outfits; the endless swapping of CDs - each one being turned up louder than the previous one; the endless procession of drinks; the constantly screamed phone-calls making intricate arrangements of where to meet various people:

"I'll see you at the second arch, stand where we went mental next to the dry ice pipe at 2.30 last time. See you there at 1!"

The endless distribution of little white or pink pills and strangely wrapped-up little packets, it seemed like we had all become Origami experts, busy making those games you played when you were children with the colours and numbers two, four, green, blue.

We're finally ready. Somewhere in the hubbub, Luke had managed to call a procession of taxis, and at midnight the cars arrive and we all start to file out. I'm last out, I leave some lights on and the telly. A final quick blast of Daft Punk's *Around the World*, and we're away.

In the cab, Lulu, who has just come back from Thailand, bounces around madly chattering non-stop. She explains to Rachel about the "journey" of the night ahead. About the drugs and their "wonderful effects"; about the DJs, "There's Nigel Dawson our favourite, Ian Ossia and sometimes, only sometimes, Sasha and John Digweed put in a guest appearance; about all of our friends, there's Northern Dave – he's the only Northern member of our gang, there's Flem who gets so excited he spits – watch out for him, and of course there's Loopy Luan – who's mad, madder than me! Ha ha ha."

Who will be there, those who unfortunately won't. Someone is being the "dutiful grandson" and visiting his Nan in Bournemouth. Someone else is in Sweden on a business trip: "Lucky cow, great job but *such* bad timing though she should have known it was the last Saturday of the month. Ha! Ha! *Everyone* knows that you keep the last Saturday of the month free. No matter what! You'll soon learn that, Rachel darling!"

Lulu is covered in glitter, especially in her cleavage, which is up by her chin somewhere. She's fidgeting and reaches over to play with Rachel's fluffy pink feather boa.

Finally we arrive at The Cross. I can see Rachel looking dubiously at the whole set-up, King's Cross admittedly is not the most salubrious of neighbourhoods, but I can't wait to see her face once we are inside. The palm trees are outside and coloured lights shine tracers up into the sky. There are lots of beautiful people standing around chatting, laughing, smoking. And a huge queue that snakes right round the club.

"God are *all* those people queuing to get into Renaissance?" asks Rachel.

"Yup. Not us tho'. It's sweet." Star smiles at her and Shannon squeezes her leg.

Straight away we're ushered inside. Everything's a swirl. Bright flashing lights; a stream of warm greetings, hugs, kisses and introductions; ordering drinks, meeting old and new friends, making more introductions. There was always a Renaissance Virgin and I tell Rachel, tonight it's her. Everyone keeps asking her if she is enjoying her night; is she OK? Did she like the club? Did she like the music? Did she want anything?

The music is loud, repetitive and rapturous, in the main room everyone is bouncing up and down in a sweaty mass: heads and arms reaching upwards, just about visible through the thick dry ice which keeps pouring out of the huge industrial pipes hanging from the ceiling. I want Rachel to glimpse a real typical Renaissance night and she is. Everyone is smiling, everyone is happy. Me, Shannon and Star give her a guided tour of the club. We show her the best spots to dance, "Now here's the best place to dance if you don't want any hassle, because it's where all the gay boys dance. Luke and Dan are always here. We like to dance over there on the step, under that pipe, that's where the dry

ice comes out, proper shoots you up on your pill," which of the bars to
queue at, "Never ever bother coming to this bar, it's always heaving like
this, always go to that one because we know Ange and she loves us and
we love her..don't we Ange?" and with that Star leans over the bar and
deposits four little pills in Ange's open hand. Kisses all round. Then it's
how to dodge the queue at the ladies by going round the brick pillar
and ducking under the heavy cherry-coloured drape which Shannon
quickly demonstrates, taking Rachel by the hand, leaving me standing
somewhat unexpectedly with Star.

"So you like her then, do ya?"

"Err,

"Dat's why we're doing all this..?" Star waves her long arms around.

"Oh come on, I'd do this for any newbie."

"Yeah, right," she smiles at me, raises an eyebrow and sucks her teeth
in one well-practiced diss. "You're gonna get hurt you know."

I am relieved to see Shannon leading a startled-looking Rachel by
the hand from the toilets.

"You ok Rach?"

"Yes, it was just quite lively in there I suppose."

"Always is, Gorgeous," Shannon winks at me.

We show Rachel the DJ booth.

"Better not interrupt him, but that's Nigel Dawson, he's our
favourite."

"I've never understood how they do that with the two record players,"
says Rachel.

"It's easy when you know how. I'll teach you if you like."

Behind me I can hear Star sniggering.

"And *that* is Renaissance!"

"Lovely, it's lovely," says Rachel.

"Right, let's go and find the others then eh?" I suggest. I can see
Luke and Dan, Flex and Max bouncing around on the main dance floor
from our elevated viewpoint next to the DJ booth. Flex does his work
and clears the way.

"Girls, let's go and powder our noses!" Shannon grabs Rachel and
Star. Just before she is whisked away Rachel grabs my arm and kisses
me on the cheek.

As soon as she grabs me I feel a familiar feeling burst over me. "Fuck me! I'm coming up. Right now!" I grab Max. A huge warm wave washes over me, it crashes through my body, I see it and it looks dangerous but I feel no pain only joy, and love. "I feel so much love for Rachel. And I want to tell her. Have to tell her. I love her and I want to tell her."

"Are you sure mate?" ask Max, "might not be the best time."

"Why not?"

"Well, you're, we're quite fucked."

"So?"

"So, it might not come out quite right."

* * *

I'm dancing with her. She is floating in front of me smiling. She is asking me if we can go and get a drink. I take her by the hand and lead her across the cobbled terrace to the small bar.

"Rachel, I feel so…"

"Alex?"

"Do you?"

"What?"

"I feel so…close,"

"What do you mean?"

"I sometimes think that what happens in this world between two people is just what life's all about. You know? That that's the whole experience," I say.

"What do you mean?" she asks again.

"I mean that some things are just supposed to happen. And that when two people are destined to be together, then it will happen eventually."

She leans in close to catch what I am saying.

"I'm not sure I understand, but I guess so, yes."

"Have I ever told you…have I ever told you …how…I…how beautiful you are?"

"No you haven't Alex…but thank you."

The moment is shattered by Rachel's mobile ringing. She fishes it out of her handbag. "It's Rupert! I'd better answer it, Alex. Sorry."

She turns away from me so I can't hear what she's saying. And I revert back to rambling about the future to the bar in general. I am so completely fucked by this point that I have no idea what I am saying, but it usually makes sense to me and tonight I feel an unusual sense of urgency. "The future is beautiful. It always looks like clouds, but not cloudy. Clouds that are clearing. Clearing fast, as if to show me a way upwards. As if to show me the future. I can see it now, all laid out for me. It's as if I've lived it before and I know what's coming. I'm not afraid. I'm ready for the future. The future is that clearing in the clouds beckoning me upwards to fly in between the fireworks and the thunderstorms. The only thing I'm afraid of is dying. I never want to die. I sometimes get these panic attacks about dying. Dying young and suddenly, and not being to tell my parents or brother in time, or say goodbye. And I think about all the things that I wouldn't have done, or done differently. Things still to do. Because I don't really believe in God or any sort of after-life or anything, I get scared and get anxious, that once you're gone, you're gone. And that's it." I open my eyes and see that Rachel has finished her phone conversation and is looking at me.

"Alex, I've got to go I'm afraid darling. Rupert is absolutely slaughtered and wants me to meet him in Chelsea. It's been a great night though. I've really enjoyed it. Your friends are *so* lovely. And everyone's so friendly. I even enjoyed the music."

I reach out for her hand. She gives it and I stroke it and then hold it in mine as I smile. I go to the cloakroom with her and get her coat. I stand in the taxi line with her, smiling in the drizzle. Pretty soon Rachel's turn in the taxi line comes and she kisses me again on both cheeks and says again how much she has enjoyed herself, and how sorry she is that she has to go. Max comes and grabs me and we march back into the club.

Here we all are again. The gang is getting bigger all the time. Some people are still drinking, most are coming up on their pills, or have come up and are taking another. We all stand around, chattering. We won't be standing for long though. We won't be all together for long. Soon someone comes up again and gets the urge to dance. Splinter groups form. Secret alliances are forged and dalliances happen that shouldn't. Secrets develop, are shared and are forgotten.

I see Richard leaning into Luke, Dan is smiling, Flex and Lulu appear and disappear like magicians, Shannon and Star are gone for hours. I don't whether to make anything of it or nothing at all.

Soon light makes images.

It's refracting.

People gurn.

Nobody notices.

Everyone screams.

Everyone shouts.

This is Renaissance.

It's easy to get addicted.

Someone grabs my arm. It's Kai, a tiny gay guy, a good friend of Richard Gardiner's. He's a hairdresser, from Vietnam, and does all the girls' hair before every Renaissance. "Alex! Come with us. I have da best chit." Richard is standing behind Kai nodding and beckoning.

Clutching a bottle of Bollinger in one tiny hand, two fingers wrapped around the stem of an overflowing champagne flute, he uses his other hand to open my palm. A clear, cling-film bulb of pure white snow is inside. It looks like an eight ball.

"What am I coming to? What have I become?" I whisper to the inside of my head as I stumble after them across the cobbles, into the toilets with the gay hairdresser and Richard Gardiner, with a bottle of champagne and an eighth of Charlie. It's very hot in the cubicle and a tight squeeze with three of us in there. We do a hit and I feel sandwiched in between the pair of them. They talk to each other, but I can't hear what they're saying. I feel them trying to reach through me, round me, into me. I'm high as a fucking kite and I close my eyes to enjoy my rush. I spin off to an unidentifiable and faraway place. It's hot, not inside-a-club-hot but dry Mediterranean-night-hot and it smells of herbs. Then I'm running down a road, running away. I am being chased.

Kai grabbing me snaps me out of it. "Alex, you ok? Strong shit, huh?"

"Yeah. I'm good. Yeah, it's good stuff."

I push past them and out of the cubicle, pouring sweat. I leave them, Kai stroking Richard's left upper-arm telling him how big his bicep is and now I'm Charlied up to my eyeballs as well as everything else that I have taken.

I see Shannon coming out of the main dancefloor and out onto the terrace. She stumbles up the steps looking beautiful, but fucked. I see Star still dancing on the floor behind her. She waves me over, but there's no way I can muster dancing now. Young Flex appears and they start dancing together, him beaming, her looking cross.

"Alex, baby, have you got any smoked salmon for me?" Shannon is asking me, she is leaning up against me, her breast pressing into my chest.

"At mine, darling. Back at mine I have. We'll have some tomorrow, shall we?"

"Have you? Have *you* got what I *need*?" she smiles and looks deep into my eyes and wraps her arms round my neck.

"Loads darling, 3 Kilos like The Progidy song."

Max spots us and comes over. He's got some female by the hand and she is following him. "What are you two talking about?"

"Smoked salmon, we're having it tomorrow," I explain.

"Ok, that's good, I suppose. Look, I want you to meet Lorraine. Turns out Lorraine and I went to the same school together in Hammersmith. And she's here tonight. Isn't that great?"

"Wow! That is! She looks lush!" Shannon beams.

I am slightly worse for wear but I lean in to take a look at this *Lorraine*. She's pretty, *very* pretty in an innocent English rose type of way. Her skin glows, she's got a trace of freckles across the bridge of her nose and her big hazel eyes give her an endearing air of honesty. I kiss her on both cheeks and present my hand. "So you knew Max when he was at school? Has he always been a posh-record-spotting-geek then?" I ask.

"Actually he has. But luckily I have a penchant for posh-record-spotting-geeks. So I have fancied him for a while. You must be Alex. Max has told me a lot about you."

"Max's other major personality characteristic is lying beyond belief." I tell her. Max digs me in the ribs. "Don't believe a word he's told you about me. I'm a really horrible person."

"Funnily enough that's exactly what he said." Laughs all round. I was sure I was going to like Lorraine. I smile. I am truly happy for Max.

"Hey. Let's go and see what Lulu's up to. She's always good for a laugh. Come on," and Max puts his arms round all three of us.

"Yeah, OK yeah. Nice one Max – you look after me don't you?" I lean on his shoulder, the crook of his neck holding my forehead. My head feels like it's about to explode. And although I am happy for Max I feel lost. I don't know which way is up. I feel like crying but I don't know why. I just know that it's getting pretty bad.

Lulu has cornered Dan whilst Luke is away at the bar. It seems she is grilling him on his drug-taking habits. I overhear her asking: "So what is it *exactly* that you *don't* like about ecstasy?" He is refusing to do pills apparently. At this point, Dan breaks his cool with a huge sniff and a wipe of his nose.

"Oh, I see, favour the Peruvian marching powder do we?" Max asks.

"Ya, I've got some Charlie – if that's what you mean?"

"Oh '*ya I've got some Charlie*' ha ha. Ya, that *is* what I mean," mimics Lulu, and then adds: "How much *exactly*?"

"Oh I dunno, quite a bit. Think I've got about a Henry left. Always have heaps on me. It's *de rigeur.*"

So Dan refuses to take pills on safety grounds, which is fair enough, although he seems to have no problem at all with stuffing half of South America's GDP in coke up his nose every night. This is the logic of the day. I know that somewhere inside my head none of it makes sense. Shannon, Max and Lorraine collapse laughing at Dan's contrary attitude to Class A drug taking. Dan looks around with a helpless look on his face presumably wondering where Luke is.

Flex and Star come back from the dance floor. Flex sweating and gurning; Star scowling at Flex's back. She grabs Shannon and hugs her and Shannon kisses her. I wonder what he did.

Richard Gardiner appears suddenly, Kai behind him.

"I'm going to get the coats," he says.

"Rich, We are *not* leaving yet," replies Shannon.

"It's nearly five though."

"It's four, not five! There are two hours left."

"Well, I'll get the coats. You'll get cold soon."

Shannon runs after Rich as he walks to the cloakroom.

Star sucks her teeth and sighs.

"Max, why is Shannon going out with such a twat?" I ask.

"He's nice?" offers Kai.

Everyone stares at Kai.

"Yeah, why?" adds Star.

"Habit," answers Max.

"I reckon she's just scared," I counter.

"Yeah? Of what?" asks Flex.

"Getting out of it. Wanting to and yet being scared of being alone. It's obvious isn't it? Just like we all are. *We'll all be alone in the future.*"

"Alex, would you shut up with your philosophical fucking ramblings about the future? Are you trying to be fucking enigmatic or something?" asks Flex with an eyebrow raised.

"No. I don't think so."

"Right, fucking shut up then coz you're pure doing my 'ed in. *And* you're blowing my high. I spent good money on these Mitsu's...!"

"Oh. OK." So I shut up about the future, even though it's all I can think about.

It's 6am and we finally all stumble outside. Me, Max, Lorraine, Star, Shannon, Richard, Lulu, Flex, Luke and Dan and Kai.

"Fucking hell. Who's driving?" I ask. This time, Lulu has driven the five of us who crammed into her Golf Julesy.

"Nobody, leave the car here. We'll take taxis and come and get it in the morning," suggests Max, the voice of intellect and reason.

"It *is* the morning," Lulu counters; "I'm driving. I'm fine."

"Lulu, you are not 'fine'!" I shout.

"Alex, I'm fine!"

"She is. She's not drunk since midnight," says Shannon.

"She is not *fine* Shannon! She's fucked. She might not have drunk, but she's done a whole lot else."

"Alex, give me my keys!"

"No. No chance."

"Alex! Yes. Give me my keys. Right now! Don't be a twat."

"Don't call me a twat. You're the fucking twat for wanting to drive, when you're fucked."

"Lulu, how many fingers am I holding up?" Max asks her. Everyone pisses themselves as Max holds up his hand wiggling his fingers in a 3-2-1 Dusty Bin routine.

"Max. Are you moving your fingers?"

"No Lulu."

"*I'm* taking a taxi. Shaz, look after *her*." I say to Shannon.

"Guys! Guys! Oi, you lot! We didn't drive here. Duh! We got taxis remember?" Thank the fuck for Star. She is the youngest out of all of us but the only one thinking straight.

"Fuck!" I say to myself. Where did I get that from? I could have sworn we came in Julesy Lulu's car.

So we join the line. I get into the taxi holding my head and half an hour later we are home. There are nine or ten lost souls who stay over at mine to continue the party into Sunday. These Bank Holidays are the most extreme for partying. That extra day just seems to get people going. It does give them one extra day to recover I suppose. The usual Saturday night shenanigans have taken place at Renaissance. Star becomes a fully fledged member of our gang, following Shannon around like a shadow; Max finally pulls; Luke and Dan are now apparently a long-term stable item; Flex and Lulu cop off regularly (although I suspect he has also tried and failed with Star) and Richard Gardiner continues to be the butt of everyone's jokes and seems to serve no purpose at all other than providing Shannon with some comfort and security – which I suppose is good. Me? Well, I got Rachel to Renaissance, and she had a good time.

Me, Flex and Lulu are collapsed onto my old red sofa. Arms round each other we sigh with satisfaction as Shannon sorts out refreshments with Star in tow as usual. "Stella for me please darlin'," I shout from my seat.

Max and Lorraine sit down together in the middle of the floor. Hand in hand, they do make an interesting couple. She looks like she likes him, and she didn't ditch him halfway through the night, which is something for Max. Maybe she could be *The One*? Star still has loads of drugs left and is trying to sell them all. All of us fucked-up people are buying them off of her. I really like the young lady who has infiltrated our gang, and it's obvious Shannon does too, the way they are constantly cuddling and whispering. On nights like this, they're inseparable. All the pills are finally distributed; cuddles are shared by platonic friends. 'Nothing'll happen. Just hold me'. 'I love you, mate'. 'I love you too.'

I decide I want a shower to get rid of the sweat that is caked onto me, force of hours of dancing. I slowly unsteadily make my way to the bathrooom, tripping and twisted. Someone sticks on *Gouryella* by Gouryella, full blast. I stand mesmerised under the huge warm beads of splintering rain that descend upon me. Each drop tingles and bounces off my back like the transfixing, crystalline, electronic sounds that had rained down on my ears hours before on the dance floor. *Gouryella*, makes its way into the bathroom and through the cacophony of the water, so I dance like a banshee in the foaming shampoo and soap.

I towel down and make my way back into the front room. It could not have been a clearer contrast to when I had left five minutes ago. Where before the crowd had been languishing on the stripped wooden floor and the sofa, nursing and managing their collective comedown and navigating the inevitable psychobabble of post-clubbing chaos, ten total nutters are now dancing around the room in the fuzzy Spring sunshine. The stereo is straining, like some machine analogue of what's happening to everyone's brains. It's a surreal scene. I stand in the doorway, watching the madness unfold and multiply in my front room and, seconds later, fall into the rhythm, whooping, yelling "Bring it on!" and dancing with nothing on bar my ludicrous bright pink towel.

I dance until the end of the song before ducking into the walk-in wardrobe to grab a pair of jeans and a t-shirt. Moving between the dancers I gather orders and empty glasses. After collecting them all I carry them very unsteadily to the kitchen. I struggle with trying to remember the orders for all of ten seconds. Then I realise I have forgotten everything. They're all having Russian Spring Punches, even the drivers, no-one's leaving. *I can't have anyone leaving yet.* A mild panic sprints across my psyche and sweat gathers on my forehead prickling me. Russian Spring Punches are the house speciality. Long glass, full of ice, double shot of vodka, raspberry puree, crème de cassis, lemon juice, sugar cane syrup, topped off with about 2 centimetres of champagne. Fucking mind-blowing. The sugar reacts with the alcohol to produce a seriously memory-lapse-inducing concoction and I always make sure to have all the ingredients in stock after Renaissance.

Once I get them all ready I run into the front-room, with the tray filled with these fantastic looking drinks.

"Wow!!! What are those, Alex?" Lulu shrieks.

"Russian Spring Punches!" I announce.

"Owwwh Mate! That's gonna kill us," Max knows there is trouble ahead. And he starts singing it. *"There may be trouble ahead, but while there's…music and moonlight and love and romance…"*

"Let's face the music and dance!" Everybody else shouts jumping up and down on the wooden floorboards.

"Right. Oi, listen up. Listen to me. I want everyone to relax. Drivers, I want you to hand over your keys, you're not going anywhere, there's loads of room. So kick back, relax, enjoy yourselves and have some fun. Star, get the rest of the drugs out! I'm buying the lot off you!"

I get up and go to the toilet. Shannon's already in there sitting on the toilet, a huge joint in one hand, black trousers and black g-string round her ankles and the other hand in between her thighs.

"Nice scene. What's going on?" I ask trying to be cool and act like this happens all the time.

"Shhhh…Help yourself to *that,*" she takes a long drag on the joint, holds the intake for ever and then nods to the glass shelf above the sink, her Russian Spring Punch, a large pile of white powder, a rolled twenty and her corporate gold card. I re-roll the twenty and snort straight out of the pile, watching Shannon out of the corner of my eye. Her left hand is a blur in between her thighs, her head is thrown back, the veins in her neck are bulging and she has the joint in her mouth sucking hard.

"Alex," Shannon reaches out with her hand for mine, "Look, put your hand here if you want." She guides my right hand in between her thighs and parts them slightly. "Good. Now slowly…gently at first, and then, when I say so, harder and faster."

I do as I am told as Shannon sighs and pulls again on the joint and takes a long gulp of her Russian Spring Punch.

"A bit faster…right. Thanks. Let me takeover. I want to come now."

I stand staring. Shannon comes, clamping her thighs tight around her left hand. I'm still staring. After a few seconds she opens her eyes, looks up at me, smiles and jumps up off the loo. We stand together at the sink washing our hands. She takes my hands under the warm tap and rubs the soap over them. "You're a lovely boy Alex, lovely," and she leans across and kisses me on the cheek as the water runs over our joined hands. She squeezes mine with hers and then lets go. We turn a tap off each and share the towel. Shannon grabs my right hand and leads me back out to the madness.

Luke, Dan, Lulu and Flex are dancing in the middle of the room and we join them. Shannon dances close to me and smiles up at me; she stands up on tiptoe and kisses me on the lips. Then she places her finger on my lips and mouths "Shhh."

The rest of the morning disappears in a hazy blur. The ceiling seems to endlessly swap places with the floor and the walls. The blinds are closed, and then are raised again a minute later. Bright sunlight is complimented by the most up-for-it music we can find: Daft Punk, hard-trance stuff like Paul Van Dyk, BT and Sasha; the Chemical Brothers; the 2nd Daft Punk album, the latest Renaissance CD. The blinds are shut again and some lovely person (Lorraine) puts the first Café del Mar album on, a true classic of our times, produced by that genius Jose Padilla in 1994. Then Flex gets bored and says, 'Let's have the entire Renaissance back catalogue on", which of course I have, so on it goes. I know that we all have at least three more Russian Spring Punches. I know that there's enough left for some of us to have four. I know that Lulu then takes advantage of a drunken Flex again, she sucks his face off for about an hour. I know Richard Gardiner tries to come onto me, which is getting a little too frequent and tiresome for my liking. I remember disappearing into the toilet with Shannon and Star although I think it was only to snort some MDMA. Lulu then gets out her pills, crushing them up and snorting them and when that runs out, Lulu gets another two grammes of Charlie out of somewhere and sorts out one huge line on the round mirror that she and Shannon detach from its place of residence in the bathroom. She makes a spiral shape, then we all just do as much of it as we want. I neither know nor really give a fuck about what is going on at this stage. Besides which, I can no longer see and at that point I pass out on my bed. I hope everyone else does so too, for their health's sake, but I'm not confident, and that's the thing about my lot, they don't know their limits, they won't stop until they fucking drop.

I doze off and Rachel is with me in my dreams, at home somewhere, not my flat; together.

"Do you want me to cook you some breakfast?" She whispers as she strokes my forehead.

"No. You don't get hungry when you do pills."

"Alex, that's not natural. Are you really not hungry? It's not healthy."

"It passes. I'll have dinner later on."

"I just wish you could stop. It can't be good for you. You don't want to though do you?"

"I do want to stop. I really do. I can. I promise. I will. Soon. I just can't let go of the feelings. But I do want to. I will soon. All I need is a good reason."

"What would be a good enough reason?"

"Hey?"

"What would be a good reason? What would be enough to make you want to give up?"

"Someone I loved or cared about, or someone who cared about me, wanting me to stop."

I truly believe it. It's just that I haven't found that compelling reason or person yet. I have talked it over with myself many, many times and I know that given the right kind of motivation, I could give it all up any day now.

We both smile. I reach out for Rachel. I pull her close and we hug for a moment. She pulls away after a moment or two. And then she shimmers and is gone.

* * *

I am awoken by this almighty racket breaking out from somewhere nearby. I still can't focus and I'm unsure where I am.

"Shannon, you've shat yourself! You've fucking shat yourself! You are never doing those fucking things ever again. You've shat yourself all over his fucking floor!"

I sit up in bed totally and utterly confused. "Jesus Christ! What the fuck, is going on?" I shout with my eyes shut. There's no answer but the racket continues and I work out its coming from the bathroom. With some difficulty I haul myself onto my feet and unsteadily make for the bathroom door. The stench of shit has made its way out into the hallway and floods my nostrils before I get there. I contemplate heading straight back to bed and dealing with this in the morning when I hear something inside which sounds like crying.

I reach for the doorknob not knowing what I am going to find inside. What I see is extraordinary. Shannon is in the bath, still fully-clothed-ish but most of her clothes are torn. Her black vest top is torn at the left shoulder and hangs open showing her leopard-print bra. Her skirt is torn all the way up her right leg. The bath has brown water in it. A bright-red, crazed-looking, semi-naked Richard is bent double over the bathtub wrestling with Shannon's clothing. Brown streaks are all over the floor-tiles.

"What the fuck is going on?!" I shout at Richard.

"I'm sorry mate. Those pills must've been too strong. She's shat herself. She was trying to be sick and lost all control of her bodily functions. We were up chatting and she went to the loo and then…"

"Look, let's just try and get her clothes off sensibly and get her out of the bath shall we? What the fuck is she doing in the bath with all of her clothes on?"

"What do you mean?"

"I mean, why, has she still got her clothes on in the bath? You fucking dickhead!"

"I'm trying to teach her a lesson."

"For fuck's sake!"

"Hunh?" He stands by the side of the bath like a plum.

"Oh fuck it! Get out of the way Rich! Listen, go and get her a t-shirt and a pair of my boxers out of my cupboard. I'll sort this out." My head's banging and I've no patience for Gardiner's shit.

"All right, all right. Cheers mate. I really appreciate this. I'll batter her tomorrow, when I get her home."

"What?! Fuck off. Just get the fucking clothes you fucking moron!"

So there I am, still fucked myself, having to deal. Shannon is in the bath, semi-clothed, shit all over her legs, shit all over her body, shit all over my bathroom, shit every-fucking-where.

I pull her up so she's sitting up at least. She opens her eyes and looks into mine. She smiles. I smile back as best I can.

"Hello babe, you've got yourself into a bit of a state, haven't you?"

"Hug me."

I do. She sobs into my neck.

I look down and I am now covered in shit too.

"I'm going to turn the shower on and get you cleaned up babe, OK?"

"OK."

I pull the plug to drain the water from the bath tub.

I turn on the shower and pull Shannon's top up and over her head. I reach round her and she loops her arms over my head and behind my neck. I unclasp her bra and lean her back against the side of the bath. I drop the bra onto the pile of her clothes. The water falls down on to her. She opens her eyes and looks up at me. She smiles, but I also see fear. Her lips are trembling. I look away and look down at her body. I bite my lip. I can feel my rage rising inside me. I smash my fist against the white tiles of the bathroom.

"What?" Shannon looks up.

"Nothing darling, nothing. You ok?"

She puts her hands on her breasts. "Yeah, ok, I guess. Are you getting in with me?"

"No darling, I can't."

She shuts her eyes and drops her hands down. She kneels up; I grip her under her armpit. She pulls her black g-string down. She starts crying. She puts her head under the shower then leans against my thigh and sobs. I kneel down and hug her. She hugs me back and kisses me on the cheek.

"What was that for? Is everything ok? Does he..?"

"Shhhh," She mouths and stretches up and kisses me on the lips and sits back down in the bath.

My head spins, I love this girl. I am too angry with Gardiner to think straight.

I squirt my shower gel into my palm and work up a good lather. I place my hands on her shoulders and rub the soap over her skin. She smiles and takes my hands as they approach her breasts. I rub the remaining foam over her thighs. She flinches. I pull the shower head down and direct it all over her body. As I rinse the soap off, I see black, blue, purple and yellow marks all over her body, all guilty, all wanting to scream out. I get a flannel and rub it gently over her arms, neck, back, breasts and her thighs. I am filled with rage and passion and am fighting every sinew in my body not to pursue my gut instinct and go in to the lounge and smash Gardiner up.

I turn the shower off and reach for a towel. Shannon is trying to get up but hasn't got the strength. I pull her up by her getting under her arms and she stands unsteadily. She flops into my arms and I carry her back into the front room where I find Gardiner collapsed and snoring on the sofa bed. He hasn't got the clothes out of the wardrobe for Shannon. I lay Shannon down next to him and go to grab a long grey jersey t-shirt from my wardrobe. She sits up and mouths 'thank you' at me and puts her arms straight up in the air. I lower the t-shirt onto her. She pulls it down and lies back. She smiles and blows me a kiss.

I turn and walk back to my room. I strip and collapse into bed. Unreal. I can't sleep and his words turn over in my head. I get up and walk to the bedroom door. I open it and look at them sleeping in the lounge. I stare at him and wonder why he's such a fucking weirdo.

He's a successful middle-manager with a consumer products firm, he tells us over enthusiastically and often and we always forget. He's the sort of guy that always tells you about his job; about how much he's earning; about how many people he has working 'under' him. He always uses the word 'under'. The sort of bloke that has to change his car every two years and thinks that's really important. The sort of bloke that has to tell you how much money, 'equity' he calls it, he's made on his property. I really don't give a fuck. He travels round the country selling tampons and other women's sanitary products to supermarkets and grocery stores. Essentially, he's a wanker. But somehow he has persuaded Shannon to be with him, to love him? They've known each other for years and he jumped in there as soon as she was free of her violent ex. He gets very jealous of anyone talking to her and you always get the impression when we're out that he'd rather have Shannon hidden away at home, sitting in front of the TV next to him; he's always trying to get Shannon to leave Renaissance before the end. Then he has this curious tendency to come over as aggressive but also homosexual when he's drunk or has been taking Charlie. The last time at Renaissance and last night at mine he was definitely puckering up for a kiss. I also think that it's weird to only realise you have homosexual tendencies when you are under the influence of alcohol or drugs. And, outwardly at least, Richard is the biggest homophobe going.

I turn back to my room, collapse onto my bed and head spinning try to sleep trying to ignore the restless and sweaty dreams that were trying to drag me under.

THE MORNING AFTER
THE NIGHT BEFORE

I wake up and my head is sawing. I reach over and grab at my pint of water. I pop two Nurofen out of the packet in my bedside cabinet. I look at my phone and it says it's two in the afternoon. I can hear the Gang Mother and Gang Daughter banging about in the kitchen. "Right, everybody. Who's hungry?" I hear Shannon shout. Shannon seems to be ok.

"I think we should go straight down to The Sun and get amongst some serious Sunday drinking; after all it's a Bank Holiday. No skool tommorrow!"

"No sk-o-o-o-o-o-ol !!!!!!" shouts Flex at the top of his voice.

"Get amongst it!" I shout.

"I've got school," says Star, bottom lip curling downward.

"What?!"

"Dad has booked me private tuition 'coz he thinks I don't go to school. I have to be back home by ten."

I want to tell her to stay, but instead I keep quiet and I make a mental note to try to be a better influence.

Eventually, Shannon's cajoling and harassing gets everybody out after an hour or so. By half-three we are on our way down to The Sun.

On the way down I drag Max aside.

"Mate, I need to talk to you."

"Yeah mate. Lorraine, carry on darling. I'll catch you up."

"There was a bit of an incident last night."

"Oh yeah, sounds fun."

"It wasn't. I think Gardiner hits Shannon."

"What?! I know he's a Dick, but that's a bit strong, mate."

"Mate, she had a bit of an accident, lost control of her bodily functions, and he told me he'd teach her a lesson and batter her when they got home!"

"Are you serious?"

"Yep."

"He must have been joking, mate"

"I don't think so mate, he said it so matter- of-fact, like she deserved it."

"Not again. Didn't the ex-boyfriend do that too?"

"Yeah."

"She certainly knows how to pick them!"

"Fucking hell, what are we going to do?"

"Nothing mate. Nothing. Don't get involved."

"What?! How can you say that? I saw."

"What?"

"I saw some bruises. We should call the police. Something!"

"Oh yeah that will look good. 'Sorry officers, so I was having this late night party back at mine, loadsa drugs, you know how it is, and this one mate of mine, I gave her a few pills, she took way too many, and made a big mess, but I hate her boyfriend and he probably hits her, so could you arrest him please?' How does that play out to you? Credible?"

"Oh yeah."

"Listen, I'm not saying do nothing, just watch out for Shannon, and we'll keep our eye on Dick."

We join the rest of the group at who are sitting at a large table in the middle of the beer garden at The Sun. Max squeezes in alongside Lorraine. He looks up at me and across to Richard and Shannon and back to me and shakes his head. Then he kisses Lorraine. I head inside to the bar to help Flex collect the Bloody Marys. Breakfast is Bloody Marys after a fine night out. Body temperatures not yet back to normal we sit outside under the fire burners and get ready for a full day's drinking.

Rachel arrives unexpectedly a minute after we emerge with the Bloody Marys. I am amazed. She's all smiles.

"Hello you," she smiles and kisses me on the cheek.

"Hello Rachel!" the gang all shout.

"You alright?" I ask.

"Brilliant," she replies, "I'm glad I came out, Rupert is off playing rugger at Rosslyn Park,"

I nod examining her over the top of my Bloody Mary.

"So I thought I'd come over to Clapham and took a chance that you'd be down here. Where else would you be?" she says. Everyone laughs. "You really need to be less predictable Alex."

She sits down next to me and Flex pushes a Bloody Mary across the table in her direction.

"You're so lucky, you know."

"Eh?"

"All this…all these people that love you."

"Love me?"

"Yes, they all *love* you, they idolise you.

"What?!"

"Yes, don't pretend you don't know, you're all so close, but you're the glue, without you they'd be lost. You have all these people around you who love you. I don't have any of this. My mates and Rupert's mates, well I don't know who my mates are any more, they seemed to have merged, they feel like they're all his. They certainly don't feel like this! All of this."

"Oh."

"I never actually even get to spend any actual time with Rupert. Not on his own anyway."

"Why not?"

"It's always with all the rugger gang, at the clubhouse, at the Fulham Tup – always there. Or else he's away travelling with work, or worse still we have to have cocktails with work colleagues. Eurgh! He is off to Brussels tomorrow!"

"But it's a Bank Holiday tomorrow."

"I know!"

"We'll probably still be here."

"Ouch! That hurts." It's an admission I know I could take advantage of. But in this spun-out state I'm not sure how to do so. I should be telling her how great she is, how lucky Rupert is, that he's a fool if he doesn't think that there aren't a million guys who would jump at the chance of being with her if he's not interested. Instead I say: "Yeah, 'Ouch', I can imagine it does hurt." Stupendously articulate.

Thing is, it actually turns out to be the best thing I could have said and as I say it so slowly it manages to sound really meaningful and as I say it Rachel clutches my thigh underneath the table, leans into me with eyes shut and plants a kiss on my lips. "I knew you would understand."

I look at her and say, "You'll just have to spend more time here with us."

"Yeah I might just do that." she says and takes large sip of her Bloody Mary.

Richard and Shannon are fawning and fondling over each other. "Stop it!" she squeals and they both look up at us looking guilty, eyebrows arched. Maybe she *does* love him I think to myself. He can be sweet and he is simply falling over himself to please her today. As she's looking at me and smiling, Dick turns away and buries his head in the crook of her neck. He slides his hand inside her jacket to squeeze her right breast. She closes her eyes.

Who am I to judge? They seem very much in love at this moment in time, kissing softly and whispering to each other, much to Star's disgust. She is sulking, looking down at the floor, picking at the label on her beer bottle and generally coming across as the sulky streetwise teenager she sometimes is.

Max and Lorraine are talking excitedly about growing up Hammersmith and mutual friends; maybe she really will be *The One*? It looks promising. I haven't seen him this happy for a long while. He looks up at me and gives me a thumbs up and a toothy grin. Lorraine kisses him on the cheek.

Flex and Lulu have been 'at the bar' for a good twenty minutes, which I assume to mean that they are in the toilets together, quite possibly taking more drugs.

And Luke and Dan well, they're just being disgusting. *Get a room...*

Flex appears from inside the bar looking flustered and flushed.

"Alright mate." He slaps me on the back, making me choke on my beer.

"Alright Flex, you look a bit out of breath, you're sweating."

"Yeah man, it's hot in there man!"

"In *where* exactly?"

"In the bar man."

"Where's Lulu?"

"Oh I left her in the toilets. She's racking up for everyone. You want one?"

"Oh so you were in the toilets with Lulu?"

"Oh fuck it! Piss off man."

"Its cool, my son!" I laugh at him as Mr Incredible gets up again and goes back inside the bar.

Shannon comes over and sits down next to me. I look over to where Gardiner was sitting and he's no longer there.

"Thank you for last night darling. I know you looked after me."

"Don't be silly."

"No, it needed to be said. You're a special friend."

"That's ok babe. I think you'd do the same for me."

"Of course I would! Of course I would."

"Not that I am planning on shitting myself anytime soon."

We both crack up and Shannon kisses me on the cheek.

"I really love you Alex. You know that? You get me. You just get me."

Gardiner appears and I am surprised to see three drinks in his hands. Shannon takes her VLS and Richard hands me a pint and holds his one up for me to Cheers. "Thanks for last night mate. Top night! And thanks for looking after Shannon. We all know she's a fackin' liability. And that's why she's mine!" he cackles and kisses her after downing a large proportion of his Stella.

Rachel is at the doorway into the bar and is crooking her finger in my direction.

"Thought you and me could do a shot at the bar, without anyone else knowing."

"Good thought."

"What do you fancy?"

"What are you having?"

"I'd like Sambucca I think."

"Two then. White though, yeah?"

"Erm, yeah."

Rachel orders.

"I can see how you love Renaissance so much now. I can see how it could be so easy to get addicted."

"It's great isn't it. I'm so glad you came. It was brave of you, I mean that lot can be pretty full on."

"I'm glad I came too. Everything was perfect. The place was beautiful and everyone was so friendly. They were all lovely to me. And it must be weird for them, a newcomer invading their gang. Tagging along with their leader."

"Oh god, not that again."

"Yes."

The Sambuccas arrive.

"So you said you might think about trying drugs sometime."

"In your dreams, Buster. Cheers, Alex. To my new special friend."

"Cheers Darling. To getting to know you better."

We down our shots and Rachel leans forward and gives me a sticky kiss. Then she turns and runs off to the toilet.

I head back outside and go and sit down with Max and Lorraine.

"What's crazy?" I ask.

"We've just found out that we used to go to the same internet café in Covent Garden."

"You're right, that is crazy," I smile at the two geeks in a pod. She may well be *The One*.

The rest of the day disappears in a pleasing haze of alcohol and cigarettes and chat. Having Rachel here seems perfect. I wish absentmindedly that it could be a permanent arrangement. Everyone seems happy. At 9pm Rachel has to leave and I know that it's to go back to Rupert. I am hurt but I draw up the protective shield of *I don't give a fuck*, and reach for a fresh pint of Stella. I'm still smiling as I know that she really does like me.

Star comes and sits down next to me and insinuates her arms in between mine and my body and hugs my arm. She yawns and shuts her eyes.

"Shall I order you a cab, Star?"

"Uh-huh. Please."

The rest of the evening is remarkable only for the fact that so many of our friends manage to make it down to the pub. Northern Dave, Flem, Don, Janey and Jade all manage to find us. It seems to be one of life's eternal mysteries as to why it's so difficult to organise a group of close friends to all be in the same place at the same time, for a spot of social interaction. But today is one of those heaven-sent days that come along so rarely that they become the stuff of legends, those rare occasions to be reminisced about when you're old and wrinkly, when they all merge somehow into one impossibly outlandishly perfect day.

WORK COLLEAGUES

Tuesday after the Bank holiday: no admonishing glances, no 'tuts', no lectures. She comes and sits at my desk and sits on a pile of my documents left there by my line manager. That's ok by me and we chat about the project and how her document is going. She asks me about a new role they've offered her as she picks at something on my shoulder. I try my hardest to engage my brain, not because I want to appear knowledgeable but because I really want to give Rachel the best possible answer. For the first time in forever I really care about something related to work.

"Well, I would think about the skills you currently have and think about what sort of skills this role would give you. Have a good think about whether they are a complimentary set of skills or whether they are just getting you to do something because you have already done it before. Be a little bit selfish and think about yourself, not about what the firm will get out of it."

"You think?"

"Yeah, of course. If the firm had their way, they'd have you doing the same thing over and over again. That way they can charge the client more for an 'expert' and keep paying you the same and yet expect you to complete the projects quicker and quicker. They rely on people just accepting that in order to make the projects more and more profitable. You need to dig your heels in a little."

"Hmm, I'm scared."

"Well don't be. I'm not saying point blank refuse things, but ask for more senior roles, or something slightly different."

"OK."

"Besides, they'll appreciate someone with a smidgeon of their own opinion who is taking responsibility for their own career development. And if that doesn't work, then threaten to tell them all the dirty secrets you know about the partners and their PAs."

She laughs out loud and then looks around to see that if no one has heard. "I really had a great time at Renaissance. Thank you for taking me."

"You're welcome."

"Everyone was so friendly and lovely, and *glamorous!* Wow."

"You said."

"But they were."

"They all loved you. You'll have to come again"

"Yeah maybe, I *did* have a great time; something different to the Sloaney Pony and the endless pints, drinking games and talk about rugger or Chamonix."

"Ah yes, rugby and skiing – riveting."

She smiles again and mouths a 'thank you' at me and then an air kiss. She gets up and turns away to go back to her desk on the other side of the project room, swivelling her hips a touch more than usual, I would say.

I smile and the fuzziness in my head is warm and friendly, not menacing. There is no acid.

DEEPER

On Thursday the 20th of May 1999, by the time the evening comes the air is still and cold. The setting is magnificent; Blenheim Palace, Oxford. The occasion is the Fortworth Consulting Annual Ball, a strictly black-tie event, full of lots of very worthy people apparently, very posh, very pretentious, and of little interest to me.

The seating plan does me no favours and I find myself sat in between Old Bore Billingham and a wannabe Mrs Old Bore Billingham, tragic she is. And two tables away but in my eyeline, is the naked back of a certain Ms Rachel Jameson. It is toned and her shoulder blades glide under her skin as she reaches for the bottle of white wine and passes the breadbasket around. Her backless black dress is simple and beautiful. It ties in a bow at the back of her neck. I am transfixed.

Old Bore tries to engage me in conversation about the project: the client's current market positioning; their marketing; their IT; the progress of the Project. My monosyllabic answers fend him off for a while, and in fact I can see that he is looking across me and down into the cleavage of the wannabe. I pour myself a large glass of white wine and take a heavy sip. Old Bore looks at me with arched eyebrows. "Oh I am sorry!" I say, as I pour a glass for him and then turn to my right to pour an equally generous glass for his voluptuous protégée.

"My dear boy, where *have* you been brought up, in a barn?" he asks as he knocks a heavy-looking, crest-embossed signet ring on the side of the smaller goblets next to the ones I have poured into. The flesh of his pinky is bulging out from all around and under the ring. "You used the wrong glasses. Leave it to the experts next time," and he beckons one of the waiters over. I excuse myself. This episode requires some emergency nose powdering. I leave Old Bore and Old Bore Mark II to chastise the waiter on his negligence at having allowed our glasses to sit empty. *Fuck this.*

The ching is good. I feel a familiar surge: renewed confidence in this unfamiliar crowd.

Two managers from the project, probably called Dom and Hugh, but let's call them Tarquin and Fuck-Face saunter into the marbled gents. I barge out past them with a loud sniff.

At my table Old Bore has helped himself to my seat and to the woman who was sitting next to me. That's ok; I don't feel like sitting down. I decide to go outside for a smoke. There are a couple of Partners outside puffing on fat Cubans, so I decide to turn the other way and walk round the building.

As I pass the rear of the building, two chefs stand leaning backs-up against the red bricks both smoking in silence. I walk past the open doorway of the lights, sounds and smells of the kitchen. Smells fishy, looks smoky and the lights are fluorescent.

I get a text. **Where are you? X** it says

Outside smoking. I was about to glass Old Bore. Come out, it's a beautiful night. I reply.

There isn't a reply. I put the cigarette out and light another as I carry on walking. Blenheim Palace is stunning, even though I'm not a great one for admiring old architecture. I hate stately homes but even the guts and pipes and innards that are round the back here have character. Soon I am rounding the side of the building, the walls are lit up by white and purple floodlights hiding in the low bushes, the lawn is shaved close and neat, the hedgerows are tended and shaped like they were poured out of a plaster caste and the gravel on the pathway is arranged as if by hand, not a single stone crossing its boundary. I think about kicking some of them onto the lawn, but I think about the work that's gone into the path. I think of the sort of person who has had to do that. Not someone like Billingham that's for sure. I round the corner of the building that will lead me back to the two puffing partners when a strong yet elegant hand presses against my shoulder. I look up from my examination of the neat and obedient gravel and see that it is Rachel's hand. She reaches down for my cigarette stroking my hand and fingers as she does so.

"Were you going to have this without me?" she asks.

"I thought you weren't going to come out." As I say this, she drops the nearly spent cigarette on the gravel between us and rolls her high-heeled foot over it. The cocaine in my head is whirling as Rachel leans forward and kisses me softly yet firmly on the lips.

"I just came out to tell you..." she says. I go to kiss her, she pulls away, "...that you should really come back inside." She turns and swivels away from me as I reach out for her arm.

I let her go for thirty seconds or so and then follow her back inside. I take up Old Bore' seat. He is still sat in mine and he doesn't even notice me. He's practically *wearing* the wannabe. I force a mouthful or two of pan-fried salmon with rocket and parmesan salad into my mouth and swallow it almost without chewing. I then push a few leaves around in the dressing and cut up the remaining salmon as if I am going to eat it. I am practiced in the art of appetite deception. Many Christmas meals and similar family gatherings have seen the same cunning tactics, especially when they have followed especially huge nights out on the amphetamines. What must my mother have thought? No wonder she felt disrespected at the big meals which usually marked a major event in our family; neither of her offspring ever ate any of her food.

In my new seat I am at a diagonal angle to Rachel at her table. She is talking animatedly to her Team Leader, a very attractive tall slim woman with short dark hair called Simone Grace. I look again at Rachel's back. She lifts her arm from her right side to rest it on the table and her dress moves away from her body. I down another glass of the Chablis and head for the gents again. There's a wait for the cubicles and I want something to do. I fish my phone out of my breast pocket.

What room number are you? I text out to her. Then I delete it. I start texting again trying to think of another way to put it, something less crass, less forward.

The first cubicle becomes free but some red-nosed old boy is hopping up and down so I let him in first.

You look

Then I delete that.

I want to

I can't say that.

The second cubicle becomes free. It stinks but I jump in anyway. I put the phone away and swap it for the wrap, a card and a note.

In a well-practiced routine I wipe the stainless steel of the loo-roll holder; insert the corner of my company credit card into the ching; tip out a little pile; line it up; re-roll my note; get ready to flush the chain and position myself above the line. I flush the toilet as I hoover the ching up with a strong, swift sniff, inaudible under the noisy gargle of the flush. I feel the buzz, the numbness, the soaring flying feeling and the euphoria; the utter confidence. I put the powder kit back into my pocket and feel for the cold case of the phone. I text out the same message I started off with. Then I shorten it just to

Room number...

Mercifully, they are clearing the dinner plates away when I re-enter the dinner hall. Rachel spots me emerging from the toilets and looks up in my direction. She shakes her head although she is smiling, eyebrow raised. I sit down again at my table and the sliding lemon sorbet soothes my cigarette-sore throat. I buzz pleasantly through the dire after-dinner speeches. Rachel doesn't turn around the whole way through. I don't mind though because I get to stare at her beautiful back. Old Bore makes a stupendously pompous speech about how great and magnificent the firm is. Anyone would think we were Amnesty International, Cancer Research and Mother Theresa rolled into one. *Cunning. Cunning stunt that, Old Bore. Maybe one day I'll be like you. But hopefully I won't.* I think he's staring right at me when he says "And we've certainly got some interesting characters with great potential working on the project now," but he's probably still staring at the breasts of the wannabe he's been gurgling away to all night sitting two seats to my left.

He announces dancing and a cheesy cover band loudly strikes up "Oh What A Night" by Frankie Valli and the Four Seasons. Then comes "Brown Eyed Girl" by Van Morrison, then the one about driving a Chevvy to a levy, which everyone bawls along to, followed by a truly appalling medley of Michael Jackson's "Beat It", Bryan Adams' "The Summer of '69", and most excruciating of all Bon Jovi's "You Give Love a Bad Name," to which all these overweight business men and women in bad evening-wear screech along and thrash at air guitars. I wonder how I got here. And I wonder how I can get out. Another line should help. As I decide to go to the gents again I see Old Bore grab Rachel and drag her onto the dance floor. She stares at me wide-eyed as I skirt the dance floor en route to the toilets. The gents are empty so I decide to set up camp in one of the cubicles for a while. I get the ching out and spark up a cigarette. I do a couple of lines, smoke another cigarette. I pull the toilet seat down and sit with my feet up on it and listen to bad music coming muffled and dull through the cold tiles, which numb my throbbing temple. Their repertoire takes some beating, Hot Chocolate, UB40, Huey Lewis, Chic, Toto, Spandau Ballet and the most bizarre of all, (considering the lead singer is a straight-looking, big fat white man), Donna Summer. There's a brief interlude and then the music starts up again although it sounds like it's definitely a DJ now, so we are at least spared the cover band. Blur, then Pulp, then Supergrass and the Verve. Christ, the DJ has really bought the whole BritPop collection, maybe NOW Cool Britannia? *Very* on-message. *Things, can only get better,* indeed.

When I come out, Rachel is nowhere to be seen. I stand leaning against a pillar staring vacantly into the mess of the dance floor. Drunk and overweight middle-aged people in tuxes thrash around like hippos in a shallow mud-pool. It shouldn't ever happen. It's a horrible scene but I am quite high now so I don't much care. I feel superb and this corporate bollocks can't touch me now.

"It's room number seven."
"Eh?"
"For reference, for later."
I smile and look around. But she's gone.

I go to the bar and order a vodka and tonic. It takes the bitter after taste of the coke away and tastes divine. I suck the lime.

I see Rachel with Simone Grace sat on high stools at the far end of the bar. They're doing shots, giggling very loudly with four men standing behind them. One of them has his arm around Rachel's neck and I want to go down there and brain the lot of them. I see myself mashing their heads against the black marble of the bar. I visualise blood and brains and mush and stuff, yellow and red, leaking and mixing and swimming over the polished surface easily in oily pools.

I hold my head and decide to go back to the hotel. In the taxi I try to remember her room number. The car pulls up to a shabby Marriott. The junior Consultants and Associates had been assigned to the Marriott Inn, which amounted to no more than a roadside motel, I had expected more of Fortworth's.

In the room I undo my tie and slump onto the bed, turning on the telly. There's nothing on. I do a line. Lie back. Stare at the ceiling. I go out onto the balcony for a cigarette. I look over the balcony ledge and look out onto the blackness of the field below. Occasionally cars and freight rush by.

Some time passes.

The dark shapes of the petrol station and services loom large and menacing and sitting like silent empty shells, waiting once more for the day to come, bringing flocks of transitory people. Grannies will buy sweets to suck on, couples will buy a baguette for the road, families will be drawn like flies to shit to otherwise unappealing offers of "Family meal for £9.99, only!"

It's half-past two.

Was it seven or twenty-seven?

'It's room number seven, of course, perfect. I order a bottle of Champagne from room service, more for the ice than anything else, and take it with me.

I don't stop to think why I am doing this.

My heart is beating hard in my chest as I pick up the bucket and stride out into the corridor. Where *is* room number seven? I clang the bucket against the corner of the wall as I turn the corner from number nine. Fuck! All I need now is for Old Bore to stumble out of Wannabe's room.

I place the bucket as gently as I can on the floor outside room number seven and take an ice cube and run it over my chest. What am I doing? I am overheating and the ice begins to melt straight away. Tiny chilled rivers trace their way down my skin. I am shocked at how nervous I am. *Chill, Alex.*

I knock three times lightly, no reply. I push the door and it gives slightly. I pick up the bucket with my right hand and with my left I push the door open. There's no one in the room. I look beyond and see the curtains moving in the summer night's breeze. A silhouette.

I take another ice cube in my hand and walk through the room towards the balcony. She doesn't move as I step out onto the balcony. I hold the ice cube a millimetre away from her skin just above the nape of her neck. An icy drop runs down her neck, down the vertebrae of her spine. She shivers but doesn't turn.

"I'm glad you came. I was starting to think you might not."

I pull her around to face me. Her breath is hot on my cheek now. In silence, impossibly close, a deafening silence filled with the sound of a million thoughts rushing through us, between us, of unspoken sentiments, of the sudden realisation of what was about to happen and the consequences it would bring for us. Our lips meet in a soft, tentative kiss. It's as if neither of us had kissed nor been kissed before. We had spoken of perfect moments and this one had the sharpness and purity of a diamond. Neither of us would ever forget it. The quiet of that fleeting moment on her balcony is exploded by the frenzy that follows; the absolute joy of discovery. Everything feels so natural and that shocks me.

At 4am, exhausted, we finally sleep. Three hours later, the sun leaking through the cheap motel blinds, I wake to find her beautiful back facing me. I pull the cover away. I run my hands over her shoulder blade. Very slowly and lightly and with only two fingers I follow her side down into her waist. I trace over her right hip and back round following the line of her body until my two fingers are lightly pressing in between her thighs from behind. She moves in her sleep. Her breathing is shallow, then deep. She moves against me and clenches her thighs around my hand, shuddering gently. We sleep again for a little while, spooning, with me behind her.

At nine we both wake. She needs shampoo. I go across the road in the cooling drizzle to the shop to get it for her. When I get back, she's in the shower so I get in the shower with her and wash her, kiss her. She gets out of the shower, pulls back the curtain, kneels in front of me and takes me in her mouth. The warm water cascades down over my body and gently she makes me come.

STAR CROSSED LOVERS

t had started off as an innocent offer: "We're going to this play, well *show,* next Saturday - d'you want to come?" I'd asked in all innocence.

"We?"

"Oh you know: me, Max and maybe some of the girls."

"I don't know what I'm doing yet."

"OK. Well let me know – it's 'La Furia de Baus' at the Roundhouse – it's supposed to be amazing. Totally mad. You go and you're part of the show. Everyone gets really wet and these dancers fly about on trapezes above the crowd."

"Oh yeah, I've seen the posters on the tube – I'll have a think and let you know."

I told her that there would be a gang of us to make her feel relaxed, but I had only ever had two tickets. And I would have given them away if she had said no; and now having a drink before the show in The Queen across the road, I feel impossibly happy.

"Alex! Don't forget to get the orange peel burnt. It makes all the difference!" Cosmopolitans. I bring the drinks over and sit next to her. Unthinking, we kiss softly and briefly. To anyone else we're just another couple having a drink in a bar. Nothing remarkable about that. Except when you consider that we aren't - aren't a couple, that is – not officially anyway. We are trying it on. And for tonight at least, it fits. I dare not look any further ahead into the future. An hour or so later we're in the thick of the show. Wet, wide-eyed and dancing.

We're pressed against each other in the darkness, sounds hitting our ears from every direction. Coloured lights and figures dance overhead. I squeeze her hand in anticipation. A hissing sound begins to make itself heard over all the others and a breeze begins to blow across the crowd of people within this fantastic theatre space. A fine mist of cold water covers my skin as slow, rhythmic music begins to play, muted drums and a faraway bass. I turn to her, her face now also glistening with the moisture in the air, my face partially lit by one of the lights. Strands of hair are wetted onto my face here and there, my eyelashes feel heavy with water. The skin on her bare shoulders is covered in goose bumps and she shivers visibly. The next moment we are kissing. We had kissed before in Oxford but this is different. Loaded with the atmosphere and thrill of the show, our senses are heightened. Mouths wide, arms wrapped tightly around each other, oblivious to the bustle and push of the crowd around us, the kiss lasts an age. It isn't the kind of kiss that serves as a precursor to sex. It's not a tender kiss, like the first one we ever had. It's a definite, strong, public kiss. It's a kiss of ownership, a claim on each other.

The crowd surges and we lose each other. The spotlight encircles me and I look up. I am blinded for a second then I see her hands reaching out, her eyebrows raised, a look of panic, then a look of reassurance as the crowd presses us together so that our bodies are in full contact, head to toe. A small girl, one of the cast, slithers past Rachel then she passes me and she puts something in my mouth, a small plastic object and grabs the other end of it with her teeth, she moves her lips forward along the thing until her lips touch mine, her wild eyes staring. It's all part of the show, the cast are in amongst the crowd dancing with the audience, kissing us, pulling at our clothes. She leaves me and jumps up at Rachel and plants a kiss firmly on her lips.

Our secret world had now extended only a little to include a theatre and a pub in a corner of our own Millennium London.

* * *

At the weekend Stella Artois are putting on films on Clapham Common. Erecting huge sixty foot screens they are showing a film each night over the weekend. On Saturday it's Romeo & Juliet, the new Baz Luhrman version that came out a couple of years ago. It's not a Renaissance Saturday so this seems a good second option. And so Rachel and me are all set to go, when on Thursday evening Rupert announces he wants to go.

"Are you fucking sure?! Does Rupert even know who Shakespeare is?"

"Yes of course he does, don't be like that."

"What? Since when does he care about romance?"

"I'll have to go with him. Are you going to still come?"

"We'll see," I lie.

So there I am, sat in the middle of Clapham Common, watching the film, whilst Rachel and The Rugger Crew are out there somewhere.

A light flashes in my hand. I look down, leaning away from the rest of the group and pull my phone into view.

"1 Message Received"

<Click>

"Rachel Mobi"

<Open>

"Hello 'star crossed lover'"

I raise my head and glance around the huddled darkness of Clapham Common. Hundreds of faces reflected the flickering lights from the huge screen in front of them. Some talking, some laughing, some apparently enthralled by the film on view. I scan the crowd. The cinematic star-crossed-lovers playing out their scene on the screen while my group versus her gang sit apart, lost amongst this sea of people like the 'two houses alike in dignity'. Our dreamy fantasy world was now clashing horribly with reality.

The film plays on. Just knowing she was there, close, somewhere, filled me with emotions I struggled to recognise or name. Rupert and his friends sitting around her. I accept pulls on the smoke as it comes around, Flex's big face in mine: "Go on ma sann!", smile when someone makes a joke but I'm not really listening, I answer robotically, "Thanks".

I wonder where Rachel is. I wonder if she is looking for me too.

Meanwhile Leo and Claire Danes are clinging onto each other, kissing fervently, looking into each other's eyes with anticipation. An illegal, unknown and potentially dangerous relationship.

I look from the screen to my phone. The air barely holds the warmth of the day as the peaty earth of Clapham Common gives out its last heat. It's getting cold. I pull my coat round my body.

Beep! Beep!
1 Message received
<Click>
"Rachel Mobi"
<Open>
"Where r u?"
I smile and reply: **"Meet me by the entrance."**
I leap to my feet. Shannon pulls at my trouser leg as I stand. She looks up at me, and raises her eyebrows. "Are you going to find Rachel?"

"Yep." I say. I look back down at Shannon and notice Richard smiling up at me nodding like a fucking toy dog. I want to kick him in the face as he pulls Shannon's hand away and forcefully puts it in his lap. Smiling at me as he rubs Shannon's hand on his crotch. Dickhead.

The only light guiding me towards the entrance is the one coming from the screen now behind me and it plays tricks on my eyes. Focusing on the massive inflatable can of Stella that I know is by the entrance and I battle through, getting the occasional heckle from the inebriated crowd. As I come into a clearing I walk straight into another person heading for the same goal.

"Sorry I..."

"Hello Ms. Jameson, fancy bumping into you here."

"Hello Mr. Greene."

We stand innocently at first, just talking. We could be two friends who have just come across each other by pure chance, catching up on news.

"Are you enjoying the film, Alex?"

"It's great. Love the soundtrack. You?"

"I love it. Who are you here with?"

"The usual. Shannon and Richard. Max and Lorraine, they're still together, Flex and Lulu, Luke and Dan. Flex is drunk. He doesn't really get it. He only perks up at the guns," I say. Rachel laughs.

Taking her hand in mine we stride purposefully away from the crowd. We're maybe less than a hundred metres from my front door. No-one will notice we're gone.

We leave work at 5pm sharp the following Friday. The air is heavy and warm, the sky bleached and hazy as we head back to Clapham on the Northern Line. I want to take her to Alba, an excellent, shabby little pizzeria in Clapham North. It's a bit of a local secret, it's on a little road just behind the tube station and doesn't look like much from the outside, but the smell just draws you in, the welcoming lights, warmth and comfort of Alba and its fried garlic aromas and sounds of opening bottles and clinking glasses.

By 6pm we're sat facing each other grinning like sixteen year olds.

"It's brilliant." she says.

I smile at her.

We eat garlic bread topped with fresh tomatoes and sweet basil and olives covered in Alba's secret dressing. Then I have a *Quattro Stagioni*, she has a *Giardiniera*, we drank a bottle of red each and then we go home and have beautiful drunk and fumbling sex.

I wonder what she will tell Rupert. I guess he must be away.

The heady rush and passion of a new relationship carries me through the daze of the days now. I live in a parallel world inhabited by only Rachel and myself. It's a fragile little world. I know it will be this way and I don't mind.

We see each other every day at work and usually once or twice over the weekend. Sunday afternoons become ours. We lunch at mine; I treat her to one of my random creations. Perhaps fried salmon and garlic potatoes. Then we go for a walk on the Common. We talk about work, our families; our fears and plans. We go for a drink in The Sun in the evening. And we always end up back at mine in bed.

I wonder sometimes what she tells Rupert. I guess he must be away.

Work is little more than an annoyance now; I am going through the motions, merely turning up, to see Rachel.

On Tuesday Rachel asks me, "Are you organising the team dinner next week, Alex?"

"Yep. We're going to this new portuguese-moroccan fusion place and then onto a bar in Piccadilly," Old Bore had found a use for me on the Project. Social Secretary. Talk about utilising my potential.

"Sounds fab. Do you think I could crash at yours for the night? It's just that, well... getting back to Richmond at that time on a Wednesday, will be a total ni..."

"Yeah, of course!" I cut in. "No worries. Absolutely. That'll be fine. Fine. Yeah. Seriously."

Then I think about it. "But it's a Wednesday. We've not done midweek before. What about Rupert?"

"Erm, I think he's away all week. I'll check."

So we suffer another insufferable, drunken and tedious night out with our work colleagues from the client Project, our minds only focusing on getting back to mine as soon as possible and pushing everything further, deeper.

I go to the bathroom, then the kitchen to fetch her glass of water. A gut-sickening thought hits me that I will only ever be 'the other man'. When I come back into the room she is sat cross-legged on the futon drunkenly fiddling with her pyjama top-buttons.

"Here you are. Have some Nurofen as well. You seem to be having a problem with your pyjama top there."

"Oh I can't get it to do up. I can't be bothered."

I'm looking down at her, smiling. I kneel down next to her on the hard mattress. Her puffy lips meet mine.

As we are lying in bed the sun seeps in from behind the blinds. I have a naïve feeling that it will always be sunny in our relationship. Rachel reminds me that we have to go to work as I slip my hand in between her thighs. "Don't you want to do *any*thing else?" Rachel asks me, pulling my hand away. I say no.

We get up. I hand Rachel various pieces of clothing, some hers, some mine, as we dress together in near silence. Both smiling, we drink, gulping at water and juice. We are late. Breakfast will be at work. Rachel will get Maccas. The two of us leave my house, unsteady on our feet, stumbling, eyes glazed and squinting at the morning sun. Letting out the occasional conspiratorial giggle, we cross the road, not considering the oncoming traffic. Fast, the horn brings us back to our senses momentarily and holding onto each other's arms we run the remainder of the way and onto the grass of the Common. It's the type of morning that July is proud of: a warm light breeze, at body temperature, so that it doesn't feel like a breeze at all but more like a gentle current of water across the skin. A pale, early sun is rising slowly but with the promise of a loud, bright day to come. We walk along in a companionable silence broken only when one of us turns, looks at the other and laughs. Still drunk on champagne, passion and the delicious secret we now share, we know the hangover will come sometime in the future, but we choose to savour this tipsy time rather than simply waiting for the sobering storm to gather and shed its disapproving rain.

I sit in my meeting, not concentrating on the Agenda or on what anyone is saying. I'm thinking about the events of last night, and the last few weeks and of those at the ball in Oxford.

It's been three months I realize but it has felt like three days. I smile. People are looking at me across the room curiously.

* * *

When she agrees to finally do it we're at Max's birthday party at his flat in Southwark. "How do you do them?" asks Rachel.

"What do you mean? You just put them in your mouth and swallow. Trust me. You'll be fine. I'll break it for you, then you get ready with your drink because it'll taste really bitter on your tongue."

"Alex, I'm nervous."

"Don't worry, these are really nice Doves. They'll be lovely, and we're only doing halves."

I take the pill out of the bag, search for the break-indentation with my fingers, place it carefully in between my teeth and bite firmly down. Half a dove falls onto my tongue and I flip it down my throat and swallow; the other half, I let fall into my right hand and manoeuvring it in between my thumb and index finger I raise it to Rachel's lips. She opens, I place it on her tongue and she quickly takes a huge gulp of her G&T to wash it down. Scrunching up that beautiful crinkly her nose in disgust. "Uuuurgh! That tasted disgusting Alex!"

"That's generally a good sign! Let's go!"

I know it will be a while till we come up so we get back to the party. Rachel makes a phone call. I assume it's to Rupert.

I'm talking to Max and Flex about Chelsea's prospects next season and Flex doesn't really care, so long as we win and we don't wear any ugly away strips. We are on Southampton's ugly away strip and Southampton's general ugliness as a team, when Rachel touches my arm. The second she does, I start to feel a familiar tingling sensation in my fingertips and toes.

"Alex, I love it!"

"Yeah?"

"Yeah. I feel great! I want to dance."

Rachel is smiling at everyone as we move through Max's flat and onto the 'dance-floor' – his front room. She keeps grabbing me as we move. We dance close and kiss often.

There is something magical about seeing someone doing (and enjoying) his or her first pill. It's a big responsibility, but it's one of young modern life's real joys, and it probably only belongs to our generation. I remember my first pill and how I felt and now I think I can see the same pictures appearing on Rachel's face tonight nine years later.

"Alex I feel really touchy-feely, do you mind if I touch you?" Rachel asks, although she already is touching me all over. "Can we stop dancing for a while?"

"Sure, let's go to Max's bedroom for a second, and cool down. I'll get you a water." We stop off at the kitchen, picking up a tumbler and filling it from the tap. Rachel smiles at everyone she meets in the kitchen. She is pouring sweat. Her glossy brown hair is wetted black on her head. People are smiling at her. In the room, she strips her top off, her chest rising and falling swiftly, the sheen of sweat catching dim light coming through the open window from the street lamp outside. It's July and the still air in the room is warm.

"Alex, take your shirt off. Let's do skin on skin, like the first time."

We sit on Max's bed facing each other. Rachel is licking my lips, her hands stroking me all over. She stands up on the bed and peels down her trousers, she lies down on me. Her eyes are watery and glazed, the pupils massive as she looks at me. We fuck fast without changing position. We are both panting, hearts pounding with the chemicals. Sweat pouring off of both of us. She comes, gasping, biting my ear; little tears running silently down the sides of her face.

A minute passes without a word. Then, "Are you ok? I feel great. Should we do the other half?" she asks, glowing in the dark.

That day should be the key to unlocking the rest of her heart, the part that she hides from me and the part that she hides from herself. The honest part she is afraid of. Instead it is the beginning of the end.

* * *

It's a warm early August evening boasting a fabulous pale blue light and crisp sky. Star and Shannon are over at mine. Shannon put in an order to Star and came round to mine with the drugs and our favourite new dealer. Shannon looks beautiful and is lounging in my warm front room on the old red sofa smoking. She's wearing light linen wrap-around trousers and a low cut white singlet. Star lies on the floor with her head resting on Shannon's leg. She is doodling in some sketchbook she carries around with her.

I call Rachel, but there's no answer. I text her: **"Evening Ms Jameson. Fancy a drink in Clapham? Maybe The Sun for a change? ;) x"**

No answer. So I rack up a cheeky couple of lines.

Rules Of Attraction is on the TV, and we're watching some of the 'making-of' section. The director, Roger Avary, is discussing the difficulties encountered in shooting the split-screen sequence when Sean Bateman and Lauren Hynde meet for the first time. Star is now sitting in front of the screen explaining that when she grows up she will be a film director and that she doesn't see why it was so difficult, and that Roger Avary can't be a very good director if he found that difficult and that she won't have any difficulty 'executing such sequences' (which are unbelievably her words), when she becomes a Director.

Shannon is lying on the sofa now, with her legs on my lap. She's smiling at me as Star gibbers on as she's doodling. We are both drinking vodka and tonics.

Star announces that she is starving so we down our drinks and head out. It's a beautiful evening, still light at half-past eight. Small groups of people are still sitting out on the Common. On blankets and sheets cheese, bread, olives and bottles of wine and six packs of beer are strewn. The more athletic Clapham-ites are playing Frisbee. A pair of boys, one in Chelsea the other in Arsenal are booting a ball between themselves. I walk through the Common content with two beautiful women by my side, another in my mind.

The walk down Clapham High Street is as eventful as ever. We witness the dregs of a fight outside the new, hideously re-furbished SW4 Bar, all puffed out threats of recriminations and stabbing, jabbing fingers; then two shambling drunks start shouting at each other from either side of the street arguing over whose turn it is to get the next four-pack of Special Brew.

"Get the cans in!"

"Yous a' fucken are gettin' 'em."

"You fuckin' get tham, ye cun'!"

"I got that last lot! Don't you cun' me, ye cun'!"

Shannon and Star get wolf-whistled at from out of the window of a passing throbbing Impreza pounding out Black-Eyed Peas so that the whole of Sahf Landon can listen; the pavement throbs; the windows are black, the bodywork gleaming white, the rims oh the rims are blinging, bwoy. The lights turn green and they're away with a screech and cloud of rubbery smoke. We have to negotiate the queues at the cash-points snaking out across the pavement; the gang of finger-licking track-suits outside the KFC; the girls with scraped back hair and gold earrings, the boys showing pants and limps; the queens lounging outside the Kasbah "Give me a hug you beast!" one of them shouts in my direction. I smile and blow the Muscle-Mary in a skin-tight black t-shirt and black PVC trousers a kiss. Shannon pinches my arse as we shimmy away to loud booing and jeering from the drunken queens. We cross the road and cut through Lend Terrace to get to Bedford Road. Shannon and Star disappear into the shop next door to Alba and get some fags and I am dispatched to get a table.

I smell her before I see her again. Amazing how strong her perfume is. It has even over-ridden the beautiful smell of fried garlic. This time it serves as a warning for me. It's a stop sign, an alarm bell and a speed-hump all in one, slowing my speed and calming my traffic. Rachel is here. Rachel. Is. Here. With. Rupert. *Rachel is here with Rupert.* She's brought *him* to *my* place?! I feel sick. On the spot I feel like I am going to throw up. She doesn't see me but I see them. I see them. Holding hands across the table, laughing. He pours her a glass of wine. She smiles. They toast each other. He leans across the table like a big stupid oaf and kisses her on the lips and brings his big stupid hand round to cradle her beautiful head.

Then a small but strong hand is pulling me backwards away and I'm falling down the stairs of the terrace at Alba. It's Star. Shannon is still looking in the window. But she comes now.

"Did you see her finger?" she's screeching.

"No," I say.

"A rock this big!" And she holds her thumb a considerable distance away from her forefinger.

I feel sick. I just want to go home and take a lot of drugs. Star makes us stop at KFC, saying she is starving. I make her a deal that we can do that if she sells me another couple of grammes. She agrees. We have a deal. I stop at the Odd-Bins and pick up another bottle of Stoli and a bottle of Schweppes' Indian Tonic Water. I stop at the Costcutter and get a few limes and a bag of ice.

Inside I rip the mirror straight off the wall in the living room and rack up two huge lines.

"Fucking bitch!"

"Alex, darling. Calm down. You don't really like her that much do you?"

"That's not the point! She never told me they were getting engaged."

I hoover my line up quickly and offer the note sniffing and blinking to Shannon.

"*Fuck!* Star."

"Is it ever not?! Chief." Star sucks her teeth at me and puts the DVD back on and starts watching the film and hunkers down over her Family Feast with coleslaw and beans.

I make a couple of stiff vodka and tonics in the kitchen. I come back into the front room carrying the two drinks. Shannon is kneeling by the table smiling up at me and proffering the tightly coiled note. I look straight down her cleavage. I put the glasses down on the table and suck up my line. And then grab Shannon and kiss her on the mouth. She looks up at me startled but doesn't say anything and just does her line.

Star tuts in front of the telly and I'm not sure if it's Roger Avary that's the cause of her disapproval again or that she's seen our reflection in the TV screen and she's tutting at us.

Shannon gets up as I slump down on the old red sofa. I look at her as she walks out of the living room. She looks over her shoulder and smiles. Star looks over her shoulder. She smiles at me with greasy lips. She raises her eyebrows to ask me if I'm all right and whether I want any KFC all in one go. I nod yes and then shake my head no, to answer both questions respectively.

I haul myself to my feet and walk out of the room to find Shannon in the bathroom applying lipstick and fiddling with her hair. She sees me in the doorway and smiles. She mouths "OK?" I nod. I come up behind her and put my arms round her waist. When she's stopped applying lipstick Shannon spins around within my arms. She kisses me softly on the lips like she is blotting her lipstick.

"You look great with that on, look," and she moves her head out of the way to let me see myself in the mirror. I look at my shiny lips.

"Shall we go out?" she says.

"Yeah, fuck it." I say. I kiss her again, our lips resting against each other. I open my eyes to stare at her.

"Alex…stop," she whispers.

I back away and sit on the side of the bath. Shannon returns to fixing her face in the mirror.

"You two gonna mess around in the da bafroom all night or come and watch the film?"

"We're going out, gorgeous! Get ready!" Shannon sings. The doorbell rings and in walk Luke, Dan and Flex.

We stumble down Clapham High Street, trying to hail a cab, and here we go again. The Sahf Landan rude bwoys are lairing fly-girls outside KFC; the crop-headed queens skipping arm in arm in ribbed black lycra to the Kazbar, there's a tiara-ed hen night congo-ing in and out of La Rueda. The lead Hen grabs Flex and makes him join the conga. Then she makes him snog each and everyone of the party. We finally get a cab to stop for us outside KFC.

Everyone else is already at the Dust Bar when we get there. I deposit Shannon on the dance floor and then head downstairs to the toilet straight away where I find Max, Lorraine, Flex, Lulu, Luke and Dan racking up the Charlie and sit down next to them at the table. I am dragged away from my fug by Max shoving his pocket mirror and a tightly rolled twenty under my nose. We do a fat line each and hug and have a team huddle which doesn't say anything apart from, "Aaargh!.. Ave…it!…Let's do it!…Wicked Ching…Raaa!..Waaaaahhheeeey!… Come on!" And we bolt back upstairs to the dance floor.

Shannon is spinning around. She swoops by and grabs me by the hand and drags me after her. She pulls me close and we dance face-to-face doing a mock tango across the lager-soaked floorboards of the Dust Bar. She runs her hands over my shoulders, down my spine and she lets her hands rest on my arse. I look into her eyes and smile; they smile back, and realising what they have done, spin away from me, still holding onto my hand. I pull her back close. I reach into the glass of VLS standing on the table next to us and pull out a handful of ice. Holding her tightly from behind, I slide my right hand down the front of her top, inside her bra, and press her left breast with the ice in my palm. I spin her around. We both lean forward and our lips meet in a wet and drunken kiss, cut short after a half second by Lulu grabbing Shannon's arm and pulling her away. I lick my lips as she is pulled away. They taste sweet and the taste makes my head spin. And she's off again, whirling round the dance-floor of the Dust Bar.

In the taxi back to mine, Flex is holding forth on how great it is to be young, good looking and free. "You see, where I get the birds is that

I'm tri-lingual. I can speak English and Croydon. That is how I get all my birds. You have to be multilingual and sensitive in this day and age."

Richard Gardiner pulls up outside my house at 4am, looking for Shannon. He's drunk and I have to shout out the window at him to get him to stop honking his fucking horn. He refuses to come inside and so eventually Shannon has to go outside to talk to him. She comes back in about five minutes later mascara bleeding down her cheeks, picks up her coat, says sorry to everyone and leaves again, slamming the door behind her. I can hear them shouting at each other as she walks towards the car, then the car door slams and Dick Gardiner pulls away with an obligatory screech of his BMW. After that the party dies and everyone leaves abruptly within 10 minutes.

As soon as they go, I dive into bed. After an hour of restless twitching, I realise I can't sleep. My head is pounding. Images of Rachel sitting across from Rupert flash and pop in front of my eyes. I feel sick with betrayal. I see Dick Gardiner punching Shannon in the ribs and I flinch. I imagine kissing Shannon in my bathroom. We fuck staring into each others eyes. I get up and go to the fridge. I get out a can of Stella. I shotgun it and go to the medicine cabinet; pop out two Nurofen and swallow those. I climb back into bed and collapse.

I am dreaming of a fire alarm when I wake up and realise that it's the doorbell. I stumble to the intercom, pick up the receiver and smack myself in the temple with it, momentarily losing track of the exact contours of my own head. 'Hmmmn….this…could be…problematic'. I go to say 'Hello', but nothing comes out. I'm dribbling, but my mouth is dry. My head is pounding.

"Hello! Alex?!" Beams the receiver cheerily and loudly. I move the handset sharply away from my ear and accidentally smack the back of my hand against the wall. I drop the handset out of pain and then realise that she has carried on talking: "…and so I thought, well I might as well, so I did". I kneel down gingerly so that I am level with the dangling receiver again. "Shall I come in? I've, brought you something round. Thought you might have a sore head this morning."

I swallow hard and try to wet my mouth with some saliva, before answering. There's a mug of tea left on the windowsill. I grab it and gag as it hits my throat, cold and tasting of ash a fag butt hits my lips.

"No, errrm, hi Rachel. ... how are you?"

"Jesus!!! You sound awful! You sound like you've been up all night and smoked twenty fags!"

"Hmmnn...maybe. Listen, give me two minutes. Just got to pop into the shower. OK.?"

"Well, just let me in at least Alex. It's pouring with rain out here!"

"Is it? Oh sorry. Come on in then." I press the button, which releases the door and wait. I am leaning against the wall when she arrives at the doorway.

"Errrm. Hello. You look...well."

Rachel bounds in and envelops me in a huge hug.

"Look, I'm sorry about the state I'm in. I must look awful."

"You look OK. I thought you'd look worse."

"Oh, it was a quiet night in the end. Just give me a sec and I'll nip into the shower and freshen up. I'll put the kettle on for you, do you want a cup?"

"Yes please. *I'll* put the kettle on. *You* get in the shower."

I start the shower, close the bathroom door and get in. I am shaking I realise. I am raging. How fucking dare she? Then I feel myself heat up and realise that its shame, shame and embarrassment. How could I be so fucking naïve? I want to be sick. The heat of the shower is doing me favours at all so I get out and open the window to try to cool down. I run the cold tap and brush my teeth. I look in the mirror and my face is blotchy red. I tie my towel round my waist and still dripping head back into the front room. She's not there. I turn into the bedroom and see her lying on the bed on her side, propped up on her elbow smiling.

I clamber on to the bed, still very unsteady. My head is still pounding.

"You're still wet. Do you want me to dry you off? You'll catch a cold."

"No thanks."

She leans over me, smiles and kisses me. She yanks at the knot at the front of my towel and works her hand in down to my crotch.

No. I'm going to be too tired to…" Rachel ignores me and carries on touching me, "I think that'll do fine," she smiles at me as I manage to obtain something approximating an erection.

"I…need to ask you…"

"What is it, Alex?"

"Well, what does *this* mean?" I'm asking like a fool.

"Hey?" she strokes my head.

"*This. Us*," I shrug.

She sighs.

"I saw you."

"When?"

"Last night. Alba. With Rupert."

Silence.

"Alex. He's still my boyfriend. But we're…"

"I saw the ring," I say.

"What ring? What are you talking about?"

"The ring. A ring."

"Alex, this is ridiculous. I don't have a ring." She holds her hand up.

"Why aren't you wearing it today? Shannon said she was it on your finger."

"Oh *Shannon* said. I thought you said *you* saw it."

"Star dragged me away before I could. We were going to have dinner in Alba."

"So you *didn't* see me wearing *any* ring."

"I wouldn't have taken you there if I knew you would take Rupert there."

"Alex, you're being childish. I don't know what Shannon is talking about." And before I can continue, she is kissing me on the forehead, telling me not to worry and I'm lying back, my head deep in the pillow, well on to the way to sleep.

When I wake up later on Rachel is gone. There's a note:

"Hello Sleeping beauty, I had to go. Sorry. You get some more sleep young man! Call you in the week. R x"

At noon and I realise I'm starving so I head down to Northcote Road market to pick up some munchies. I reach the bread stall in the market contemplating a brie and salami baguette or a ham and cheese croissant to fill my churning stomach when I spot the Oakley shades perched atop his head about four stalls down. He hasn't seen me yet. They're at a stall selling huge candles and huge candle-holders. He looks happy, relaxed, beige, very beige. Beige chinos, British racing green Polo shirt. I think I might vomit. No, actually he makes me want to go up and grab his fucking-Oakleys and scream to him. "Put them on! Put them on, or put them away. Just do not perch them on your fucking head like it's OK. Because it's not! It's offensive and you look like a dick. I mean, do you have eyes in the top of your head?! No! Didn't think so!" Maybe they're still on his head from January from when he was in Chamonix and he hasn't taken them off. Or was it Meribel this year? Oh I don't know, somewhere in Les Trois-*fucking*-Vallées at any rate. His hand is on her fucking shoulder now. He's bored of the candles. He's staring up in my direction but I don't think he'll recognise me. We only met once, very briefly. Rachel looks up, she stares right at me. We're maybe twenty feet from each other and there are lots of people between us, but she makes eye contact and stares right through me. Nothing, not a flicker of recognition, nothing. *Nothing!* I raise my hand to wave but stop myself just as soon as I've started because I'm not waving but drowning. Drowning in a sea of shit.

The next day, I don't go to work,. That night I am walking round the Common towards Max's when my mobile goes.

Rachel <<calling>>

"Hello." I say.

"Where are you?"

"I am on the Common, sitting on a bench on the Common. I was just out walking."

"Alex..."

"What?"
"Oh God, I don't even know where to start."

Silence.

Breathing.

Silence.

"I think about you all the time Alex."
"But you will never, ever leave Rupert, Rachel."

Silence.

Breathing.

Silence.

Quiet tears; hers.

The outside sound of Clapham Common and of a thousand thoughts battling to come to the surface and the sudden, deafening realisation that I must break this cycle.

I call Max, my friend. Help me, friend. "Max, it's me. I need to talk, can we go out and get smashed? I need to cut loose. I was going to come round, but can we go out and get fucked instead?"

"Meet me at Cannon Street at six; I'll get one of my brokers' expense accounts. True to his word, Max is waiting for me, beaming at the tube, with a friend/trader of his who happily hands over his AmEx and various VIP cards. He's more than happy to shell out on us as Max has just passed a lot of big numbers his way. We thank him and head for the nearest bar which is a Pitcher & Piano. Max orders a bottle of Bollinger.

"So, what's up?!"

"Rachel, doing my head in."

"OK, tell me all about it. I've got some important news to tell you too – don't let me forget – but tell me what you're going to do now, first."

I tell him I'm not sure, I just want to change so many things in my life. I don't know where to start.

Shots.

More shots.

We chat it through vaguely as two male best friends making zero progress and decide leave happy with our chat. We're outside at ten-thirty after a few more bottles of champagne, trying to hail a taxi to take us to L'Equipe Anglaise – an awful champagne/ poseurs bar frequented by City types, wannabe gangsters, small-time drug dealers and Lebanese princesses. However, that's where the VIP cards are for so our hands are tied. We arrive and as we enter the club, our jackets are taken off us and replaced in our hands by a bottle of Bollinger each. We head for a side-booth where we sit down and smile at each other. Max orders every shot they have behind the bar to be delivered a pair at a time. Goldschlager, Tequila, black and white Sambucca, Jagermeister, AfterShock, until we're working our way through the flavoured vodkas. When we're out of the club at midnight, extremely drunk, we get poured into a waiting cab by the doorman and we share a taxi.

We're both asleep because neither of us have ordered or taken any drugs, when the taxi stops in Tanner Street in Southwark to drop Max off. The taxi driver is impatient and grumpy and almost drags Max out of the cab. Max does his usual trick of banging the back of the car as it heads off. Only this time he appears to be hanging on to the rear window too as the impatient taxi driver accelerates down Tanner Street and then turns very sharply into Tower Bridge Road, and I am looking out the rear window, becoming concerned as Max tries to keep up with the increasing speed of the taxi. His legs are pumping furiously away and the expression on his face is growing more alarmed by the milli-second. Suddenly he disappears from view. I think Max just fell over; the cabbie turns towards Clapham Common and I fall asleep again.

I get home twenty minutes later and am rummaging around in the kitchen for something to eat when my mobile starts ringing. I assume that it's Rachel so carry on hunting the booze-food. It stops but then rings again straight away. I fish the thing out of my right trouser pocket and just about see that Max's name is blurrily flashing at me.

"Yello, mate. You all right?"

"Ma'e. You go'a come an' 'elp me."

"What?"

"I fell over. Ma teef."

I can hardly understand a word of what Max is saying. His words are slurred, but I can tell that something awful has happened. His tone is worrying and I think I can hear him sobbing at the other end of the phone, although I can't quite be sure. My mind starts spinning, I see him running after the cab; the cab speeding up; I see him falling, arms and legs a blur trying to reach out. I flinch as I recall the image. *What the fuck was he doing?*

I agree to go and meet him and put the phone down. I call a taxi and try to sober up as I wait for it to arrive. On the journey, I fall asleep again.

The future is beautiful. It always looks like clouds, but not cloudy. Clouds that are clearing. Clearing fast as if to show me a way upwards, towards my future. As if to show me the future that is undoubtedly up there somewhere.

I am awoken by Max calling again to tell me he'll be at the Royal London Hospital on Whitechapel Road. I wonder why he has gone to Whitechapel Road when he lives in South London. When I get there I give the bloke £30 for the £24 fare and run inside. It's dark and empty and I think I'm in the wrong place, but I keep walking until eventually I see Max sedated and half asleep on his back in a grim-looking dentist's chair in the middle of a dimly-lit and draughty room. It's so cold in the room that I can see my breath when I exhale, but Max is dressed in only his shirt and his trousers. And I see the front panel of the shirt is completely ripped away from the neck and is hanging off to one side, flapping gently in the draught. The whole scene is beyond macabre and I can't work out why there is nobody looking after him. As I approach him I begin to see the damage that has been done to his face. His mouth is hanging open like he's stupid. His thin pink lips have been replaced by two crimson balloons; swollen like some disgusting collagen operation gone horribly wrong. He has no front teeth on the top row; the skin above his top lip is torn away and his t-shirt is covered in blood. Whilst I am staring at all of this, a short, pale and unshaven man in baggy jeans and a grubby, off-white smock appears from the shadows behind Max. Without looking at me or saying a word he produces a needle and thread and begins sewing the two flaps of yellowing skin that constitute Max's top lip back together. Max flinches but his eyes remain closed. I gag, but keep watching, trying to count how many stitches he is having sewn into his lip.

"Err, excuse me," I say. The 'surgeon' ignores me. "Look. I'm…er…a friend of this guy. Is he ok?"

The 'surgeon' turns finally and smiles faintly. He has finished his sewing I notice, and Max now has some very attractive black stitching across his top lip. I count six stitches. He pockets the needle and thread. "Does he look ok?"

"Err no. Not exactly."

"You're one of his *friends* then?"

"Err yep."

"Brilliant. Who needs enemies eh?"

And with that, he disappears back into the darkness from where he came.

Max opens his eyes. He waves his arm in no particular direction.

Now someone else appears from the shadows and tells me I can take him home. Max asks me to stay at his, "just in case". And we get a taxi back to Tanner Street. In the taxi, my head is throbbing as my hangover really kicks in. I sleep sketchily on the couch and am woken by Max's mum who arrives at 8.30am with coffee and croissants for me. A nice touch, but no Nurofen. Ouch. Not nearly as "ouch" as Max though. When he wakes up, he looks a million times worse than last night. Both his eyes are black; his top lip is so swollen by the stitches it nearly meets his nose; his mouth is a gaping black hole and now I can really see the damage done to his front teeth: the two central ones have been ripped away from the root out; the one to the left is a jagged little stump; the one to the right is cut clean in half as if it only ever grew that long. His bottom lip still looks like a collagen-nightmare, but now in the daylight you can see how the thin, bright-red skin is stretched across the bloated bruise underneath. It looks like some sort of hideous fucked-up toy balloon.

I am sent home to collect my car and I spend the entire day driving Max and his mum, neither of whom can drive, round several dentists. None of the dentists seem to want to treat Max even though this would clearly be several thousand pounds worth of work. I am eventually excused after securing the services of an expensive dentist in Knightsbridge. Max's mum will look after him tonight. Max doesn't want to tell Lorraine until he's had some work done on his teeth. I drive home and order the curry I have been dreaming about all day. Just before going to bed I phone Max to check on his well-being. They have cleaned out all the half-bits and he can speak more easily and have given him a stack of anti-inflammatories to bring his lips back down to normal shape and size. I feel guilty about it all because it was my demanding that we went out but then I again I did want to ask Max what the fuck he was doing chasing after the taxi and holding on. He had mentioned wanting to tell me something important. But I decide not to, in case it's something ridiculous and I don't want to make him feel even worse than he must do already.

TWO-MEN-TERRA

"Mate, let's go on holiday, I have to get away. *We* have to get away. You cant go to work like that anyway. Have you got any holiday left to take?" I ask Max.

We're having breakfast, his mouth, his face in general are healing brilliantly.

"Loads. I've not had the chance to take any yet this year."

"Right. Let's go. Let's just go somewhere. It's so obvious that we both need to get away from it all. Somewhere nice and relaxing. Chilled. You all right with it just being me and you?"

"Yeah why?"

"Lorraine?"

"Yeah, she'll be cool. She'll understand. She's a dream."

"You're right. She is."

"What about you and Rachel?"

"What? There is no me and Rachel!"

I wonder how it's happened that Mr. Max Campbell has landed himself a woman like that, a woman that cares for him; loves his quirky ways and exalts in his geeky commentary and his eccentricity; an intelligent and generous woman who positively beams and glows when she is with him. And I always hoped that he would find someone like Lorraine. I truly did. It's nothing more than he deserves. It's just that I assumed I would always have to be on the look out for him. That he would be searching a lot longer than I for his soul-mate. But there he was, happy as Larry. And here I am, the Other, alone and confused.

"I know this place," Max says, "My parents used to go there in the sixties. It was a hippy hangout. They used to go there and do nothing, just chill, smoke some weed and re-charge."

"Sounds perfect. Where is it?"

"It's this place called Formentera. We should have gone there last year really, but we were too busy clubbing or recovering from being fucked. It's next to Ibiza."

"Oh no…we don't need *that* mate. I am not going *any*where near Ibiza!"

"No, no it's nothing like Ibiza. I promise. It's much smaller, there are no clubs and hardly any English go there. It's too complicated for most of them to work out. You can't fly direct. You have to fly to Ibiza, then make your way to the port and catch a ferry over. And then the ferries aren't that regular either. And they stop at 8.30pm. So all in all, that means that the clubbers and mentalists don't tend to go there and it's too far off the beaten track for your average lager lout to bother, either."

"OK. I'm trusting you on this. Let's do it."

So I arrange two weeks off for myself off from Fortworth. It's not difficult to persuade them to let me go. In fact, they almost seem happy to let me go.

That Friday night, the 15th of August, we are on an Easyjet flight from Gatwick to Ibiza, both happy and relieved to be getting out of the country and the madness for a while.

The flight is a nightmare if only because of the fact that it reminds us of everything we are trying to escape from. A group of six lads from an indeterminate spot in the Midlands occupy the two rows in front of us. They are steadily drinking the plane out of booze and are getting louder and more obnoxious by the minute. To my left, a couple are brazenly counting out their pills on their meal tray. "These are those Mitsubishis, I was telling you 'bout, Trace. They're wicked. Got twenty of 'em. They come up really quickly. Not too 'ard though. And they're nice 'n' dancey. You'll like 'em you'll see. Not too mongy. Perfect for you."

"I don't mind mongy."

Yeah I'll bet you don't Trace, I think. I *am* getting jaded. I shut my eyes and try to block out an Essex-meets-Ibeeeeefa! chorus.

We land a little over two hours later and Max and I are off the plane mercifully quickly. We shouldn't have checked any bags in though, because although we reach the correct carousel early, we are soon surrounded by the familiar drunken, cackling, hordes. Each and every single one of them turning their mobiles on. Beep-beep. Beep-beep. Beep-beep. Beep-beep. Beep-beep. Beep-beep. Beep-beep. Beep-beep. Beep-beep. Beep-beep.

Text messages arriving from the Spanish mobile companies. Beep-beep. Beep-beep. Beep-beep. Beep-beep. Beep-beep. Beep-beep. Beep-beep. Beep-beep. Beep-beep. Beep-beep. Beep-beep. Beep-beep. Beep-beep. Beep-beep. Beep-beep. Beep-beep.

"Look I'm a 'Movistar'!"

"Yeah right. Me too. Look."

Beep-beep. Beep-beep.

"Well I'm on 'Airtel'."

That's Airhead, Trace. Air-*head*.

Beep-beep. Beep-beep.

"Oi, John. Whachu on? I'm on Vodafone Es-pag-na. Izat good?"

Beep-beep. Beep-beep.

"Mate. Get us to Formentera, before I kill someone," I am desperate. It's strange and I feel hypocritical because I know that in reality I am not that different to these people. I know that I am capable of behaving in a far worse manner. It's just that I think that I have reached my limit this year. Something has to give but I don't know what it is. There are cracks appearing all over my life. And I have been papering over them, battening down the hatches whenever a crisis looms. But really, really it's time I was honest with myself. But what is it that I need to confront? At the moment I just feel a fuzzy unease. That's all I can say. I try to take the pieces of my life in turn.

My job – hated. It makes me feel sick just thinking about how I am wasting my days working for tossers who I don't like, on projects I don't care about. I mean do I really give a fuck whether or not UK Gas or any other fucking company manage to implement their new customer billing system on time and on budget?! No, I don't think so. And why do I do it? For the money. And that fact in itself makes me sick. Sick with myself. I never thought I would do that: sell out. But I have. I am a prostitute. I am the veritable Corporate Whore. And the tricks I am expected to perform are no longer worth the money.

My relationship – confused. Rachel? I am fuming. So angry with myself. So naïve. I have never felt so stupid. Then again is that a sign of being really in love? I realise I don't know. Do I honestly see any future at all in that relationship? There is none and I need to get out. Get rid. I need to get to grips with that and be happy with that decision. Shannon? She is beautiful and more like me than anyone I know. She is in my heart and a kindred spirit. Why the fuck is she with Richard Gardiner? Why won't she leave him?

My drug-taking – out of control. Fucking-well out-of-fucking-control. What the fucking hell am I doing? The problem may be that I am addicted.

My friends – great. Christ I'm lucky. I have the most patient friends in the world.

So I make a mental deal with myself to do some thinking about all the main aspects of my life that I do not like and to make some resolutions to do something about them when I get back to London.

Finally our two bags arrive and we join the queue for a taxi, which will take us down to the harbour. We have to wait until the ferries start running in the morning, but given that it's already 3am, it surely can't be that long a wait. Besides, the time gives Max and me a chance to talk and have a few beers at the quayside bar.

We walk in stickily and plonk our bags on the off-white marble floor. It's hot, the air is heavy. The light above the bar is blue white. A fan drones lazily above our heads, barely making the still, thick, hot air move. A fly, too lazy or hot to fly around the blades of the fan, hitches a ride on one. A short, unshaved but amiable looking man is wiping a tiny brandy glass behind the counter. Sweat has collected above his eyebrow. He smiles and it slowly rolls down his cheeks. He is unfazed. He points at the stereo and cuts his throat with his hand and creases his face up apologetically.

"I don't think their stereo is working," I offer.

"Dos cerveza, por favor," says Max in an impressive guttural accent. I look at him.

"Que?" he says.

"Nothing, nothing at all," I smile. "I'll get a table outside."

Beside the quay, the various sized boats line up. I position our bags and ourselves at a table well-placed to keep an eye on all goings on. And we settle in for a couple of beers until the first ferry starts running, which Max tells me will be at 6am.

"Thank God for that!" I sigh, slumping into my chair, large beer in hand (an indeterminate size somewhere between a pint and a litre – they don't serve pints in Spain and the small beers are the size of shots). "I'm so glad we are out of there. And it looks like you're right; no-one from the airport is here." Max and I make up the only clientèle of the bar, apart from four locals, presumably workers or taxi drivers in an animated discussion about the football on in the far corner of the bar sitting under the TV which is attached to the wall and showing a game.

"See I told you. And Formentera will be nothing like Ibiza. All your worst nightmares will be well on their way to San Antonio right now."

"Well thanks, mate. And Cheers!" We raise our glasses and sigh and relax and drink our way through the three hour wait until our ferry is ready. At 6am a large catamaran starts up with the rising sun.

The crossing is beautiful. It's colder than I expected, although we *are* out on deck in the day-break breeze. The night light stays with us and the sky is navy blue, lightening to turquoise all the time. A vague mist lifts suddenly like a muslin shawl being removed to reveal a beautiful face. The sun starts to come up as we move across the short three mile stretch of water south to Formentera. Brooding, dark land masses become inviting lush green islands. The dark teal of the sea turns light blue; sandbanks show themselves in the shallows; beautiful greens and deep blues combine, as I stare down intently at one point a huge shoal of brightly coloured fish gather turn to face us and then disappear. After twenty minutes, the island moves gradually into view through the evaporating early morning fog, clearing as the sun begins to warm up the day. It's green and gold; you can pick out the tallest palm trees, shiny strips of bright sandy beaches and the white froth of breaking waves.

"Mate, I fucking love it," I shout across at Max, my words struggling to make themselves heard in the wind, "I can feel myself unwinding already."

"Yeah? You'll love it. You'll see, you'll unwind really quickly. You know what, I'll bet you're unwinding already."

I smile at the deaf bastard. Too much standing near speakers in loud nightclubs, that.

The small harbour comes into view after another five minutes and we begin to slow down. It's picture book. The white-fronted shops and bungalows catch the sun's bright rays and palm trees line the entrance to the harbour. As we collect our bags, a small, smiling figure is waving at us from the quayside. It turns out to be our 'rep' – for want of a better word. I say that because she doesn't really look or act how you would expect a holiday rep in the Balearic Islands to look or act. *She's* definitely *not* been caught on Ibiza Uncovered, shagging the clientele after ten tequila shots. She's older, maybe late thirties and as becomes apparent through her chat as she drives us to our villa, well educated, very polite and very friendly.

She escorts us to the villa with our bag of welcome groceries and wine and then she's gone; "Let me know if you need anything at all, boys."

The villa is not luxurious, but then we weren't looking for that at all. Just lots of tiles, lots of white and orange tiles.

It's getting warm, so we leave the unpacking until later, and head down to the sea which is a hundred metres away from our villa. The village in which we are staying is called Es Calo according to Max. It's small, even by Formenteran standards. The capital, San Francisco is four times as large, has a church and a town square, then there's San Fernando, which is where the islands' workers predominantly live and Es Pujols, the tourist centre of the island with its cafes, bars and souvenir shops. We pass through the lane down to the seafront. The buildings in the village are painted white or beige, and every person we pass offers a smiling "Hola" or "Buenas Dias". I'm smiling as the sea comes into view. It's a glittering vision of deep blue, interrupted only by glinting bright-white flashes at moments when the sun catches the top of a wave. The cove forms a perfect semi-circle; to our left are five launching ramps for the local fishermen. They look so rickety that I think they might collapse at any moment, but Max tells me that they are in full working order, and only empty now because the men are out at sea.

"This is nothing, you wait until you see the other side of the island where the *real* beach is," Max tells me.

"Well," I reply, "I haven't seen the sea for a year, so this is good enough for me".

"Let's go and sort out some scooters, then we can get around the island easier."

We pick out two mean-looking machines from the scooter and car hire shop in the village, fill out the necessary paper-work (none necessary) and set off with our polystyrene helmets bobbing about in the approximate vicinity of our heads, at a blistering 30kmh, completely in touch with our slow-paced new environment.

Max is a terrible scooter rider and wobbles wildly around in front of me, especially when being passed by one of the island's taxis. They don't give us much of a wide berth and Max screams obscenities into the dusty air in front of him.

"Relax, mate! We're supposed to be chilling out!" I bawl at him, pulling up alongside.

"Yeah, cool. Shall we go and see the beach my mum told me about, the one they used to go to in the sixties?"

"Yep. Let's do it."

We swing round at the next turning and head for a small stretch of yellow marked on the map he bought from the scooter man. Max points at a spot: Playa Migjourn. "That's the place."

We're riding for about five minutes, before we turn left off the main road, following a barely tarmacked track we put our faith in the map and Max stops at a faded and dusty brown sign promising "Playa – 200m". We bump off the tarmac and smile at each other and shrug. I am willing my scooter to go faster. It won't, of course. We're on a dirt track now, trying to pick our way through jutting rocks and the large roots of the olive and fig trees lining the track. The hot air is thick with smells of other, as yet unknown herbs and plants, overpowering even the stench of unburnt petrol spilling out of our inefficient mopeds. We head down into a dipping hollow for around fifty metres and as we emerge upwards, the scooters struggling to carry their passengers' weight and make headway in the sand, the path widens, and we come to the brow of the hill. Max has stopped up ahead; when I catch him I see why. For nearly one hundred and eighty degrees in front of our eyes, is pure azure. The sea's colour is truly beautiful. The light blue near the shore indicates a depth of a few feet, ten feet maximum. That shelf protrudes out for at least eighty metres evenly out into the sea, whereupon the colour darkens dramatically and suddenly to a dark turquoise, and then as far as the eye can see, it's beautiful, flawless aquamarine until the horizon. Two small, but bright white triangular sails indicate two yachts sailing right out at sea.

"That's fucking beautiful."

"Yeah."

At the entrance to the beach flutters a skull and crossbones flag in the breeze, marking the Pirata Bus Beach Hut.

We head for the flag and park up the scooters nearby. As soon as we cut the engines a soft melodic tune wafts through the air towards us. Like Café del Mar, but unrecognisable. "Mate, what *is* that tune?"

"Dunno, don't recognise it."

"That's strange."

"Yeah, it is," he says, "Wicked though. You fancy a beer?"

Max points at the bar, this little shack where the music is coming from, a slanted straw roof which almost comes to the ground and looks to be holding up the rest of the bar. Under the roof we discover two large tables, benches on either side. A couple are playing backgammon on a fading and sandy board, others are playing cards. Behind the bar are a man and a woman. They have clearly been here a long time. I'm not sure yet if they're together, although they *do* treat each other with that sort of vague, absent-minded familiarity that all long-standing couples do. They both have tans that look like they've been ingrained so deep in the skin; they wouldn't fade if they lived in Iceland for several years. They look very friendly and smile broadly at us as we plonk ourselves on two of the high stools in front of the bar.

"Errm, hola. Dos Cerveza, por favor," Max asks the man. "Y dos vodka y tonica."

"Hallo. Wilkommen."

"Ah. You're German?"

"Yes. You are Englisch."

"Yes, yes we are. Errr...I...err...sorry about that," Max replies, pulling out his best Hugh Grant impression.

"No, zis is not a problem. But not so many Englisch come to Formentera."

"Yeah, um. We got lost on the way to San Antonio?" I suggest.

"No really, we don't like that sort of thing. We are looking for a relaxing time really. We have very stressful jobs in London. We just want to chill out. You know?"

"Yes, yes. *Ich verstehe*. Formentera is the right place for you!" he says casting his right arm out over the bar, over our shoulders, and out to the blue yonder. We turn round 180 degrees on our stools to see what he's gesturing at.

"I am Gunther. Please, enjoy and respect to the island."

We sit down and inspect these dangerously strong-looking generous drinks. I cannot actually get any tonic into my vodka.

"Christ, this is beautiful mate. Thanks for suggesting this place. It's going to do the trick I can tell," I pat Max on the shoulder. He is staring calmly out at the deep blue sea like me.

"Alright?" I ask him.

"Thinking about Lorraine. What did I do to deserve her?"

"Are you kidding? She is lucky to have found you mate! You are a top bloke, the best mate anyone could have, it's just supposed to happen mate. Maybe you're just due some of the good vibes for once? But don't fuck it up. She is *gold*."

* * *

In the morning I'm still asleep when Max comes back into the villa whistling. He bangs about in the kitchen, which I ignore, but then he pokes his head round my bedroom door. "A glass of freshly squeezed orange sir? Or should I say: '*Zuma de naranja?*'"

"Trez bon Rodney. Trez bon."

"Ah come on Alex, got to get into the lingo."

"Ah, ok. Right. What's Spanish for yes?"

"Fuck off, it's *Si* you dick."

"*Si*. Ah, cheers mate. *Si, si senor.* Yeah, orange juice would be wicked. Nice one. Where you been?"

"Down the local *supermercado*. It's great. Got everything. I got the News of the Screws and The Observer."

"Nice combination!"

"Well, you know. Creature comforts. Can't give up on blighty that easily. Don't you want to keep up to date on the latest transfer gossip? And the red-top's got the full season's fixture list in. Guess who we've got first match."

"Man U away?"

"Yeah, how d'you know that? Ah, anyway, you gotta see this little shop, the little woman in there is *so* friendly and helpful. I'm gonna practice my Spanish on her."

"Yeah you do that Rodders," I grunt, engrossed now in the sports pages.

"Oi! Take that down the beach, you can read it there. Come on, let's go. Do you know it's eleven o'clock?"

"Max, we're on holiday!"

"No. Come on. You *have* to see this island. You'll relax more by being out and about. Come on, let's go and lie on the beach. And in fact, leave the papers."

"All right, all right," I say. "Well, get outta the room then. I wanna get up."

"Go on then."

"I'm naked under here."

"What?!"

"I always sleep naked when it's hot, and if I'm not mistaken I've got a rather impressive piece of morning glory going on."

"Christ! Are you sure you should be getting a hard-on reading about Gianfranco Zola? I mean he's good, but not that good, surely. I'll get a beach bag together." Max leaves the room chuckling to himself like the strange boy that he is.

"Yeah, you do that you nonce!" I shout after him, "Don't forget the total sun-block cream your mummy packed for you." The fair-haired boy would be a lobster by the end of the day I reckon.

"Shut up!"

"Yeah, yeah. I *know* she did! Or was it your *girlfriend?*"

"You're just jealous!"

"You're right, I am." I really, really am. I have a fleeting thought of my own mother, distracted and vague on anti-depressants and sleeping aids and I am suddenly filled with a horrible sadness that makes me want to just stay in bed all day.

"Just put some clothes on and let's go," Max shouts, "It's a beautiful day!"

That makes me look out of the window and I see that the sky is blue, I feel the air is warm and although I miss her and my heart is broken in two with uncertain love, misplaced trust and images I can't replace I feel that the sun may just bleach them out. I trust Max and his process and everything feels better in an instant and I jump out of bed naked. I put on my blue Diesel swimmers and my best Antoni Alison black t-shirt.

We head back down to the Playa Migjourn. It's near deserted and we pick a spot in the middle of the beach, sort of equidistant between the sea and the back of the beach and the bar. It's just before mid-day and starting to get hot. I'd say around twenty-eight degrees. And we pretty much sit there all day. Not moving much; gradually the beach fills up, clearly these people have been out later than us last night; I love the sea so I'm in and out all the time; I sneak out the News of the World (I packed it in my bag without Max seeing) and continue with the sports pages. Max sits in his funny straw hat and his total-block sun cream and reads his book – *American Psycho* by Brett Easton Ellis. Strange choice for holiday reading, as I am thinking this, he lifts his head and looks across at me. But he doesn't say anything. It's like he's in shock.

I guess he's reading the Coat Hanger scene.

"Tonight I, ah, just had to kill a lot of people!" I shout this across to him.

"Yeah," Max lowers his eyes again; clearly he has just read a really horrible scene. "This book is fucking gross man. Some of the things in here are disgusting."

That literary stumble apart, the day passes in a glorious sunny haze. Occasionally one of us goes up to the bar to order a couple of beers, usually *Estrellas*. The beach fills up some more at around 2pm: a gang of gorgeous Italians play volleyball, well. We watch people playing Backgammon at the bar. I love the game and want to join them, but can't quite fathom the courage; my mojo is gone temporarily and I see Rachel everywhere, eventually sunset comes. We head up to the bar. Gunther greets us. He's not been there during the day, but greets us like long lost brothers now and dives behind the bar to make us two of his special sangrias, which he hands over to us thirty seconds later. "I hope you like. Now please, sit and enjoy ze sunset."

Max and I do as we are told and choose our perch on the rocky headland in front of the bar. We are facing west towards the far end of the island where a long strip of land heads out into the sea. The sun sets directly behind it, and as the sun touches the horizon, the Balearic chill out tunes are replaced on the sound system by an operatic number. Sarah Brightman and Andrea Bocelli, *Time to Say Goodbye* (Con te partiro).

I think about Rachel and it's funny because I actually struggle to fathom an image, a scenario I want to think about. Instead I see her and Rupert in Alba and I smash it. I feel angry. I clench my fists and I sense Max at my shoulder with a drink.

Both Max and I are staring at the horizon, as are about another hundred people - basically all of the people from the beach plus some others who have just come down especially for the event. It's hard not to feel emotional as the bright orange disc is swallowed by the dark earth. I'm getting drunk and the opera tune is playing on my feelings. It's only a sunset and presumably it happens every day as it does in a lot other places in the world but for some people it's too much. I look around and lots of people are crying. Some people, I think Italian, are hugging on my right.

"It is their last day on ze island," confides Gunther, appearing from nowhere, he pats us on the shoulder and hands us two more sangrias. "Some people find zis very...how do you say...?"

"Emotional?" I offer, the hairs on my neck standing on end.

"Yes, very emotional. You will be the same after two weeks. You two are Englishmen. You will not see this yet." He raises his glass to ours in turn and moves off in and out of the rocks, collecting glasses, tripping over his flip-flops, and cursing in the über-language.

We turn back to the sunset, not long now before the sun completely disappears behind the headland. So beautiful and so simple. I ask myself when was the last time I saw a sunset? I can't remember. Of course it happens in London every night, just as it does everywhere else in the world. And sunrises? Well they were ten a penny. But it's impossible to see the real horizon in London.

Gunther's wife, Marianne, brings the tune to a roaring climax just as the final shard of sunshine disappears from view behind the headland. Perfect. A rapturous round of applause, loud whistling and cheering greets this exquisite piece of timing. Basically, the place goes nuts. "Apparently this happens every night," Max shouts to me, smiling from ear to ear. A minute or so later, the music comes on again, louder and livelier; again we don't know what it is, but it's European, Balearic and everyone is dancing, so who are we to criticise? "I've got to get hold of some of these tunes!" says Max. "I've no idea what they are!"

Within half an hour it's completely dark on the beach, save the moonlight dappling the waves out at sea. Italians are dancing on the tables, everyone is drunk or stoned and we are in heaven. My stresses and worries about Rachel, working in the City and the stress and mess of my life may as well be a million miles away.

We're not very adventurous and every day of the entire first week passes in pretty much the same fashion as the first day. One of us wakes up first to go down to the *supermercado*. You put on yesterday's salt-encrusted trunks, not noticing this yet because you're hung-over, and mosey on down to see the little lady. *"Hola…Buenas dias"*. *"Un poco de queso, jamon de Serrano, y pan. Gracias. Adios"*. And that's Spanish. There you go, all you need to know, bar the *cerveza*. And everyone knows how to say that. We get down to the beach at about one-ish. Pick a good spot; a very strategic activity this. A good spot, next to some beautiful girls but not hemmed in; with options; get a sandwich and a cold beer from the Pirata Bus.

* * *

We talk rubbish to Gunther over sangria and the odd spliff.

"Gunther, how long you been here?"

"Seventeen years."

"We're not even seventeen years *old* Gunther."

"Oh come on. Yes you must be! My daughter is seventeen, and she kills you at backgammon. Come on! You must be nearly dirty!"

"Yeah. You're right! We *are* dirty. Very dirty."

"Come on Meike! Come and whip me at backgammon!" I shout at Gunther's beautiful daughter Meike who is clearing the tables at the Pirata Bus.

"For sure, I will," she smiles. "I vill beat you, *sehr gut*."

"And after zat, you go make ze rumpee-pumpee, humn?" Max snickers into my ear.

I punch him so hard he spits his olive out.

"Ouch!"

"Respect the island." I say.

* * *

We watch Balearic sunsets: "Fuck me. Look at that. Shit! Look at that!"

"Oh fuck."

"Fuck."

"Fuck."

"You got the camera?"

"Fuck no."

"What?"

"Fuck."

"You fucking twat."

"What?"

"That needs filming. That's what. You twat."

"Oh fuck."

"Yeah, 'Fuck'."

"That's fucking beautiful, man. That's why we came here."

"Yeah. No shit!"
"Now I see. Max, this was a good fucking call."

And we relax.

Relax.

Breathe.

"Don't get the papers, today."
"Yeah, I won't. Good idea, I was just thinking the same thing, actually."

"About the papers?"
"Yeah."
"Yeah, no need."

On the Friday afternoon, exactly a week into the holiday, we are sitting on the beach, doing nothing as usual. But I'm thinking. I am relaxed, but thoughts are drifting back to London. Back to Rachel. Back to Fortworth. Back to the *real* world; how I hate to say that. I think about how happy I am here, and how unhappy I am at home.

"Max?"

"Yes?"

"Max, I've decided. I've decided to resign from Fortworth when we get back. I've had it."

"Yeah? Really? Can't say I'm that surprised really mate. It's been coming. You and Fortworth is not a match made in heaven is it? You just needed some time to step back away from it, to see. You want a San Miguel? You don't fit in there. None of us do. You think I'm happy at my place? No! Do you think Shannon is happy at Digitech? No. Do it. Quit! I'm going to get a beer."

"Good decision"

"Right, decisions: San Miguel or Corona, or Estrella though?"

"I'm serious."

"Me too, now which beer?"

"God. I don't know. You decide. Estrella?"

Two minutes and Max is back with a tray with two of each. "I couldn't decide mate, so I got two of each."

"Great, thanks."

"The problem now of course, is which one to have first."

"Hmmmn. Yes, true. You should have asked Gunther for his advice, he would have given a good logical German answer to our dilemma."

"Anyway, have you decided what to do after leaving Fortworth? I mean, if you are going to make that decision – and I *do* think it's a good one – then you might as well look into something you really like doing.

"Huh?"

"What I mean is, don't just leave Fortworth and jump straight into some other consultancy job. They'll all be the same. Do you know what I mean? I mean, if I could leave Parks', I would get into music. You know, electronic stuff."

"Yeah, coz you're a geek!"

"Charming. I am trying to help you, make a suggestion…"

"Well why *don't* you leave Parks and get into some geek music?"

"Look, don't start with that. OK? We are trying to sort *you* out. I'll get out eventually, but I'm OK there for a while. I need the money. But you need to ask yourself what it is that you want to be doing with your life."

"Right. OK, so…what is it that I like doing? What would I like to do?"

"What? Are you asking me? 'What do I like doing?' Don't you know? What do you feel passionately about?"

"Errm…well…it's difficult. You're putting me on the spot asking me like this."

"Well, I thought this is something that's been bugging you for a while. Thought you might have had some thoughts. That's all. Some answers. That's all."

"Well I like Art…"

"Uh-huh."

"Errm…"

"Yup."

"Well, you know, painting..."

"Yes. Yes I know what art is! I meant go on. What do you want to do in art?"

"Well, how should I know?"

"Are there any artists you admire?"

"What?"

"Fuck me!"

"Rothko?"

"Yes. Good. And?"

"Oh fuck I don't know!" I shout back at Max, hurt by the dawning realisation that having managed to take some sort of decision about my job, I don't know what else it is that I'd rather be doing and it seems that I am already staring at a dead end. Having waited all these years to be free, I don't know what free actually looks or feels like.

I quickly turn away from Max and pretend to survey some girls from under my large black sunglasses.

But I *am* resolved to leave Fortworth, I *do* want to feel passionate about something that I am doing. I want to not have to suppress my true self when I get up and go to work in the morning. I must do something more creative. I do feel that I will no longer be the Other man in the Rupert Rachel relationship.

An hour passes easily between men reading the newspaper. Max says nothing as he gives me some space. He eventually pipes up with:

"Mate, do you fancy a trip over to Ibiza? Renaissance is on tonight at Pacha," Max is reading out from DJ magazine, "We could get the last ferry at 8pm, get some dinner, then go to a few bars and head down there 'round mid-night, then catch a ferry back in the morning. What do you reckon?"

"Yeah. Fuck it. Go on then."

We pack up there and then and head back to the villa on our scooters. We put on the Renaissance Mix Collection Part 3 CD - Dave Seaman; classic to get us in the mood, whilst we shit, shower and shave.

At around six in the evening we're sat on our balcony, vodka-and-tonics in hand, toasting the night ahead.

"Let's make this a good one hey? Because I reckon we'll only do one big night this holiday."

"Yeah, I agree, I'll go a bit mental tonight, but that'll be it. Take it easy after that. Just need to freak out a bit tonight."

The ferry crossing to Ibiza is the reverse of our journey on the first morning. Sunrise is replaced by sunset but it's just as beautiful, if not more so. The sun disappears behind the hills on the western side of Ibiza. When we dock its getting dark; street lamps night up the blackening sky. It could not be more different to the tranquil of Formentera. Neon lights advertising clubs and bars throb provocatively; there's a McDonalds' next to a Burger King, next to a Lotto shop, then there's a sex shop, a Murphy's Irish bar, and the pavements are crowded with pre-clubbers and flyers. We struggle through the mad people until we reach the old town. Here it becomes a bit easier to make your way down the street, and the place starts to feel like a Spanish town rather than another part of London / SoHo NYC / Oxford Street / Carnaby Street. We stop at a restaurant that looks somewhat authentic, and sit down. We order some fresh fish, drink a bottle of rosé wine each and generally take our time over dinner as we have four hours to kill before we go to the club.

"This is all right mate," I say raising my glass to his. "Quite nice really. We didn't do any of *this* last year."

"Well last year, it would have been inappropriate. We weren't that interested in food last year as I recall. Everyone was always fucked. A few too many of the amphetiminos."

"Ha, ha. True enough. Is that why you didn't mention anything about Formentera?"

"Well, yep, it's not exactly a 'let's go mad' place is it?"

"No. Glad you didn't actually. Our little secret then." We 'cheers' again. "Do you think we've changed then since last year?" I ask him.

"No, not really. I think we needed a break, so maybe we're a bit quieter; and well, last year there were thirteen of us, so *this* type of thing would have been a bit difficult. I'm enjoying it like this; just you and me, mate. Let's have a large one tonight. One to make them jealous when we get home and tell them about it. I mean, come on: it's BT and Sasha tonight. BT's bound to play *"Loving You More,"* and *"Embracing the Sunshine."* We gotta get some good pills. We'll have a fucking blinder.'"

"Yeah. Cool. Let's get the bill then."

We pay and leave. As we make our way round the port Max disappears into an old shop front with someone who looks like Jesus for a minute. When he reappears he simply whispers "Pills!" into my ear. The Manumission crew parade along the terrace, through the bars, advertising their 'Sail the Seven Seas' night: beefy oiled-up sailor boys, naked bar their hats and trunks, dance with beautiful tall girls in pleated white mini-skirts and white bras. Mike and Claire Manumission lead the show as usual, tossing paper boats and hats and confetti into the crowd. People are coming up to them stuffing things into their hands; trannies with huge, back-combed hair-dos and thigh-length patent boots squawk across at each other from one bar to another, their faces powder white and their lips scarlet pouting. All around confusion reigns, tiaras are tossed, feather boas are unfurled, turquoise and pink and snatched.

The anticipation of the night ahead coupled with the hot, dry, Mediterranean air and the vodka is making my mouth dry.

"Shall we bosh a half of these then?"

"Yeah. What are they?"

"Look like classic Mitsus to me. Wanna see?"

"Nah. Just bosh it.

"Urgh! Tastes rank! Must be good," Max says as he boshes his pill.

A few couples 'lobstered' by the sun, try to make their way through the throng, faces shining, holding hands and scared, they have spent too much time outside during the day. Poor English-rose skin.

It's midnight and we decide to head to the club. It's a walkable distance, and we decide to take that option after inspecting the taxi queue which is least one hundred metres long and snakes round the corner and out into the street beyond the KFC. It's a hot night, and I'm sweating after two minutes of walking. "Aaargh! Not going to pull now! Had that garlic paste, and now I'm sweating like a pig," I say.

"*Alioli*. And you *are* a pig," replies Max.

"Ah thanks, mate. I know I can always rely on you when I need a compliment."

"What do you want? A fucking wet wipe? I'm sweating too. Pacha's air-conditioned inside, it'll be cooler in there."

"I know that," I say.

It takes us fifteen minutes just to walk round the port and then through this no-man's-land docklands but we know what we're doing as we've done this walk several times before. Eventually Pacha comes into view. It's a great club; probably one of my favourite in the world, and definitely my favourite in Ibiza. It's not as big as Privilege and may not get the same DJs as Space; but it's one of the originals. It's a proper Spanish nightclub, you get less English there as a proportion of the crowd. It's one of the rare nightclubs that stay open even after the Summer madness is gone. It's a place where the locals come, long after we've gone back to London.

There's a scrum at the door (at a more English-dominated club there would be a queue – even when we're fucked, we can queue), and our advance tickets count for nothing.

"Spot of rugby scrummaging tactics?" I say to Max.

"Yeah, why not? Put that public-school education you hated so much to some good," he replies.

I lead the way through the jostling crowd. It's true, I had been quite good at rugby as a schoolboy, representing the county at open-side flanker, here in this scenario, it was all about the push and soon we are close to the front, waving our tickets in the faces of the door staff, our tactics having been deemed entirely acceptable by the rest of the scrum. I reflect momentarily that such behaviour in London would have caused a fight. We're inside within a couple of minutes, a long white-walled walkway leads you into a square-ish pre-hall. Latino lounge lizards in white shirts, unbuttoned at the top and at the bottom lean louchely against the walls. Glamour Queens totter around giggling and flirting and looking tanned, long brown limbs crossed and uncrossed, high toothy smiles and air kisses are given and taken easily and unvalued. Northern English lads mill about in groups of fives and sixes supping beer and surreptitiously counting pills, all in nice shiny shirts and loafers. Everyone smiles, many wear shades. The air is thick with familiar aftershaves and perfumes all vying for attention – D&G, Gucci, Armani. We stride through and up three steps and we're into the first bar area of the club. The throb of the music makes the butterflies in my stomach turn excitably. A familiar sensation of anticipation floods me. I turn to Max and smile. He's smiling and rocking his head back and forth, unfortunately out of time – but I don't tell him; I can tell he's trying to figure out what tune is playing. As yet it's a little muffled as we're not on the main dance floor.

"It's…it's…I'm sure it's some version of…No way! They're playing the dub mix of *For What You Dream Of* by Bedrock! Christ! That must mean a Renaissance DJ is playing already."

And he's right, the geeky-bastard. As we enter the main room, the tune is in full motion and even *I* recognise it.

"Right, let's go and get ripped off at the bar shall we? A few drinks? I ask.

"*Vodka y tonica para ti hombre?*"

"Err, Vodka and tonic for me please mate."

We get ripped off at the bar, then do our usual tour, trying to suss out the crowd, trying to work out who's DJ-ing when, trying to spot dealers for when we need them. Pacha is a big club, and you can get lost in there quite easily. There is a large, sort-of-circular dance floor in the centre. It's the lowest part of the club and on the dance floor it feels a little like dancing in a big pit; the rest of the club looks down and into the dance floor, watching the show you're putting on. You have to climb three steps to leave the floor on any side. There are loads of different levels, little platforms and stairways and the place feels like it has grown organically and that they have added pieces one at a time as it's expanded. Leaving the dance floor to the right, we follow its contour round until we reach a set of stairs; we make our way up, turn right at the top and we're above the dance floor, looking down. The place is filling up nicely; hands are in the air, and the bar areas are heaving. We walk along the first-floor balcony, at the back of which a young pale looking couple are already slumped on the couches, looking tragic. At the far end is the door that leads to the stairway to the roof terrace. We decide to have a look around. It's still muggy and the warm air of the night hugs our faces as three girls swing the door open, running inside giggling.

The change in temperature brings me up on my pill and I want to go back inside to the music. The hairs on my arms and the back of my neck rise and I get a tingling sensation in my toes and fingers and arms like a million tiny bubbles are bursting as they fall and touch the skin all over my body.

"Mate," I say to Max tapping him on the shoulder, "You coming up yet? Because I am. I'm getting the first tingles and feeling dancey. Can we go back inside?"

"Yeah, same here. Fingers and toes? Yeah let's go and check out the dance floor."

Trisco's "*Musak*" is thumping through the sound system; the dance floor resembles some glowing mass bouncing in rhythm. People are blurring. The throb of the bassline marking time. Heads jumping, arms waving. All the colours of the rainbow are being reflected off the crowd, their arms throwing shapes and spinning out arcs of laser lightning. It's like watching the Northern Lights (even though I've never seen those for real). Orange clouds mingle with blue mists and green laser lights strike through, cutting shapes out of the sky. Once again I am reminded of beautiful astronomy as she casts her spell, showing me the Big Bear, then dropping me out of the sky. I fall through the clouds. I am suddenly totally fucked and I dance like a madman in the crowd for what must be an hour or more. People grab me and pull me as I dance. I scream my joy to the DJ. I whoop, in time to the beat. Sweat is pouring off me and I decide to take a breather. I'm at the bar and see Max coming back from the toilets. I shout over to him:

"I thought my life was in a pink dildo."

"What?!"

"The Pink Dildo."

"Oh yes of course, how silly of me, The Pink Dildo."

"What?!"

"Your money. YOUR MONEY! You carry it around in that pink dildo," he says pointing at my groin.

"Max! I am fucked!"

"Or a Black mamba."

"What?! A BLACK MAMBA?!" I shout at him, "Oh yeah, did I ever tell you about that night, when this girl came up to me, asked if I was Indian and then proceeded to tell me about how she liked using black mambas? Big huge ones. Even in her arse. Did I?"

"What?"

"Did I ever tell you about that night, when this girl came up to me, asked if I was Indian and then proceeded to tell me about how she liked using black mambas? Big huge ones. Even in her arse. Did I?"

"Err, yeah. Wasn't it last New Year's Eve?"

"Nah. No. No. It was *last* New Years Eve. In err…Stoke-on-Teeside."

"That's what I said."

"You didn't say Stoke-on-Trent. You said…What *did* you say?"
"Unnnnh…what *did* I say? I didn't say anything really…When?"
"You did."

"What? Not about the venue."

"What? No…But about that thing. You said…that you said."

"I said?"

"What?"

"What the fuck are you talking about?"

"What? Anyway, that's not important. What was I saying?"

"Dunno."

"Me neither."

We look at each other, smiling; it's lingering, as looks do at 2am, even between two blokes; his pale grey eyes looking into mine, telling me to go on; to relax; to enjoy myself. It's saying: 'I understand, I know what you're feeling, I'm feeling it too, I know where you are coming from, I know where you are going.'

"I'm going to the toilet," I say to Max.

"You want me to come with you?"

"No you stay here and look after the club and all the dancers."

"OK."

I stumble into the steamy toilets. I stand at the urinal, and stare at the tiles, the hubbub of mixed languages burrs happily in my ears. I turn and look at my face in the mirror. I smile, I think. A voice in my head. "Hello darling, you having fun?"

"Yeah darling,"

"I wish I was there,"

"Do you?"

"Yeah, I'm sorry I was so vague. So rubbish."

I reach out to touch her face and my hand touches the cold of the mirror.

Max grabs me and leads me back outside to the bar and places a drink in my hand. I look away and someone with a huge horse's head walks by. I look down at my drink, raise it to my mouth and slurp bitter, fizzy tonic water. My brain tells me again that someone has just walked past with their *head* replaced by a horse's one. Equine-head.

The horse walks through the crowd calmly, shaking its mane gently and neighing at people. It's a beautiful deep-chestnut mare. I rub my eyes. I turn back to Max to tell him: to warn him. The only problem is that Max now has reptilian scales running all the way down one side of his face and down his neck. So I decide not to bother him with it as he probably has enough on his mind right now.

But then I change my mind.

"Max. Has that bloke over there got a horses head on, or am I just hallucinating with these pills?"

I turn his head around pointing in the direction of the equine featured-man. It's just he's not there any more. In fact I can't point him out because I just can't see him at all.

"What?"

"There was a geezer walking through here a minute ago with a horses head on, only it was a woman-horse though, I swear."

"You hallucinating again?"

"Yeah. Fucking hell *am* I?!"

"Weird. I never get that. What's it like?"

"Well you see people walking round with horse's heads on for starters!"

"Hmmnnn. No. Definitely never seen that. You must have extra sensory vision my son."

"I think I do," I say, sighing.

"Nope. Not me."

"Shit! Shit! Shit! The worst I ever did was when my Nan was putting out the washing then calling us in for dinner, then I went in. That was bad because I was never hungry, but I had to eat because of my Mum, you know. I *had to*, couldn't let her down, but my stomach was so small coz of the speed we had all took. Then, when Sundays were over we could have permission to run around after and me and Luke could let rip. We would sprint after the sheep in the fields. We chased them till we caught them and puked up over them. Covered them in gravy."

"Er…"

"You never did that?"

"No."

Whilst Max is getting the waters in, a newt strolls past me on his hind legs and offers me his girlfriend – who is also a newt – and his drink at the same time. I try to ask him how he got hold of a ticket – being a newt, but he just brushes the question aside, suggesting he's here on GQ's account, and if I had any logistical questions I could speak to Anna Quirlemioni on + 44 (0) 207 790 4678. He repeats: "Anna Quirlemioni on + 44 (0) 20 7790 4678', he was very particular about the plus four fours. 'Good luck buddy!"

So I take the newt's girlfriend, and his drink, and lead her onto the dance floor. We are dancing there when three Spanish fly-guys come up to me and mutter some words in my ear as I am trying to snog the gecko. There are tongues everywhere and I can't hear what they are saying because of the music, and then that's irrelevant anyway because I can't speak Spanish. So even if I could hear them, I wouldn't be able to *understand* them. So I actually don't know that they are Spanish, but I assume that they are Spanish because they *look* Spanish. One of them grows and grows and grows until he is a towering Tyrannosaurus Rex. He is growling looking down on us. So I decide to close my eyes and focus on kissing the newt or lizard. But it always seems like she has too many tongues. (I am confused dealing with all these tongues in my mouth). She clearly likes me though and is rubbing her belly up against me. Her hands run down to my crotch. And she starts moaning as we kiss. So, I am in the middle of this really wet kiss with her, and then he - Tyrannosaurus Rex - is trying to grab me with one of his massive claws. So I carry on, trying to ignore him. Me fucked and the newt, she is getting really horny. Rubbing herself all over me. It's wonderful, feels fantastic and I feel like a child again.

All around me there are fireworks and Ferris wheels, bright lights and happy, smiling faces. The fireworks give out with small warm explosions sending millions of sparks flying off in every direction. All around me there are fireworks and Ferris wheels, bright lights and happy, smiling faces. The fireworks give out with small warm explosions sending millions of sparks flying off in every direction. All around me there are fireworks and Ferris wheels, bright lights and happy, smiling faces. The fireworks give out with small warm explosions sending millions of sparks flying off in every direction. Catherine wheels spin spraying fantastical spirals of every conceivable light and colour. Then I'm in outer space it's nearly all black apart from thousands of beautiful twinkling stars which are fairy lights being turned off and on by a huge fat lady in an overflowing pink satin dress who is standing in the doorway to the room with a big flashing control pad for all the lights in the Universe. I lick her dress and suddenly I have candy floss in my mouth and I am back at the fairground and a clown is laughing at me, mocking me, bells are ringing loud, and all my friends are behind him pointing and sniggering their faces all distorted and mis-shapen they look like a pack of hyenas.

I feel a huge spike into the middle of my back, a horrible stabbing, ripping sensation and I'm forced to stop. For a moment everything goes black.

* * *

I'm running down a road. I'm naked, I don't know why but I notice that my bare feet are hitting the warm tarmac with a slap. It's pitch black apart from the moonlight catching the cat's-eyes in the middle of the road. I'm holding my trousers and my shirt in my right hand. They're soaking wet, whipping back at me as I pump my arms. And sweat is pouring off me as I run. But why the fuck am I running? I turn to look behind me and three men are running too. But then maybe they're not men. I look again and they're the Spanish lizards and geckos from before, in the club. The three fat cunts are running behind me. One of them is huge and I think I recognise him, but I don't stop, because they might still catch me. I think about it though and reassure myself in my hazy logic that I am fitter and faster than they are and as long as I keep running, they will tire before I do. It's true. I am. I've been doing my press-ups all holiday and going for the occasional run on the beach. They're maybe fifty metres behind me I guess, although its difficult to be precise as my vision is a little hazy and it's very dark. The Tyrannosaurus Rex is really struggling with the pace – I thought they were fast fuckers, terrorised the rest of the dinosaurs and all that. Maybe tarmac is not his track of choice. And his little arms are useless, just hanging there, as his legs labour to carry all his weight unaided. My mouth tastes salty but the air tastes sweet and heavy with the scent of herbs the way all hot Mediterranean nights seem to. The muscles in my legs are burning and my head is pounding. I make another mental push and try to sprint even harder. I'm not sure how much longer I can keep this up. I hope that they will stop chasing me soon. When I look behind me again only the very tall man is still running. But I can see that the other two have stopped and are calling him back. My Spanish is not good and I am fucked but I can understand that they are trying to call him off. I look down because I feel a cold wet sensation between my legs. In the moonlight, I can just make out that blood is streaking down my thighs and on my right leg it's reached all the way down to my ankle. It looks like blood, but it's so fucking dark that I can't be sure. I feel nauseous. And so I stop.

* * *

When I wake up it's dark.

I feel like I have been hung, drawn and quartered. My head is pounding, and I realise it's not only a hangover, when I lift my hand to my forehead and come across a huge bruise where my flat forehead used to be. My mouth tastes disgusting. I have no idea what has happened. I'm not entirely sure where I am, but I assume it's the villa. How did we get home? I'm in bed, and then I recognise the faux-Picasso prints on the wall. I am in my room in the villa. I feel relief but there is a black hole. Something ominous tugging at my consciousness.

I reach onto my bedside cabinet, where I keep my mobile in order to check the time, but its not there. My watch isn't on my wrist and it's not on the bedside cabinet either.

"Max! Max!…Max! You there?"

Nothing. I crawl to the door and open it whilst kneeling. I can see Max's silhouette on the terrace. He's drinking what looks like a bottle of wine and smoking. Then I can hear him talking softly although I can't make out the words. He's on the phone. Must be Lorraine. Of course. He sees me and makes some very hurried excuses and hangs up.

"Mate. Get back to bed! What you doing up?" Max jumps up out of his seat, chucking his phone onto the table. He helps me very slowly to my feet and guides me back to my bed and lies me down.

"Mate. You gave me a fucking scare."

"I feel shocking mate. I feel...dead...I...feel...nothing. What happened?"

"Pretty fucking scary mate. Do you not remember?"

"Not a fucking thing. The last thing I remember is being out on the roof terrace at Pacha."

"Mate, that was last night, about twenty hours ago."

"Shit, what happened?"

"I don't know. All I know is that I couldn't find you at the club when it finished. So I presumed you'd pulled. I tried texting you but you didn't get back to me.

"Where's my phone?"

"I don't know. Shit, have you lost it? You should phone Vodafone and cancel it. Bar the calls."

"No idea where it is."

"Fuck. Anyway, so I went down to the port to get the first ferry back here and there you were. Looking like shit, but there all the same. What did you get up to?"

"No idea. No fucking idea."

I am seeing flashing lights, grabbing hands. Everything's a blur. Single-frame snapshots are exploding in my mind like the burnt out flashbulbs of dozens of old cameras guilty and explaining.

"Don't you remember?" Max asks me

"Nope."

But I do. Darkly I remember dancing. The song was "Silence" by Delerium. I remember being with this beautiful tanned woman. She had short black hair. The whites of her eyes were really white. Really, really white. Her boyfriend was watching.

"Your foot was covered in blood. Did you cut yourself? You must have."

He was standing by the side of the dance floor as we danced. His girlfriend turned into a newt so that her boyfriend wouldn't mind. He didn't. He just kept pulling us back close to where he was standing so that he could watch. He was smiling as his girlfriend rubbed herself up and down against me. I was getting hard. He saw that I had a hard-on.

"Dunnno. Where are my shoes?" I ask Max to keep him busy as I try to remember more.

"How should *I* know?" Max asks me incredulous, eyebrows arched, creases in his forehead.

"And then what?" I try.

She pushed her hand into my trousers and felt for me. Grabbing me, pulling me out of my trousers, guiding my hand to her cunt. Her boyfriend kept nodding. Smiling.

"Well, we got the ferry back. You were fine all this time. Talking bollocks, but fine, nothing unusual. When we got back here we went straight down the beach. You insisted."

"What?! And?"

"Well, I don't really know. To start off with you were fine; just mucking about, drinking beer, sunbathing, jumping in the sea, whatever. Then I'm lying down, having a nap…and you come r-r-u-u-u-nning out of the sea, well stumbling really, kicking sand all over people, and you're just about reach where I am, you fall to your knees and just start puking, weird stuff. Not just normal stuff, like food. Well we hadn't eaten for ages anyway, so there wasn't much of that, but there was this like…bile. Weird. Yellow and foaming, and…mate, maybe, no definitely, a bit of blood.

I was jostled over to where the boyfriend stood grinning, dribbling and frothing. His fly was open and three pairs of hands guided my hand inside his fly. I tried to resist. It was impossible. Large hands were on my forearm forcing my hand inside his shiny trousers. The girlfriend was rubbing the head of my cock trying to coax me to touch her boyfriend.

And you were mumbling. Something about running, *'gotta keep running'*, *'gotta keep running or they're gonna catch me and…'*, and you were humming that "*There may be trouble ahead*". Then suddenly you stopped and lay down. You seemed ok, so I left you alone for a while – you know, to sleep it off. But it got really hot around twelve-ish so I decided that we should come back here. So I tried to wake you up but I couldn't. You just wouldn't wake up. Nothing. Whatever I tried you wouldn't come around. I was throwing water on you, ice, everything. The group of people next to us looked up and stared at us. Then they moved away. I started to panic, but then Gunther turned up and we got a lift from Gunther, who was lovely and concerned about you.

I tried to kick at whoever was behind me. My hand felt sweaty pubic hair. Coarse pubic hair. A tiny penis, wet, sweaty and hot. My hand was being forced up and down by the two huge reptiles towering over me. They were roaring at me to do as I was told. I reached for his balls and grabbed them as hard as I could.

Thank fuck the Travel Agency Rep – that Eleanor – didn't turn up. She would have wanted to take you to the hospital."

"Fuck that! Thanks mate. I couldn't have gone to the hospital. How did I get this fucking massive bruise on my forehead?"

"That? I have no idea. Although I seem to remember that you had it at the port so maybe you did it when you went AWOL during the night. How does it feel now?"

"Fucking painful to touch, but ok I guess."

I heard the scream, his, in my ear. And then I felt the needle in my back. It had to be a needle. A needle with some sort of tranquilliser in it because the next time I was conscious I was outside with these three goons being raped by the side of the road.

"Mate, it was pretty grim stuff on the beach."

"Sorry."

"No don't be sorry. I was just worried. What on earth happened to you? Did you get into a fight?"

"Not sure. It's all a bit hazy?" I realise my hands are shaking and I sit on them.

"Well if you can't remember from when we were out on the terrace last night, that was about midnight. And now its nine o'clock. That's twenty-one hours. And what was that about the running, and why were you singing "*There May be Trouble Ahead*?"

"I couldn't tell you." *I wish I could but I can't. I know but I can't say. You're my best mate but I don't think I can tell you this. I'm not really sure if I've told myself yet.*

"I think you might have been snogging someone's girlfriend," Max offers helpfully. He could be right.

"Yeah - I was snogging someone. There were these three blokes. They were dancing really aggressively in front of me, making fists of their hands, and throwing them towards my face. I was snogging this newt, well, bird. You know…"

"What? You were snogging a newt? Were you hallucinating again?"

"I don't know. Sorry. It's all really…really…vague. Must have been I suppose."

"Sounds weird. What about the blood? Are you cut?"

"No, can't see anything. The very last thing I remember was dancing with that cute bird that looked like a newt and snogging her. Then I came up and I was fucked. I mean fucked. Really fucked. Seeing stars and all sorts. I came up really strong on my pill. I started hallucinating again and these three guys kept trying to grab me. I think they wanted pills. Or they wanted to buy me a drink."

I had one of the goons below me trying to lick my balls. Someone was behind me fucking me. It didn't hurt though. My sphincter felt numb. Two people were beside me. I couldn't quite see who they were because it was so dark. My eyes were still adjusting and I was still feeling groggy. But by the noises I could tell that they were fucking too. There was a woman's high pitched squeals and a lower pitched grunt, which I assumed was coming from a man. I turned my head to look over my right shoulder. The girl/ newt from earlier was bent over double with her feet and hands on the floor whilst someone male, not her boyfriend, fucked her from behind. I looked further behind me to see who was fucking my arse. It was her boyfriend. I tried to assess the situation. Her boyfriend gave me a toothy grin as he rocked back and forth. I felt nothing. You won't hurt me you fucking cunt. You won't hurt me. But I will hurt you. I will hurt you.

"What? What three guys?"

"I dunno. These three guys. I was hallucinating again."

"I don't remember them."

"I don't remember *anything*! Max, I've got to stop this. Something's happening in my body."

"Could be an idea mate. At least for a week or two."

"No I mean forever mate. Give them up."

"Hmmn, don't over-react, though."

"I'm not over reacting mate. What's the point if you can't remember a thing anyway, go missing for half the night, puke bile up and wake up with a massive bruise on your head? Is that a good fucking night? That's fucking grim. And sad. What's it doing to us?"

"Maybe you just need to take a few less. I mean you do take quite a few, really quickly. Or just take a break."

I returned the boyfriend's ugly smile with one of my own. He decided to get up from behind me. He came round the left side of me. The fat man had stopped trying to lick my balls from underneath and was trying to direct me towards his own nether regions and I saw my chance. As the boyfriend positioned himself helpfully in front of my face so that I could access his genitals I reached down in between the other guy's legs. His body relaxed. The boyfriend's cock was in my face. I raised my fist and brought it down as hard as I could on the balls of the guy below and in the same movement I swing it back up. I grabbed and squeezed the boyfriend's nuts. I lurched forward and butted him in the stomach bowling him backwards onto his arse. I saw my clothes; at least some of them strewn on the ground grabbed them and ran. Ran and ran and ran.

* * *

"You all right mate?" Max asks me. "Looks like you've drifted off. I think you should go back to bed."

"Yeah I will in a bit. I'm all right though. How many did we have?" I ask him. It's a redundant question.

"Well, I had six, but I reckon you had more. Maybe eight, maybe even ten? And they were strong too."

"Fuck. No."

Max's mobile vibrates. A text. He doesn't say anything. I see his face screw up. Max hands me his phone in disgust.

"It's a text. For you. From Rachel," he says, "she wants you to call her."

I ignore him and take the phone. It just says.

Max pls pass this onto Alex. Alex, are you having fun? I miss you. I'm sorry I've been rubbish. Pls call me. R. X

I delete the message.

"She is leading you on mate."

"Look, you don't know anything about it ok! So just fucking leave it out all right?!" I spit these words out and Max looks shocked.

"Alex. Calm down. Look, I'm just saying that I don't think it's going to work out well for you, that's all."

"I…I know."

"She would have split up with Rupert by now mate." He's leaned forward and put his hand on my knee. I flinch and feel like I want to punch his lights out. *Punch my best mate's lights out.* "Mate, I'm gonna go to bed. I feel tired."

As soon as I shut my eyes I am assailed by images of the night before. *I see huge bulging penises in my face, purple veins bulbous and popping; sweaty, gurning, leering faces spit at me and explode in front of my eyes. I see the dark gravel of the road and I see myself being dragged. Burning scratching skin. Raw and bloody wet flesh. I see rivers of molten pus flowing like an erupted volcano. I see my own hand disappearing into a seemingly dark and never-ending hole. I feel cold clammy snakes and worms. My hand is severed at the wrist. I pull it out and stare at the spurting fountain of blood shooting from the stump of my forearm. Pills are being poured into my mouth. Bitter, chalky pills, crumbling and making me choke. Tens, hundreds, thousands are being forced in by big muscular hands. One is holding my bottom jaw open like a clamp, one my top jaw, another holding my nose. I can't breathe; my vision goes cloudy; my eyes are streaming; I see reptiles' scales. I am choking.*

I wake up coughing, gasping for air and drenched. I feel like my gut is about to fall out of my arsehole. Spitting and dribbling bile out of my mouth I head for the bathroom, naked. My feet are slipping on the cold tiles because they are drenched in sweat. I slip and land hard on my right knee,

"Fuck!" I scream, as a jolt of pain shoots through me like a huge electric shock, and decide to continue the rest of the way on hands and knees. I look behind me and see that I am leaving the human equivalent of a snail trail of mucus, bile, blood, sweat and saliva on the pristine tiled floor of the villa en route from my bedroom to the bathroom, like I am Jabba the Hut. I start spewing as soon as my head is hung over the side of the bowl. It's a dead weight and my burning cheek rests somewhat soothingly against the cool porcelain. My stomach wretches painfully again and my body swings up involuntarily to heave another litre of stinking liquid down the pan. I feel my sphincter loosen and warm mucus leak down and out onto the shiny white tiles of the bathroom floor. Red flecks and streaks make pretty patterns in the pale yellow slime. My eyes are burning through crying and I am letting out huge sobs as my face burns with a thousand pinpricks of bursting capillaries and blood vessels giving out through sheer humiliation and degradation. I am exhausted and I don't want to be sick anymore. It's too painful. I turn and sit shambling in my own excretions. Through glassy, blood-shot and beaten eyes I see Max standing in the doorway.

He looks as white as a sheet. Surely he must see now this has to stop. He is nodding his head. How can I ever tell him?

* * *

We leave the following day and land at Gatwick, an hour delayed and in a sinister replay of the scene in Ibiza airport, the baggage reclaim hall is filled with the 'beep-beep' of texts arriving on people's phones. We're back in Not So Cool Britannia, I realise. Yeah, thank *you* Mr Blair. Things can only get better.

HAPPY BLOODY BIRTHDAY

t's 8.30am on my birthday, a Saturday two weeks after we have come back from Formentera and I am fielding and replying to the piss-taking and well-wishing texts beep-beeping on my mobile. In fact I am trying to reply to just one such text from Flex whilst having a piss when the front doorbell rings. I stop pissing. I put the phone down and wash my hands.

The man from DHL offers me a cardboard box. Could it be something from Mum and Dad? I did mention the Global knives last time we spoke. Or will it be more boxer shorts and socks?

I sign his little handset thingie Hugh Jarse, which I think is not a bad joke seeing as I got it from George Michael. I heard he used to check in to hotels as Mr. Hugh Jarse. The DHL man doesn't notice, in fact he doesn't say a word and he has headphones on and is chewing gum.

This is exciting! I honestly have no idea what it will be and am shocked at how excited I still get at the age of twenty-nine. I go back inside and I rip the thing open. It's a parcel, from Rachel, wrapped in expensive-looking grey paper. It says "From Rachel, with love…?" on a small plain tag taped to the top of the box. I feel myself frown. I feel empty and blank. I open the lid of the box and inside is a beautiful set of two chrome mugs and saucers. I sit back on the old red sofa to contemplate them. They mean nothing to me and I get up quickly and walk towards the kitchen. I send the entire box sailing through the air and it smacks through the swing lid and hits the bottom of the bin.

Lulu is in charge of the evening celebration logistics and she's decided upon a huge meal in La Rueda, the Spanish tapas restaurant on

142

Clapham High Street, followed by everyone getting up to mischief back at mine. So we're standing at the bar having a few drinks while we wait for our table. Luke, Dan and Flex are getting loud and lairey, and it's only nine o'clock. Some idiot orders Russian Spring Punches.

"How do you spell playa?" Max is asking me., "A-L-E-X G-R-E-E-N-E. That's how!" And he splatters my cheek enthusiastically with spittle without pausing for breath with his new teeth.

Luke looks like he spoiling for some argument or other with me. "Hey Big Brother, who's it going to be tonight then?"

"Hey?"

"Don't give me that. Will it be Rachel, or Shannon or maybe someone new? Eh?"

"Jesus. What's your problem? Can we have this moral lesson some other time please? I.e. *not* on my birthday!"

Luke looks at me with daggers and stomps off to the toilet, it would seem, just after Richard Gardiner.

Shannon bounces over and gives me my birthday card, and a big kiss on the lips.

"What happened to your face? How did you get that graze?"

"Fell off the moped, no biggie," I smile and kiss her back, I hold her for a second and press close into me. She smells good. And she whispers "Happy Birthday Gorgeous Boy!" into my ear and pulls away.

Max passes me a dangerous and dodgy looking concoction that he and Flex have been in a conflab about, deciding upon ingredients. In the end it looks like they have gone for every ingredient behind the bar. They've been shouting instructions at the barman for ten minutes. Quite rude, as they are all highly qualified cocktail-makers in here.

"Here you are Lairey-Boy!" And he thrusts this pint of thing, all multi-coloured and foaming into my hand.

"Ah, cheers, Posh-Boy. And what's in this?"

"We'll tell you when you've downed it son! Waheeey. Get it down yer." Flex has his hand behind my head shoving me nose first into the drink.

"What *is* this?"

"It's Your Birthday!"

I down the concoction in three slugs. I raise my glass high in the air to applause and stereophonic cheers and laughter.

"Barman! Another six of your finest Russian Spring Punches please!" shouts Flex.

The night hurtles along. It seems like everyone just *has* to buy me a drink. And it seems that each one of these drinks has to have the most alcohol in it ever. It's like they're competing to see who can win some perverse competition to see what is the highest alcohol content possible that you can fit into a pint glass. Oh yes, they're all pints. Russian Spring Punches, Bloody Mary's, TVR's, VLS; Absolute Shambles; Champagne Bellini's; apart from the shots: Tequila; Absinthe; Abortions; B52s. Copious cigarettes. White shirts far too inviting to remain white for too long. "No, honestly. I think the red cocktail is actually a great accessory to your white top, Shannon, it adds character."

"Really?"

"Yes really."

"You fucking bastard!!! I can't believe you just did that."

"It looks good! Let me lick it off!"

Flex lifts his glass fast to mine and they both smash. A huge roar goes up from our party and a round of applause from the rest of the restaurant. The meal drags on in a haze of lairey toasts, tapas and too much red wine, sangria, tequila and absinthe. Eventually I hear Max, Flex and Luke conferring, before Max climbs on the table to announce:

"Right, we are adjourning to Okeover Manor, Clapham Common North Side. Party! Any questions?"

Once inside, the drugs do not take long to come out. Luke has bought me a couple of grammes of uncut charlie as my birthday gift and we decide to get stuck in. He gives me a hug and gets his wrap out. We barge into the bathroom. Luke does the honours, lowers his head, rolled-note in his right hand. I'm so pissed I don't know if I'm going to get the line up my nose or spill it all down the sink, when it comes to my turn. Luke too, by the looks of him. Laughing, he manages to get most of it up one nostril. As he stands up he hands me the note. "Aaaaah. That was good." By the look in his eyes and shaking body I can see he got an instant, massive hit. Must be good shit. He rocks back on his heels, making way for me to get to the sink, but unbalanced by chemicals and booze he leans too far backwards and falls, grasping at the shower curtain as he goes, into the bath, full of ice and lager cans and bottles of champagne.

"Woaah there little bro." I try to grab him, but miss.

Sitting there, presumably freezing his arse off, he's cackling away like a madman, something about Star and the drugs, which I can't work out. He looks like Casper the Friendly Ghost because he's brought the white shower curtain down on top of him. I leave him there, little ghostie, safe in the bath - I've got Charlie to polish off. Which I do successfully. But then I decide to join him in the bath. Sitting down next to him, both of us dangling our feet over the side, arses wet and cold.

"Ha! Ha! Ha! What a load of charlie we've got. Where's Flex? *He'd* enjoy this gear."

"Dunno. He's not in here is he?" He looks under the shower curtain.

"Not likely."

Shannon enters the bathroom. Fed up at waiting for the two of us, bladder bursting, she hitches up her skirt and plonks herself down on the seat.

"Hey! *We* were in here first," Luke screams.

She remains seated, carries on pissing. She laughs at us.

"Aren't your bums getting cold?"

"Oh yeah! Fuck!" Let's get out of here bro!"

Laughing and sodden, Luke and I leave the bathroom, arm in arm.

I grab Max and shout at him. "Mate, let's go back to The Cross again. I feel like getting totally mullered!"

"Are you sure? I thought you were going to take a break."

"Just one more big one. Fuck it, it's my birthday!"

The combination of absinthe and coke has got me talking to lizards and other reptiles inside my head again. It makes me wonder what we have just snorted. It doesn't really feel like coke.

I feel lethal, on the verge of frenzy. I feel like my mask of sanity is about to slip.

The lizards keep appearing in front of me, dancing and offering me small jagged daggers to use, very sharp little daggers. Although one insistent little bugger keeps trying to get me to go outside and build a snow-man. I wouldn't mind, but it's not even snowing, nor has it since February. Max orders the taxis and in a narcotic whirlwind I gurn and swirl and spit obnoxiously through the taxi ride there, talking to Pterodactyls and Lizards and Iguanas. I'm telling them that it's my birthday and I want to get trashed, fucking fucked, trucking fucking fucked, trashed! And that's what we tell the door-whore when the seven of us blaze into The Cross. They let us in for free and we walk in and almost don't recognise the place. Not because we're so inebriated, but because since the last Renaissance barely a month ago, they have totally re-organised the layout of the club. And not just that, it has doubled in size. They have taken over the rest of the railway arches behind King's Cross station. It used to be four arches and now it's eight. The atmosphere of the club is gone. Gone, gone, gone. We don't know where we are. And I've lost Max, everyone.

I move. I am stopped by a very polite but nonetheless insistent reptilian, who won't let go of my hand; a lizard I think, although I can't be sure of this. Where *is* Attenborough when you need him most? *Fucks sake.* Some people call them geckos. At any rate I'm not in any state of mind to discuss which side of the greater iguana family she is from. I say *she* because this lizard / gecko / whatever is definitely female. I mean, what I actually *mean* is, is that it, sorry, *she* has breasts. Or at least it *had* them. Now they've disappeared. Christ! *I am mullered.*

The lizard says to me:
"Oh my God! Excuse me. Can I ask you a question? I mean I'm sure you're not. But are you? I just wanted to say: You look like Huey from the Fun Loving Criminals. Has anyone ever told you that before? You so do!" She's an American lizard?! How do they do that? She stands upright on her two hind legs, balancing cutely on her tail. She's holding a VLS in her right...her right...err...what are they called? I mean what are lizards'...'hands'...called?

Hands? They don't have hands you moron. Morning moron. Moron. Moroccan Moron. Mormon. Moomin. The Moomins. Movenpick ice-cream. You scream, we scream, we all scream for ice-cream. The Scream by Edvard Munch: good painting, that.

Do they have hooves or claws?

Oh fuck it.

or pincers?

Yes, pincers.

"And the male gecko expands its pincers."
Thank you Mr Attenborough.

Wait. Hold on a second. Focus. What *am* I supposed to be doing?

I don't know. Wow look at *her...*

Wait…lizards…pincers? Mandibles. No! That's the jaws…and that's locusts, grasshoppers, crickets. That's just not cricket.

No, look you're supposed to be doing something Alex.

You fuckwit; concentrate.

Fucksake. Concentrate. Orange juice. Without bits. Bytes.

Oh yeah, hold on, I'm supposed to be looking for Max; everyone.

…………………………hmm.

"Thanks love. Sure, I'll let him know. What? What did you say?" *Who on earth am I talking to?*

I want to go home, I want my Mum.

I don't know where I am.

I don't recognise this place.

I want my Mum.

This isn't my club.

Am I not happy?

I am not happy.

I want my Mum.

The thick velvet drapes dividing up the club, creating intimate spaces, have gone. The brick walls have been painted white; it looks like IKEA. It's too bright. The industrial pipes have disappeared, replaced by discreet air condition vents in the new false ceilings which makes it look like an office.

There are people just milling around, mostly just wandering about looking puzzled. Looking for their favourite spots, which of course have been moved, or simply do not exist anymore.

"A refurbishment! There's the lounges, there's a chill-out zone. Well? What do you think, guys?" asks Marcus Jones, one time punter at The Cross who used to get fucked with us and lose his shit on the dance floor to Nigel Dawson like the best of us, now manager of the London franchise, as it says on his badge.

"Oh my god," shrieks Luke. "What have they done?"

I, Max, Luke and Flex are stood arms by sides, askance, distraught.

"Max. Fat-boy wants to know what we think about the new refurb," I shout out to Max, with Marcus Jones well within earshot. "He wants to know our opinions, as 'valued and regular punters' - his words those, mind you, as to what we think about the changes!"

"No. It's no good!" He shouts back. "They've ruined it! Tell him to put it back to the way it was before."

"Nah. It's no good." I shout at Marcus. "You've ruined it! Put it back to the way it was before. You cunt."

"Why?"

"It's not the same now. It's not as intimate. What's with the white fucking walls for starters? Is this a bistro? It's too fucking light. This is a nightclub! Nightclubs are dark. You go there at night. We can't chat to Nigel. We can't hassle Brian into letting us have a go on the lights."

"So, you want it back the way it was so that you can do the lights?! Fuck off."

"Fuck off yourself, you fat knacker. You asked us. That's what we think. And don't call us 'punters'. We've actually been coming here longer than you have! Which is presumably why you *did* ask us. Actually, why the fuck *did* you ask us? I mean, what I mean is what can *you* do about it anyway?"

"Yeah, what can *you* do about it, you fat shit?" shouts Flex.

"Well, you've been coming a little while now, and we like to keep in touch with the average punter. What the punters like…"

"What?!!! What the fuck was that?! What the fuck did you say? The 'average punter'?! Do you know what, fat-boy? You cunt! You fucking slag! Don't you call us 'average punters', you fat cunt!" A Lizard is trying to crawl into the left corner of my left eye. 'Fuck off! *Not now, please!*'; fucking reptiles never know the time nor place: no fucking manners. Just like this fat cunt in front of me. He'd have to be taught a lesson.

"Look….I, I don't want any trouble f-f-ffffrom you l-l-l-lot…" stammers Marcus.

"No. *You* look, you fat cunt. You *are* a fat cunt. And an arrogant, ignorant one at that. I've been coming here longer than you have been licking Chapman's hairy, spotty, pink arse. We are not fucking 'punters'. We *make* this place. Without us, this place is nothing. Without us, *you* are nothing. No, in fact, you are nothing anyway. You're nothing but a little arse-kisser. And you've got no real say in what goes on here anyway, you little shit! Without *us*, Renaissance is dead!"

"Right. That's it! You lot: OUT! Security…I need some back-up." Marcus bends his fat neck to his collar so he can speak into his security headset.

"Fuck you, fat-boy!" And with that, I swing for him.

It's just like I'd imagined it to be. Hitting Marcus I mean. It's hilarious. After his face has collapsed to absorb the blow politely and like a well-made blancmange, Max and I just stand there in silence for a full second or two before bursting out huge bellows of roaring-lion-like laughter. The fat franchise manager lies on the cobbled terrace spluttering, scratching around for something. None, of us can quite work out what it could possibly be.

"What's he looking for?" I ask.

"Oi, what you looking for, you fat cunt?!" Flex shouts.

"Food probably."

"Yeah. Or his pills," says Max.

"We should have ripped his arms off and battered him with them," decides Flex.

"Yeah. Too right," I agree.

"Right. Let's go and sort Mr. Chapman out." Chapman is the guy that runs Renaissance. It's his baby, and presumably his idea to make these changes.

"Right!"

We turn and head for the office. Not sure what for. The lizards are clouding my vision now and I can't see much apart from scaly skin coming in from the corners of my eyes to cover my whole retina.

"Shit!" What's going on?" I hear Lorraine ask as we storm past.

"Nothing! Fucking nothing!" I shout.

We storm past the rest of our gang, I am flanked by the most terrifying flying lizards and dinosaurs. I egg them on *"Come on! Now is when we dance!"*

"Oi! Chapman! Chapman!"

"Chapman, Chapman, get out here you cunt."

"You lot!" Ben, the head of security bellows at us. "What do you want? Jake ain't around."

"Yeah right! Come on Chapman! Get out here. We need a word, son."

"Yeah. We need a fucking word!" Flex backs me up.

"Look, I told you he's not 'ere. Now fuck off. He ain't 'ere! Go on, fuck off! Or you will wish you 'ad."

"Fuck off, cunt! What do you mean he's not here. Get him out here now!" I scream.

Jake Chapman appears on the terrace: "What's going on? Oh, no it's not you two again."

"Ha! Ha! Knew he was 'ere you fucking lying bastard, Ben." I point and scream at Ben like a maniac.

"This lot have just beaten the shit out of Marcus," Ben reports.

"Oh, fuck off. One punch. He was being a cunt an' rude!" explains Flex.

"What the fuck is happening to our club?!?" I shout.

"What do you mean *your* club? You little fuckers. Who do you think *you* are?"

"We are," I say, swaying on the spot I am standing, puffing out my chest, "Messrs Maximilion Campbell and Alex Greene Esquire. The finest clubbers in the land and your most loyal servants sire."

"You are mad mate. You need 'elp. Are you on drugs?"

"Course we're on fucking drugs Loads of 'em."

"Tonnes," Max corrects me.

"Tonnes," I agree. "Your Star gets some good stuff."

"Oh, you little cunts! You leave her alone! I *know* it's you she fucks off with all weekend! You leave her alone. Do you know how old she is?"

"Oh fuck off will you! What? Are you accusing is of being paedophiles now are ya?! Do *you* know how old she is? Do ya?! It's *you* that should be ashamed of yourself. Having her flog your drugs for you. You dirty old cunt!"

"You're a fucking disgrace Chapman. You know that? We used to have real respect for you. You know that?" says Max.

"You'll not see her again you cunts!" he says.

"How you going to stop her Jake? You can't just take control back whenever you want you know. Once you've lost it, you've lost it."

"You'll leave my niece alone or you'll wish you never met her," he says.

"I wish I'd never met *you*." I say back to him.

"We're not scared of *you* Chapman," Max adds, although I'm not sure I agree with him.

"Jake, please just tell us why you've fucked up our club. Sorry, sorry sir, *your* club? Where the fuck are we going to go now?"

"This isn't *my* club you idiots, just as it ain't yours!" He looks frustrated with us. I think he can see how desperate we are. Maybe, just maybe Chapman understands how we feel.

"What?!" we all say.

"I don't own this club. Someone else does, these Chinese bought it a couple of months ago. I just put on Renaissance now."

"Who owns it then?"

"I can't tell you that I'm afraid. They don't like people to know."

"So you didn't have anything to do with the re-furb then?"

"Nope. I already told you. Not my venue. And you want to know what?"

"Yeah, what?"

"If I am being totally honest with you, I don't like it either."

I am feeling sicker by the second.

"You want to know something else?" Jake asks us raising his eyebrows, grim-faced and sitting down on the steps leading out to the terrace.

My heart sinks. I'm numb. How can it get any worse? How could they make it any worse? Could they maybe be changing the music policy to r'n'fucking b'? Could they be introducing a dress code of chinos and white slip-ons? Could they lose their late license and shut at 2am?

"What?"

"The owner has 'suggested'" and when he says this he makes those inverted commas signs with his fingers, "that we have the night every week."

"No way! Do *not* do that. Promise us you haven't agreed to that! Promise, please!"

He doesn't answer, his head is in his hands.

"Jake! It won't be the same. You can't do that. It'll kill the spirit. It's a once-a-month only thing!"

"I'd love to agree with you boys. But it's all about money. The owner sees it's a success and wants to cash in on it every week. And he's right.

He's expanded the club to get more people in and by doing it every week, he'll make so much more money. You know it's the best night around. It's in all the magazines; got the best reviews in Time Out, that's why you come, and it will be full every week."

Me, I am livid. I can feel myself shaking inside. I am building up to a frenzy. I look down and my fists are clenched so tight that my knuckles have gone white.

"Aaaaaaaaargh!" I run full pelt at him. He looks up like the quintessential rabbit-in-the-headlights. I am still screaming as I fling myself at him and hit him hard. I knock him off the steps and then we're rolling down them. I get in two good hits on his stomach that knock the wind out of him. He lands on top of me, with his knee in my balls. But then Max is kicking him hard in the ribs and he rolls off me. Ben grabs Max and one of the security guys thumps Max in the stomach, which must fucking hurt. He 'oooofs' out in pain like they do in comic books. I can see the speech bubble hang in the air like a balloon. Flex rescues Max and drags him away. A flurry of kicks and punches rains down on me. I dodge them all or else I block them. All of them are mere glancing blows. The pathetic enemy scores no direct hits at all. I am invincible; impervious to pain. And then two fantastical huge lizards appear at my side and begin to smite and strike out at the attacking hordes. Bodies are thrown hither and thither like matchsticks. They swing their huge powerful tails and take out twenty or thirty of the enemy at a time. They roar tremendous and terrifying roars breathing fire and cleaving heads clean off torsos with mighty sweeps of their gargantuan claws. I turn and run.

Only when we get home do I discover there have been *plenty* of direct hits. Oh yes, plenty. My right eye is a beautiful shiner. There's a comical egg-shaped bruise above my left eyebrow. My ribs kill and my legs are black and blue with bruises from where I've been kicked. Shannon, Star and Lorraine coo and fuss over us. Star is beside herself that anyone to do with her family could have done that to us.

Turns out we actually have Star to thank for calming the situation. Star appeared pretty much after I jumped her Uncle and she started screaming and crying. Jake ordered a halt to the proceedings. And she, lord bless her, told her old man what lovely, charming peaceful people we were. How *he* should thank *us* for looking after her. How he should be grateful for us. How she hoped she would know us forever. And with that we ran, ran like we've never run before and made it to the taxi rank. The security staff made to run after us, but Jake called them off.

* * *

Max and I are whispering, sitting huddled together on the old red sofa.

"Boys? You all right? Ok?" Lulu comes up and asks us, offering us a small mirror with some white powder on it.

"Dunno babes. Can you leave us for a bit? We're trying to work it out. Thank Star for us. Get yourself a drink darling. And Max and I will have V&T's. Cheers." I turn back to Max, "Mate, you know what? That's the end for me."

"Hmn, that's the second time you've said that to me in the last fortnight?"

"I mean it this time, that's the end for me. I've had enough. I can't keep doing it. Turns me strange. It really fucks me up."

"Yep that was extreme."

"Yeah. I wanted to get it on. Really want to start a fight. I feel lethal. I feel like, like, like a fucking reptile. You know I see all sorts of weird reptilian stuff when I'm fucked. Scaly skin everywhere, its fucking scary."

"Yeah?"

"Yeah," I rub my forehead and sigh. I stand and point at the curling, yellowing postcards hung in a little column on the wall, in between the two large sash windows.

"You know, I used to really see the images on these postcards: Spring – tiny, growing quails eggs full of life; Summer – fully grown butterflies, a dozen, every imaginable colour and pattern; Autumn – a beautiful green turquoise and purple peacock feather; Winter – cold shiny wet twigs. The end of life, back to the ground. I haven't turned to 'Autumn' yet, but it won't be long coming. The year is turning. I trace around the words: Summer, Autumn, Winter, Spring.

"Were they just taking the piss out of us? Did anyone else feel this? Did anyone else see all these things? *This* was everything to me. They fucking sold this bollocks to us didn't they? This whole crap about hu-hu-hu-how clubbing was going to be different. How it was going to be about beauty, love and belonging. Bollocks and cunts. Sorry about my language but I feel betrayed. Used. It's all about money. They don't care about us. They don't care about the spirit, the feelings. They just want big clubs, with massive bars, to take loads of money and now they want it every week!"

Silence.

The room seems eerie, almost empty. But it's full of people, supposedly my friends, it's just that they're all sitting in silence. Dumb fucks. And *these* are my friends?
Everyone is staring at me, not nicely.
There's Max, his eyes all shot to pieces, Lorraine asleep dumb in her stupor in his lap.
There's Flex gurning and sucking face with Lulu, not listening to me.
There's Star – God bless her, she's too young to be getting like this. It shouldn't happen. I shouldn't let it happen.
There's Luke lying on top of Dan, finishing off the bottle of poppers. And there's Shannon, sat touching that disgrace of a human being – Richard Gardiner, still with him. Christ I can't stand it.

It becomes light outside, it jars and irritates me further. Bright sunlight bouncing on the white walls. Shadows of the trees move in random patterns on the walls as they blow in the wind outside. I realise I am terrified and tears start to run down my face.

"I had the maddest dream last night," pipes up Shannon suddenly. "My boss, Mike, yeah? Is a crazy Man City supporter right, and, in order for City to get promoted to the Premiership they have to beat Blackburn Rovers tomorrow. So in my dream, Mike and I are at the game standing on the side-line watching the game bellowing at City in full support, as you do. The nearest player on the pitch is giving me the eye big-time. It's David Beckham! Sorry, Richie baby." Richard Gardiner shifts uneasily in his seat. "But it *was* David *Beckham*!!! He looked so fucking gorgeous, I was mesmerised and it was like magnets drawn together. He was running past and just had to run over to me and he simply squeezed my hand and look right into my eyes, right into my soul and heart. I forgot where I was and when I realised I looked across at Mike, my boss, who was giving me that look like, oi-oi, you've done it again Shannon! I then remembered the crowd in the stadium and looked up all around me and there were myriads of faces analysing what was going on here. Half time whistle was blown and David came running over and said that he would spend half time with me because nothing in this world is more inspiring than me. Wow, wow, wow! Instantly fallen in love. He tells me that he has seen me so often before and so wanted me and has decided that he is going to leave Victoria to spend the rest of his life with me. Thank God he didn't really have that crap girly voice as in real life. It was really deep. I was in love, head over heels! He goes back on and scores two amazing goals in the second half. This is when it all goes wrong. I roll over in my scrumptiously comfortable bed with a big smile on my face thinking about David, I nuzzle my head in the pillow then I realise it was totally a dream. And then I wake up."

"Errrrrrr. Thanks for that Shannon", I say in the most cutting, spiteful, sarcastic voice I can muster. The others are giggling, but stop when they realise the ice has *not* been broken.

"What?! It's true! I dreamt it!" Shannon says.

"Oh fuck off Shannon!" A gecko stomps angrily across my vision as I take a big hit of amyl that someone has passed to me. "Beckham plays for Manu U. United, not fucking City."

"Don't tell me to fuck off. I was trying to help, lighten the mood. *You* need to take yourself less seriously Alex."

"'Myriads of faces'?! It's a 'myriad'. 'A myriad'. You fucking thick bitch! Christ! Why don't you fuck off?!'"

"Hey, Alex fuckin' shut it will you! What's the matter with you?! Calm down!...Just calm down!" says Richard intervening on the side of his girlfriend, even though she's just told everyone about a fantasy about fucking David Beckham right in front of him.

"Well, you know what Rich?! You can fuck off too! You fucking tosser. Go on fuck off! The pair of you. In fact everyone Fuck off! Now! Get out! I've had enough! Just had enough. Leave me alone. Leave me-the-fuck alone. That's it! JUST ALL OF YOU, FUCK-RIGHT-OFF!!"

Max jumps up and shepherds everyone out into the hallway, but I can still hear him say,

"Listen everyone, just leave for now. You all know that he doesn't really mean it. He's pissed off about Rachel and that. I'll stay here for an hour or so and try and calm him down and get him to go to sleep." I hear some whispered words from the others and then the front door slam shut.

Max comes back into the room, "Mate. You were pretty harsh on that lot."

"Hunnnh?"

"Well, what's the score mate? You OK?"

"Yep, fine, just wanted someone to agree with me that we'd been fucked by those cunts. You give your life - your youth - to some club, and then, it turns out that some cynical middle-aged, in-the-shadows cunt has been fucking planning it all along, and knows just when he's gonna pull the plug on you. Fuck you right up. It's all so cynical. I feel used. Fuck it. Fuck it all."

"Listen mate, why don't you try to get some kip? Ehh? It is really late. Or very early."

"Yeah. OK."

"You might think about stopping. For a while…?"

"You're right Max, I might."

"It'll be hard."

"I know. Thanks. Want to shine any more fucking revelations on me?" I feel like being sick.

"How you going to go clubbing?"

"Don't know. Maybe I won't."

"What do you mean? Not go to Renaissance again?" Max looks at me incredulous, like I'm mad. I know what I have just said has shocked and disappointed him and I feel upset that I have let him down. But he just can't see what I've just seen.

"After last night? Will you? For starters, I don't think we'll be welcome back there again."

He nods.

"Look, I don't know. I just feel like it's out of control. I don't know what I'll do. But I know I've got to stop taking pills. This psychosis is doing my head in. I don't know who the fuck I am any more."

"Look mate, I've got to go. Lorraine's waiting for me."

"Oh Fuck off. You can fuck off as well then. You and your little Lorraine."

"Oi!"

"Go on!"

"Fucking stop it, Alex!"

"Yeah? Cool mate. I'm really happy for you mate. With Lorraine I mean. She seems great."

"Don't do this Alex! Go to fucking bed."

And he goes.

"It's 8am." I'm talking to myself and I can't even see. "Or is it 9am? I've stayed up with the amyl bottle on my own. And shots of tequila. And vodka. And there's coke, I think, it could be K, all over the place and I'm dabbing it because there's no way I can roll a note. The phone. The phone. I need to phone Rachel. Must phone Rachel. I need to phone Rachel. Rachel. Rach?"

...

...

"Hello?"

"Rach. Hi it's me. Good morning. Except it isn't. 'Good' that is. As in not good. I'm fucked. I'm sorry. I miss you. Where are you? Can you come over?"

Silence.

Breathing.

"Rachel…I need you."

"*I can't talk!*" she hisses. And the line goes dead.

I fall back on the old red sofa and bite my lip. Blood oozes into my mouth and not noticing the pain I suck harder and stare at the ceiling, which is blistering and popping and moving in front of my eyes. It spins and looks like a Bridget Riley, which is unhelpful. Blood drips out of my mouth, down my chin and onto my white t-shirt where it dries, hard.

I sleep all day and night.

When I wake up on Monday morning I phone Max to check they got home ok. They did. After that I phone Billingham's PA and explain that I am sick, very sick indeed.

COLD TURKEY

go to the doctors the same day and after looking at me for all of two minutes, Dr Henman declares me exhausted and prescribes me amoxycillin and codeine and advises bed rest for a week.

"You're diet's fucked right?" he interrogates me in his thick Northern Irish accent. I half expect him to say; *"I know where you live!"*

"Err,"

"You're stressed at work? You went to Ibiza this Summer? Partook in a few of the party favours?"

"Eh? How did you know?" I try to laugh it off.

"You can't do it all mate. You need to rest. You're getting on," and he laughs.

"There you go," he hands me the prescription "and go and get this now from Boots across the road and go home and go to bed."

"OK."

"You're going to go to work, aren't you?"

"Well…"

"Go home."

"OK."

In reality I am glad and I leave, collect the prescription and head home and I go back to bed. I truly am exhausted, shattered and confused all in one bundle and even though I only went to the GP to get the requisite paperwork it is the best thing I could have done and I needed it.

I spend the rest of the week in bed.

* * *

On Friday afternoon I send an email to the Clapham High Way gang inviting them all over. I need to apologise. Twenty minutes later Shannon is at the front door with bottle of champagne.

"Hello babe. You bored?"

"Thanks. Listen…I"

"Shh," and she places a finger on my lips, "Max explained everything. Glass of your favourite?

"Uh-uh. Where's Richard?"

"He's at home sulking. We're not getting on that well at the moment, to be honest."

She swings the bottle up for me to inspect.

"Bollinger, nice."

Shannon fetches two champagne flutes from the kitchen whilst I check for more emails – none yet - and plonk myself down on the trusty sofa.

Rachel <<calling>>

I hit ignore. Shannon smiles at me. I shrug my shoulders. The phone goes again. I ignore it.

"Do you think anyone else will come round?" Shannon asks.

"Yeah, why not? Max and Lorraine will. She's good isn't she?"

"Yeah, I'm so happy for him."

"I'm just amazed they're still together. I thought he would have fucked it up by now. Done something dumb, you know."

"He's not the idiot you make him out to be, you know. He's very funny," smiles Shannon as she takes another sip of Bolli and looks away.

"He is?" I ask incredulously. Not because I am jealous. But because I suppose if totally honest with myself it's that I always thought of Max as a bit of a buffoon; my best mate but still a bit of a buffoon. And that's where I had happily pigeon-holed him. That's where it was comfortable for me to keep him.

"Yes! And she's perfect for him. She likes all the things about him that you think are nerdy and geeky. She's patient with him," Shannon smiles at me.

"You're right. Absolutely right. I do like her. I just want it to work out for him," I say.

"It will. It will work out for all of us one day," and she pats me on the knee and leaves her hand resting there. She squeezes my knee and somehow, for some reason this makes me feel uncomfortable. I stretch up and her hand falls away. "OK. We should do something, it's Friday night," I sigh.

"But you're not 'partaking' any more are you?" she asks back reaching for the bottle of Boli again and topping us both up.

"Yeah. Going to try not to. I should be all right. I'll still go to the clubs."

"Without taking anything?" Shannon asks me, her eyebrows raised.

"Yeah. Why not?"

"Well. Good luck".

"Thanks. Doesn't sound like you have any faith in me".

"I do, *I* just haven't been able to do it before. I tried it a couple of years ago, and lasted about half an hour after we got in the club!"

"Ha! Ha! Why doesn't that surprise me?"

On the old red sofa together we finish the bottle of Bollinger and watch some old videos. Rachel calls twice more and I ignore the phone on both occasions. I show Shannon the phone both times and she simply shakes her head slowly from side-to-side to indicate a firm 'no'.

She takes the phone, presses the red button until it turns off and puts on the floor. After that she takes off her high-heels and lifts her feet up under herself then stretches forward and puts her head in my lap and continues watching the video.

At seven pm Shannon's phone rings.

"Hello. Max?...Yes I am. We're watching videos. No his phone's not on. I'm screening his calls for him...Ok we'll see you in a bit then."

"He is plastered and on his way round with Lorraine, some more Bolli and some vodka. I told him to come over. OK?"

Shannon gets the door and Max and Lorraine join us on the sofa.

"What's the story for tonight? You got any flair?" he asks Shannon and I as he fills us up.

"I quite fancy going clubbing," I offer.

"What?" Max asks.

"Yeah. I want to know whether I can do it or not."

"I think that's very brave of you," says Lorraine "And we should all support you. We could the same thing darling," she says looking at Max and reaching out for his hand.

"Ok then. Actually yeah. There is supposed to be this great new night on at Heaven starting tonight called 'Dirrty Weekend'," says Max. "Shall we go? You can see whether you can go clubbing without taking anything. And Shannon, Lorraine and I will go and get fucked. Who else is coming?"

"I've invited everyone, so we'll see."

Before 8pm Star, Luke and Dan and Flex and Lulu all turn up at mine to join Max, Lorraine, Shannon and I for the evening's entertainment. Star has a new haircut. She has had a neat little bob done. Exactly like Shannon except that the fringe runs in a diagonal, higher above her left eye and meeting her eyebrow on the right. She looks older with shorter hair. I tell her and she is happy and says thank-you. She says she would offer me some gear as a freebie but she knows I don't want any so she won't. She kisses me on the cheek.

The taxis are ordered; the drugs are handed out; nobody can believe that I will make it through the evening without taking a pill or having a line of charlie. Should I blame my friends for their lack of support? Should I feel hurt by their lack of faith? Probably not. I reflect that I have given them such an image of me that they cannot see me having the discipline and will power to stick to my decision. They see me as weak-willed. But I *know* that I am changing. I *am* changing, but I am battling against years of baggage; a self-created image and reality that I now hate.

We hit 'Dirrty Weekend' – a new night on the London scene. Tall Paul is the main DJ attraction and he does a decent enough job, but to be honest I don't have a good night. So determined am I not to succumb to taking drugs that I forget everything else. My friends are dancing like idiots; their faces all go horribly out of shape; they all look so stupid. I cannot get drunk however much I drink; the music doesn't make sense – I recognise some of the tunes, but they don't have the same effect they normally do. They don't make sense. I feel a horrible unease that this is actually only any good when you are chemically altered. I try to talk to

Star about it, but she is only interested in dancing with Shannon. I buy her an exotic cocktail, which she sniffs at and takes two sips of. Then she slides off the stool, thanks me and is lost to me in the dancing, sweating crowd. I spot her newly bobbed hair bouncing next to Shannon's a few minutes later.

But, and this is a big but for me, *I do not touch any narcotics.* I think idly about what Rachel is doing whilst sipping my seventh vodka and tonic. I imagine her shopping with Rupert; choosing Labradors; choosing curtains; choosing cutlery sets; choosing which items to put on their wedding list; choosing, choosing, choosing the items to fit into her life. I don't know why but I always imagine them doing something very domesticated. But, I *do not* ring or text her.

My head hurts so I make my excuses and leave early. Max pats me on the back and says well done. Shannon comes up and kisses me on the lips, but they are really both interested in getting back to the dancing and getting the next pill down their necks. So I go. Terrible things, really: drugs.

It's 11am on Saturday and I am lying in bed, contemplating the shenanigans that the gang would have got up to last night and taking two Nurofen to ease my banging head, when my mobile rings.

Rachel <<calling>>

Rachel <<calling>>

Rachel <<calling>>

I let her ring off and then delete her number from my phone. I sit up and I then go through my Recently Received Calls list and purge that. I double-check that she isn't in my Recently Made Calls list. She is not. I then go into my Saved Messages and delete the **I LOVE YOU MR GREENE. X** message she had sent me one drunk and lonely night. I hadn't believed it then and I certainly don't believe it now. And with that deletion goes all trace of Rachel from my mobile. A very modern deletion. Now, I cannot get in touch with her, which I was pretty sure I wouldn't do anyway, but just in case. I never learnt the number and I am glad of that.

Gone.

She doesn't ring again. I get up and go for a walk around the Common. I come back and read a book. The day passes with me reading the paper, watching some more television and making some pasta before going to bed. I watch Match of the Day at 10.30pm and go to sleep straight afterwards. She doesn't ring on Sunday either. I wonder idly how the gang are faring. None of them ring me either. All day though, I want to ring Shannon. Random feelings of jealousy attack me at surprising moments as I contemplate Friday evening. None of them have rung me. I fall asleep on Sunday night with a frown on my face.

* * *

When I wake up on Monday morning I am filled with a strange and inexplicable yet certain resolve that I am going to resign from work. I don't know what else I will do, but I feel the beginnings of successfully making changes in my life and I want to build on them. In any case, I tell myself, they will probably ask me to work my three months' notice period, and that basically gives me three months to look around for something else and actually decide upon something else.

Chef? What about a chef? Masseur? Football manager?

I dress quickly and efficiently. I sling on my favourite grey suit with dark red pinstripes; white shirt, crisp and spotless. I slip a collar stiffener into each of the collar-tips. Tie, dark blue, grey number. I slip on my black leather brogues, still remarkably well polished after all this time. I look like I'm trying to make an impression on my first day, not at all like someone who is resigning, but then again I like catching people unawares. As I stride across the Common I feel good but I don't know why; clearer in my thoughts somehow. The weather seems to agree with me that it's going to be a good day and the sun comes out from behind this bank of rapidly receding cloud and shines on me for a minute before I disappear underground at Clapham Common.

When I get to work I decide to wait until eleven. I don't know why but I do. I think it just sounds like a good time to resign. Time to burn, as they say. I will ask my Team Leader for 'a quiet word'.

I slip out to the Prêt across the road to grab a mid-morning Mocha and gather my thoughts, prepare my speech: "Well, it's like this you see Libby. This company is a piece of shit; its run by an arrogant stuck-up bunch of wankers like Billingham and populated by an arse-licking jumped-up bunch of hoighty-toighty, narrow minded little creeps... like, well...you." Yeah, that should do it. Yeah right. I am pondering re-scripting my speech when a familiar smell fills my nostrils, a light touch exerts itself on my shoulder and a heavy breast-like shape presses into my shoulder-blade. I don't need to turn around.

"Gotcha!" She says trying flirty familiarity.

"Hi..." I hadn't considered the possibility of running into Rachel at all.

"How are you?"

I want to play a straight bat, so "Fine thanks," is my reply.

"You're ignoring my phone calls!"

"Err, yes, it's over, right?"

I knew there would probably have to be another meeting at some point. But seeing Rachel had simply not registered as something I had to do today. And I was pleased at this. She was slipping from my consciousness already.

"What?!"

"I don't understand. It's for the best isn't it."

"Well yes, but..."

"Look Rach, can we not do this *now*? I've got something important to do. I'm seeing Libby at eleven."

"And? So? About what?"

"Well...to resign."

"What?!" She replies in amazement.

"I'm resigning. Leaving." And I tap my right foot loudly on the floor. Damn I am happy. This was definitely the best decision ever. "I am leaving Fortworth." It made me so happy to say the words! I almost wanted to tell the whole of Prêt. Stand up on the fucking Head Barista's shoulders and announce to all the Fortworth employees in there and all the other City suits: "I'm leaving! You can all rot in hell you cunts!

You deserve each other!" But I don't. But I *do* imagine it all. And it feels good; damn bloody good. I am more than certain that I am doing the right thing. I smile. Rachel is still talking, as usual.

"When? What? You didn't tell me! How? You can't."

It's true. I hadn't told her. Sub-consciously or not, I hadn't told Rachel. My one time confidante and lover. Not whilst I was away, not since I cam back. I had simply not thought to tell her. I smile again. This is good, this is progress.

"Didn't I? Sorry I could have sworn I did. Well you know, I need to do it. It's not me, this…this…" I gesture around me, "Is it." And I don't ask her, I tell her.

"I can't believe you didn't tell me Alex." She looks cross and hurt.

"I only decided whilst I was away. And I only decided to do it this morning. So…I've pretty much got to go. And do it."

She was welling up now which was not exactly what I needed.

"Oh Christ. Please Rach. Don't cry. I didn't mean anything by it. I just didn't get round to it that's all. I was going to…" I am so weak and I grimace at myself for lying to her. Damn! Why can't I just tell her: *"I'm over you, you bitch. And I don't give a fuck what you think anymore. That's why I didn't tell you!"*

"You…"…sob…

"used to"…sob…

"tell me…everything"…sob and a big sniff.

I reach for the Prêt napkins and pass a few to her. I still haven't ordered my Mocha and the clock is ticking. I want to catch Libby before her eleven o'clock.

"Rachel, I have to go. I have to do this now. I need to get to Libby before she disappears into a meeting. It's the right thing for me. I really thought I'd told you. Sorry."

I push her gently away from my shoulder. I check the lapel of my suit for snot. None, thank god. I look her in the eye and smile and leave, without my coffee.

I catch Libby coming down the stairs as I start bounding up them. I have second thoughts as soon as I see her. If I'm honest, she's a decent person, tries to manage me well and tries to do the right thing. But I have little in common with her and the rest of the company. It simply not at all what I am about. I am wasting my life, my brain. My heart and soul is being forgotten, I have to get away. I remember this and my resolve is restored. I'll do it. And I do, do it. I ask her for a word. She tells me she is late for her eleven o'clock. I tell her that it'll only take a minute. She senses what it's about and asks me not to do it now. I shake my head. She asks me if I'm sure and I nod my head. She asks me if there is anything that will change my mind and I shake my head again. She asks me what I'm going to do. I shrug my shoulders. She huffs, raises her left eyebrow and turns to carry on down the stairs. I stand there dumbstruck at the nature of the interaction – I never thought it would be *that* easy. Libby gets to the bottom of the stairs, turns looks back up at me. With no visible emotion she says, "Clear your desk Alex. We won't need you to work your notice. You can leave today. Contact HR and arrange your Exit Interview. Hand in your laptop, you'll be on gardening leave." Nothing else. No good-bye. No thank you for all your hard work, not that that would be applicable. However, she could have understood and thanked me for wasting my days and my intellect away in pursuit of the bottom line. No 'do stay-in-touch'. No, 'see ya'. No 'Good luck Alex!' Oh well, what *did* I expect? All a bunch of cunts.

I whip out my mobile and call Max.

"Parks, Miller and Schwab, Foreign Currency Derivatives Desk, Good Morning Max Campbell speaking."

"Shut it you nonce! They're fucking letting me go straight away! Aaaaaaaaaaaaaaaaaaaargh! I've just done it."

"What?! Aaaaaaaaaaaaaaaaaaaaaargh! You cunt! You fucking cunt! You're joking?!"

"Nope. I thought they'd make me do the three months. But my manager just said they'd let me go today and I still get the money."

"Fucking hell. Mental. You can't have been doing anything that important then?!"

"Guess not. Got to do a bit of gardening that's all."

"Right," says Max, "let's go out and get cunted!"

"You at work?"

"Yeah, course. Where do you *think* I am you fucking idiot? *Sometimes*, Alex, I do worry about you."

"Well, I mean, it's just you're swearing like a trouper."

"De rigeur my boy, de rigeur, they all swear like fucking cunts in here."

I meet him outside his office on Ropemaker Place at 6pm sharp. He is beaming from ear to ruddy ear. And in his right hand he is holding a bottle of Bollinger.

"Where'd you get that?"

"Err, work bar. Don't worry, it's a freebie. I closed some big numbers today. And I told them your news, they hate management cuntsultants here!"

"Let's go."

We head for Two Brydges, an excellent quirky little members' bar just off St Martins Lane. It looks posh and serious at first glance, all oak panels and crimson carpets and hunting scenes on the walls, but it really gets debauched in there, quite down and dirty. The toilets are well set up for drug-taking and the attitude of the staff is laissez-fair to accommodating. However, the ease-of-drug-taking-facilities are of little interest to me now although I do notice them, so I concentrate on getting drunk.

"Mate, me and Lorraine, you know, it's getting serious."

"Yeah I can see that mate. You only just noticed? I could have sent you a postcard. She really likes you."

"You sure? What makes you think that?"

"Well the fact she can't stop talking about you, being with you, all the time."

"She isn't here now."

"Don't be daft! You know what I mean."

"That's great news, because, I really like her. I think she might be the one. I think I may be in love with her. I haven't told her or anything."

"You should."

"That's what I was thinking, but I didn't want to push it."

"Push it? She's waiting at the door mate. It's an open door; push it! If you don't, it might close. I can't believe you can't see that."

"I don't want to fuck it up."

"You won't. She loves you. You should tell her how you feel. Just don't do anything too cheesy – I know what you're like."

"Fuck off!"

"You are and you know it. Come on, drink up."

"You know what you're going to do yet?"

"Nope."

"Brilliant."

"I'm fine with that."

"Good, send me a postcard when you work it out."

"Will do."

* * *

In the morning, I am rooting around in the kitchen, actually munching stale pappadums from the curry I ordered last night when I got in last night when my phone goes, a familiar number I can't quite place. I ignore it in favour of hunting down the chutney in the back of the cupboard to make these pappadums more palatable. Today I would normally be getting up and going to work, suiting-up to make myself more suitable for office work. Work as a very serious, high-minded and professional consultant, but today I'm not. It's nearly ten o'clock and I haven't really got up yet. I've not shaved and nor is it likely that I shall. I am having pappadums for breakfast. I may have a bath rather than a shower, *I may well part my hair behind*, then I may go for a walk, maybe buy the newspaper. What a luxury it will be to have time to sit down and actually read the newspaper instead of catching the headlines via news feeds online at work. I shall need a coffee whilst I catch up on current affairs. Maybe I should go out for a coffee? Or maybe I should go to Borough Market, buy some proper quality coffee and then come back, make a fresh cafetière's worth and sit down and really enjoy it; spread the paper out all over the floor and read all the bits I really want to read but never have time. The editorials, the columns, the letters, the sport section, the *arts* review.

The doorbell rings.

I look outside. It's Rachel.

Fuck.

Fuck.

Fuck.

Fuck.

Fuck it!

Fuck her!

I go outside into the building foyer because I don't want her to come into the flat. I open the front door. I stand there looking at her standing at the door, her collar pulled up against the cold. It's become late October. It's raining hard and behind her leaves scatter and whirl; people are battling across Clapham Common with dogs in tow, or vice versa. A couple are flying a kite, nutters.

I don't move aside to let her in and she doesn't walk away. Eyes locked, I remember the times we had often stood like this - except *then* it was different - holding onto each other tightly, squeezing each other, looking out onto the common. The precious and fragile world we had created over the summer was long gone now though. Biting back tears in gasps, Rachel is finally turning away but says, "I know what you said, but I had to come. So much has happened - I can't begin to tell you - but life is just not the same without *you*. I need…" She raises her right hand to her cheek to wipe away tears and rain. I can feel my eyes widen. I am raging now.

"*You* need? You. You. You! This has always been about YOU! - do *you* realise that?! I needed this. *I* did. *I* needed this *distance!* It's too *late!*" I shout these last words. My hands are clenched in fists at my side. A woman walking past hurries on, head down.

She gasps: "I'll go I…I'm sorry…." She stumbles backwards away from the doorway, out into the pouring rain.

"I have made resolutions to stop taking drugs; to resign; to do something creative; to rebuild some bridges to my parents again."

"I can help you with all of that."

"No, thanks." I turn away wondering what I will do. The door slams shut on its spring. I don't bother going to the window to watch her drive off.

* * *

At 3pm I decide to order a pizza. The Super Supreme arrives thirty-five minutes later, a two-litre bottle of Coke, garlic bread and some chicken wings. It's not that I'm hungry, just bored and indecisive. I am munching my second slice of pizza absentmindedly when my mobile goes. My heart sinks. I assume that it's Rachel. I really really do not want to talk to her again. I look at the phone. It says

Max <<calling>>

And this is the terrible thing. I let him ring off. I decide I will just finish this slice off and then I'll call him straight back. It can't be an emergency. He was ok when I spoke to him last night.

I finish the slice and then demolish another one. Maybe I *was* hungry? I consider doing another when guilt gets the better of my appetite and I decide to call him back. After wiping my hands on the back of my jeans, I pick up the phone. I dial 121 and listen to his message.

"'Ello mate. Only me. Mate, I need your help. Again. Sorry about this. I am leaning on you a lot at the momen'. But this is very serious. I need your advice. Lorraine, well, Lorraine…I don't really know how to say this…Christ. It's so unbelievable. I never really thought this would happen to *me*. Well, Alex, mate you're just not going to believe it. You must call me as soon as you get this."

My heart sinks again. What horrendous misfortune has befallen my haphazard and un-coordinated best friend now? With what evil arrow has Lady Luck wounded him this time? I have never encountered a man so prone to accident and misfortune as Max.

I dial his number and wait. Nervously. It rings several times before a female voice answers.

"Hi Alex. It's Lorraine! Max is just coming. He was in the toilet. Here he is."

"Alex."

"Mate."

"You all right?"

"Yeah, superb."

"Really?"

"Lorraine's pregnant!"

I am dumbfounded.

"Hello?" he asks.

"Is it yours?" I had to. I just had to.

"Course it's mine you fucker," he laughs.

"We-h-ell, I think it's you that's *the fucker* don't you?"

"Well, yes. I suppose in a way I am. Yes," he replies sounding very pleased with himself.

"Well fuck me. That's mad. Brilliant! Congratulations. Wow. Well I mean; I hope it's brilliant. You're both happy about it aren't you?"

"Alex, you *can* be a tit sometimes. We're chuffed. Definitely. She just turned up and told me."

"Amazing mate."

"Amazing."

"Right, shall I come over for drinks then? Or we off out somewhere?"

"Err, well I thought we'd get a take-away. You know, Lorraine can't drink. Pizza or curry and Mum's got some special bottle of wine or something. But yes come over, there's something else I need to talk to you about."

"Cool. Right, I'll be over in half an hour. I haven't had a curry or pizza in ages!"

"Cool."

Fuck me! As I shower and change I think about it: my mate Max, a *father*? Surely not? It's not time. Not him. Surely not? He's not a *Dad* is he? Max, a *father*? Well, I think. Why not? He *is* twenty-eight, he's got a well-paid job; he clearly loves the woman and she clearly loves him. Well yes why not? It's just so soon. So rapid. Before me!

But there is something *else*? What the fuck does he want to ask me? Ah, to be the Godfather. Of course! Always fancied myself as a bit of a Don Corleone. Yep. *"I'll make him an offer he can't refuse," "Michael, don't ever take sides against the family,"* and all that. Smiling and content and overjoyed for Max and for myself, I step out of the shower and towel off.

* * *

"I want to ask her to marry me," he says to me. He is shaking; his hand, holding his Coke, is no nearer to his mouth than when he picked it up a minute ago. His eyebrows are arched so high I am wondering how he has the muscle power to keep them that high, they are almost in his hair. It looks painful.

I am sipping on a bottle of Peroni at the point when he drops this bombshell neatly into my lap; I splutter and spit everywhere. A good deal of it goes up my nose, which is painful. And a good deal goes over Max, which is funny.

"You do?" I cough.

"You don't think it's a good idea? I knew you wouldn't be happy."

"No, listen. I didn't mean it like that. You just surprised me. That's all. It's fair enough. I just didn't really know that you were religious. I mean I still associate marriage with religion and I didn't think you were into all that crap. If *I* ever feel strongly enough about someone to want to have some public affirmation of our love I don't think I'll choose a marriage ceremony. Do you mean as in a church, white dress etcetera?"

"Yeah, why not?" He looks crestfallen. He puts his drink down and stares at it. I have to recover the situation quickly.

"No reason. Just asking."

He brightens a little. "Well I think Lorraine would like it. And Mum definitely would. I'm easy. I just want to make the two women of my life happy."

It was astounding to hear Max talking like this, and it was actually touching.

"So? Do it!"

"Well, I wanted to check with you."

"Check what with me?" Sometimes he could be the most cryptic of people. "What do you mean check with me? Check *what* with me?"

"God, for an intelligent chap, sometimes you can be the most obtuse of people. What am I, being cryptic?"

"What do you mean?"

"What I mean is, are *you* going to be all right?"

Fuck me! Was *I* going to be all right? Fucking joker. It was me that looked after *him*.

"Mate, I'm over the moon for you. Course it'll be all right."

"You tit. That's not what I meant. I mean, will *you* be all right on your own? You're going through a tough time at the minute. You're changing a lot of things in your life and you're being very brave, mate, but…"

"But what?"

"But…"

"Just fucking say it! *But-fucking-what?!*"

"Well I'm worried about you."

They did. They all fucking did. They all thought I was a loser. To be worried about.

"Fucking hell. Are you serious?"

"Chap, listen. It's not meant like that. I just wanted to check with you first. That's all."

I don't believe him for a second. But what can I say? I can't ruin his moment. I will ponder it later. "Mate, thanks for your concern and all your help over the last few…weeks, months, whatevers… It is always appreciated and you're my best mate and I'll love you forever. Don't worry about me. I'll be fine. Besides where are you going to go? It's not going to change that much just because you're getting married."

"And having a baby," he adds smiling, like he was correcting me. *Surely he hasn't forgotten already?* I could see him thinking.

"Sorry, yes of course. Yes, the baby."

"Well I don't know. We may try living abroad or something. Or move out to the country. But I'll just have to tone down the party lifestyle a little when the baby arrives. Help Lorraine out a bit I suppose. You know with…things…"

"Oh I see, yes, the *things*."

He's rambling and mumbling a little and I can sense he's embarrassed. He really wants to be proud of what he's saying and feeling. *Am I really that hard to talk to?* I nod when I feel it appropriate and try to get the right mixture of seriousness and happiness on my face, even if deep inside me there is an element of disappointment. I don't want to let it show. I want to make this easy for him but his unease is palpable. He mumbles on a little more, something about "shared responsibilities". I nod again and give him a broad smile. I lean forward and put my hand on his knee. I decide to cut in because now he's just getting embarrassing. "Mate, I am chuffed to bits for you. The pair of you. I *will* be fine. We will *all* be fine. Whatever happens we *will* be fine. Yeah?"

At this he rallies and his whole face brightens as if a light has just gone on inside. He's remembered something: "Good, good," he says, "because there is something else I wanted to ask you the night when I ran after the taxi."

"Oh?"

"What?"

"Nothing, I thought it was the pregnant thing."

"No."

"No?"

"It's something else,"

"Oh, Christ! I'm confused, but go on."

"Yeah!"

"Well, this had better be good…go on!"

"Err…"

"Well…?"

…

"Well,…?"

"Erm, well, if you're all right with it, I'd like you to be my Best Man. Would that be ok?"

"Mate. I'd be honoured." I honestly feel choked up.

"I know I should really ask an old school friend, or a member of the family. And I know we've only known each other a few years; but after all we've been through together; and we've become such good friends; I couldn't really think of anyone else I'd rather have next to me on the day and, and…"

"Mate…" I grab him and hug him. "Wait, you've been sitting on this since August?"

"Yeah. I didn't know how to ask you."

"You dick."

We raise our glasses together both grinning like idiots. I down the rest of my beer. Max sips carefully at his Coke.

"When you going to ask her?" I ask him

"New Year's Eve I thought, at the party. What do you think?" he asks, eyebrows again looking painfully arched.

"Cheesy."

"Oh cheers. It *is* Millennium Eve, don't you think she'll say yes?"

"What? Are you serious? Oh I don't know, a good-looking chap like you. Why not?"

"Fuck off."

"Jesus Max. You are having a *baby* with the woman. She is clearly mad about you. Of course she'll say yes. You fool! And *you* worry about *me*? You're not right you aren't."

"OK. Sorry. It's just, well, she *is* the one. You know."

"I know mate, I know. She's the one. But if she doesn't turn up soon with that curry, I'll divorce her for you, before you've even got started. I'm starving."

And with that there's a clatter of heels up to Max's front door, much rattling of keys in the lock and in burst the two women in Max's life, beaming, fragrant of curry and laden down with what looks like all the food in the sub-continent. All through the messy, congratulatory meal I keep looking at Max, wondering how all of this happened to him so quickly. Had I missed something? I always only thought about these things for me I realised. I wonder when my turn will be.

And I keep reminding myself that of course Lorraine didn't yet know about the marriage thing. That was to be after all, a surprise, even if a cheesy one. And Max's Mum looked so bloody fulfilled; her only son, happy with his lot.

In the taxi on the way home, I think to myself, *oh well, I didn't bag Godfather, but Best Man is a good consolation prize.* When I get in, I go to bed and fall asleep, smiling.

* * *

I continue to aimlessly look for a job with all the urgency of a sloth. Some of the lack of motivation comes from the fact that Fortworth are still paying me my gardening leave. They are paying me the same amount of money to do nothing for the next three months that they were paying me to do quite a lot for last month and the month before that. I look in the papers but I don't find anything inspiring. I also sign up with a few Recruitment Agencies but I don't hear anything back from them. Useless tits they are, Recruitment Consultants. I really do not know what I want to do. I honestly have no idea what I want to do with my life. Should I?

On a whim on a moody Tuesday I decide to go to an art gallery. That is the sort of thing civilised and cultured people are supposed to do when they have time on their hands isn't it? I decide upon the Tate Modern for no reason other than that I have a vague notion that I want to look at modern art and it's not far away. I have to ask the man at the tube station how to get there and he doesn't know. After much cack-handed investigation I am told that Southwark tube station is my best bet, but from there they haven't got a clue. Cheers. Christ, how hard is it to get culture in this country? I get to Southwark tube and ask the woman there. Clearly she hasn't a clue either. Luckily a very pretty French girl tells me that she is going to the gallery to see Rothko. And that I can follow her. As we exit the tube station, a gaggle of six or more French exchange students greet her and they trot off, gibbering away loudly in French. I follow. Soon we are walking up to a concrete ramp to the massive front doors of this industrial looking power station type-thing. Then I am wandering down the slope inside, wondering where all the paintings are.

I leave the Frenchies to it and decide to meander around at my own pace. I don't want any guides or brochures or any of that crap. I want to discover this place on my own. I take the lift and randomly decide to get out at the 3rd floor.

I wander into a large room. It's dimly lit, sombre almost. There is an atmosphere to this room. The walls are covered in these gigantic pieces. Mostly dark reds and earthy, humid browns. I love it. I love the whole feel of the room. No-one is talking, a few hushed whispers. I read the plaque by the entrance. "Mark Rothko." Hmmn. Yes of course. I remember the prints from books at school. But from the prints you have no idea what the paintings are like live. The reprinted colours were a poor imitation. But now, wow. I like these.

The scale is amazing. Just huge. They are all at least twenty feet wide. It just had never occurred to me that art could be so *big*. The simplicity of a few similar colours painted in blocks adjacent to each other accompanied by the sheer size of the things is actually shocking. I read the information about how he painted them for a New York restaurant, but then changed his mind. But I don't much care. I just keep getting sucked into looking *into* these paintings. They seem to me like giant portholes to another world, or at least to another emotional dimension. I suddenly realise that I am very tired and I take a seat in front of my favourite piece, a black rectangle with a red one and a brown one above it, all on a dark red background. I stare at this thing for I don't know how long, fifteen minutes or more; I lose track slightly. I feel strange and then I realise that there are tears rolling down my cheeks. I rub them away quickly.

I get up there and then with this ridiculous idea in my head to go to The Clapham Artist & Students Supply Shop on Lavender Hill and get some paints and give it a go. Just throw some around.

When I get in, I have a selection of student acrylics. I am advised by the man who works there that these dry quicker and are easier to manipulate than oil paints. He also tells me to get some cheap hard board from the DIY shop and prime that up first before spending too much money on canvas. I think he senses my naivety, but again I don't much care. I am driven with this amazing enthusiasm to give it a go. It's a feeling I haven't felt for a long, long, time. I remember it vaguely, from my childhood, from wanting to be the best. I am eleven years old, playing football with my Mum and Dad watching and cheering me on from the sidelines; so keen to impress, so keen to be involved, so keen to master a new art. For the first time in twenty years I feel enthusiasm.

I spread pages of yesterday's newspaper out on the floor and position the larger of the two pieces of board I have on them and lean it against the wall. I slop the primer on with indecent haste and then sit about impatiently waiting for it to dry. I cannot wait, I want to be able to get on with it. To test myself. I just have this feeling that it's going to be good. Eventually the board is dry. Sod the primer next time. No, do it the day before. Plan things. The new me would plan things.

I squirt a few paints, mostly reds with incredible evocative names, *Vermilion (Hue)*, *Red Ochre*, *Quinacridone Burnt Orange*, *Venetian Red*, *Crimson Cramoisi*; and some browns, *Burnt Umber*, *Burnt Sienna*, out onto a small piece of off-cut board I had persuaded the old man from the DIY shop to give me as a makeshift palette, and I start painting. What will I paint? It strikes me that I have no idea. A huge wall throws itself up in front of me. I feel sick. I don't simply want to ape Rothko. And I'm sure I don't want to do something representational. I cast around for inspiration. What will give me inspiration? What do I *love*? Clubbing; drugs; Renaissance. I'll paint that. Max has taken loads of photos, they are bound to give me some ideas.

I dig the pile of photos out and start to go through them. The memories come flooding back. Happy smiling faces in every one. All right, the faces were gurning and not that attractive. But we were having a good time. And we were *thin*. "Food is the enemy of fun!" we used to sing. I can almost feel myself coming up again as I look through these images. I remember the feelings. Then I see it, a crowd of arms, blurred in the dry-ice. A bright white light; red lights; shards of reflected lasers, twisted shapes, iron, the pipe-work of the club, clouds of dry ice. Atmosphere. There is atmosphere in this photo and that's what I want in my painting. I will paint the atmosphere and the feelings. It'll be abstract *and* representational. I lean the photo up against the mantelpiece. I decide to paint the entire board red and then go from there. I push the paint around and soon have it covered. I put on a Renaissance CD, 'Renaissance Presents…' by Ian Ossia and Nigel. I put on the second CD, Nigel's; it starts with the Miro track *Paradise*, and I turn it up. Loud. I close my eyes. I am in the club; I am fucked. Max is there laughing, dancing. Shannon is bouncing up and down trying to lead me onto the dance-floor. Flex is shouting in my ear that we need to go to the bar again. Star slouches, awkward-looking, beautiful and young. Luke and Dan are dancing, throwing beautiful shapes. I open my eyes and stare at this now bright red painting in front of me. I pick up a large brush and spoon it into the dollop of white on my pallet. I sling it onto the board. I jab and point. I just paint with the feeling and the sounds going on in my head. I dance as I do and I try to turn the random strokes into arms, waving in the crowd. I look at the photo for guidance, but not too much.

The thumping bass of Dominion *Lost Without You* makes me put down some thick slabs of dark red and maroon. The melancholy threat of Mantra *Snake Charmer* sees some black spikes introduced. I carry on in this way for over an hour. I look at the thing and I smile. I like it. I have created a painting. I am sweating. I am covered in paint. I am *ecstatic*.

* * *

Max turns up early in the next morning to show me the engagement ring he's just bought for when he asks Lorraine to marry him on New Year's Eve. He's chuffed with his ring and he shows it to me with touching care and pride. I have to admit it's an impressive piece of kit; a large simple diamond on top of a platinum crown. "Not bad son. Not too shabby at all. How much did that set you back? A week's wages?" I ask. "Few grand," he answers off-hand.

He's looking at the painting, which I have moved to above the mantelpiece.

"Where did you get that? It's nice. Is it an original?"

"What?"

"That." He points at the painting.

"I did it."

"Yeah right."

"I did."

"You never did."

"Yeah, yesterday."

"*You* did *that*?"

"Yeah. Don't sound so surprised. I did it."

"Come off it! Where did you get it?"

"I swear, I did it."

"That's fucking brilliant mate. *You* seriously did that?"

"Straight up, look at my hands, look here are all the brushes and paints."

"It's wicked that, Alex. Really. That the first one you've done? I'd buy that mate. It's fucking brilliant. I didn't know you could paint."

"Neither did I!" I exclaimed. I really didn't. And as for it being good…I had enjoyed painting it and I personally thought it wasn't bad, but I didn't think anyone else would like it.

"Is it a clubbing scene?" he asked. "It looks mad. Feels really familiar. It reminds me of going clubbing. Like Renaissance off it, on one. You know!".

"That's exactly what it fucking is!"

"Seriously? It's great and that is just what it evokes."

"Yup! Wow I'm so chuffed, that's wicked."

"It's brilliant, I knew straight away."

"That's why I did it," I said, "the old feelings were an inspiration. I chucked on one of the old CDs and got down to it."

"Alex, *that* is wicked! There, you don't need a job. You *are* an artist!"

"You seriously think it's that good?"

"Absolutely mate. Definitely. It really is. I'll buy that one off you right now."

"*If* it's for sale…" I said. I had a plan.

"If it's for sale," he conceded. "Sorry mate. But you *could* sell it. If you wanted to…"

"I'll do you another one for your wedding present mate. Now let's have another butcher's at this ring. How much did it *really* cost you?"

* * *

December comes and it becomes apparent that the only other job that I have of any consequence is to arrange the Millennium Eve New Year's Eve party. I abandon looking for a 'real' job entirely. I do a few more paintings along similar lines. I mine all the pictures and feelings and memories I have. I realise suddenly that I have hundreds upon hundreds of images from which to draw inspiration, lasting the last ten years of my life. I outpour all these years of images stored in my clubbing memory bank. It's a cathartic experience. And although I am not deliberately trying to purge myself of the past, I feel it coming out of me and onto the boards. Huge shards of colour and emotion flow out of me.

Not convinced by the quality of the paintings, I am still painting on primed hardboard. I have become good friends with the owner of the Clapham DIY Centre on Acre Lane, a kind old Jamaican guy with three or four really impressive and jolly teeth, the rest not bothered with recently. He laughs at me buying so much hardboard.

"What are ya up to boy?" he roars, presenting his gappy smile, "Are you in a war or sumtin? Are you building a *barra-kyade, m-a-a-a-r-r--n*?" He laughs at me every time I go in, asking for a larger piece of wood and I smile back wishing I had the time to explain everything, but I don't.

"No, no. Not at all," I reply, "I'm pulling them down, mate. I am trying to pull them down."

GREAT PARTY

S tar and Shannon come round a lot; they love the paintings too. They know what they're about straight away. They are my main helpers for the party now. Star takes charge of DJ bookings. She says she'll ask her Uncle about booking a Renaissance DJ – *the least he can do*. Max is happy, overjoyed in fact at the prospect of having one of his heroes playing for us. "Anyone will do!" He beams, "but NIGEL would be extra special."

"I'll see what I can do," Star winks back at him.

Shannon is on the case with the invite list and the booze. Between her and Lulu they are sorting out the drugs. It is one hell of an order and I don't even want to think about how much it'll cost. "Just make sure there's enough," is all I say on the matter.

Luke is in charge of décor, glam but understated, glowing and twinkling and warm without being trashy or looking like Santa's Grotto.

Christmas comes and goes with Luke and me at our parents' house in Wimbledon. My Mum looks sad in a way I can't recall and much more frail than I remember. We *"haven't been to visit"* and we *"don't call to see if everything's ok. Just a telephone call…would be enough…"*

She struggles with the cooking, so eventually Luke and I take over. We sit Mum down on the sofa in front of the telly with a glass of wine.

For the first time in years, I am really hungry on Christmas Eve, and really looking forward to the turkey the next day. On Boxing Day I devour the honey roast ham and left over roasties in one sitting by myself. We don't even have to go to church like we used to and so we spend the evening drinking, whisky for me; Luke gin & tonics; Mum and Dad, sherry. We chat and talk about things for the first time in years.

Nothing ground-breaking, not the topic we should be discussing, but we do talk a little and that's good. I tell them about the painting. My Mum loves the paintings I have brought down and calls me *Picasso*. But she is worried about me leaving Fortworth and doesn't manage to suppress the fact that her eyes are welling up.

Preparations for the party continue and are desperate and frantic. The mobile rings and beeps constantly. My father 'tuts' at me every time it goes.

Star rings to say that her Uncle may well be able to get us Nigel Dawson to DJ for us. It was looking good because his gig in Brighton had been cancelled. It would cost us two-and-a-half grand but I decide it's worth it. It is Millennium Eve, after all.

We head back up to Clapham two days later and start getting the house ready for the party. Luke and Dan come over first thing in the morning with an unimpressed-looking Flex in tow. They immediately set about staple-gunning and tacking paper snowflakes of all different sizes hanging from the ceiling on translucent threads; hanging, pasting and re-pasting silver paper, giving mirrored effects to doors and sections of walls. I think it looks like a mess to begin with but Luke assures me he has a plan so I go with him. Besides which, I have very little choice. It's his design or nothing. After a while it starts to take shape. The early confusion gives way slowly to an icy and sparkly white and silvery heaven. Everywhere you look there are snowflakes of some description or size. LEDs twinkle in amongst the white powdery mist. Winking at the promise of the hazy, crazy night to come. Somehow they have hung cotton wool, thread and polystyrene balls without it all looking disastrously cheap and tacky. It gives the impression of a beautiful fucked-up mist. I smile at Luke and hug him. I admire *his* creativity. The place looks gorgeous. Much better than I thought it would. And it looks better and better as the day goes on and gets darker. The lights become more pronounced; the translucent threads from which the snowflakes hang which were visible during the day disappear from view completely in the becoming twilight. I look up at the ceiling in the main room and see that they have hung a white cargo net of fairy lights. The net hangs low in places like low-lying clouds, billowing down, catching you up in its magic. It really is like looking up at the night sky. Or at least it *will* be to a lot of chemically adjusted people later on in the evening. And I am reminded of a night not so long ago when I last saw astronomy on the ceiling.

I turn the telly on to BBC1 and a reader is saying:

"Today, the last day 1999, the UK prepares to celebrate the end of the millennium.

Britain is gearing up to join a global party in a spectacular array of revelries to welcome in the third millennium.

The scale of the celebrations ranges from large organised events, to street parties to an evening at home watching television footage from around the world.

Despite predictions of rain, millions are expected to pack the banks of the Thames in London Thames for funfairs, music, and street entertainment from 1100GMT until 0200GMT New Year's Day.

Celebrations around the world will kick-off at 1000 GMT as the Chatham Islands, Tonga, Fiji and Kiribati experience the new millennium first.

The people of Samoa will have to wait 25 hours more as the millennium arrives there last.

In between, festivities will be staged around the world.

With Britain's capital as the home of time, eyes turn to the Queen's official opening of the £758m Millennium Dome, in Greenwich, south London.

She will arrive by boat along the River Thames to join 10,000 invited guests including 6,000 members of the public - who have not all received their tickets yet.

Celebrities and politicians including Prime Minister Tony Blair will attend.

In a blow to the celebrations, the Millennium Wheel will be officially unveiled but will not take passengers due to a capsule failing a safety check.

At midnight, a 60m high "River of Fire", created by pyrotechnic candles, will light up along the Thames in 10.8 seconds - as fast as the earth rotated into a new age."

Max turns up with the sound system at around two. He has hired three sets of 1210s, Numark mixers, NAD amps and an impressive looking collection of literally dozens of BOSE and JBL speakers. He sets about directing the team of sound engineers he has also hired for the event, telling them where he wants everything set up. He knows exactly where he wants every speaker, the position of each of the DJ booths, the type of music to be played in each one and the set-up needed to make that happen. He really is a geek. A genius and wicked bloke but a geek nonetheless. As usual Lorraine is standing on the sidelines smiling and watching the love of her life organise affairs.

My rules for a having a great party are as follows; they always have been, they always will be: ensure a massive over-supply of drugs; ensure a massive over-supply of booze. Ensure quality music. Ensure people dance and talk. Mix, stir and enjoy. Sit back and watch the fireworks.

At three, Flex is relieved of his decorating duties in order to go and get the booze. He has a budget of £2,500 and he does well. He comes back with two cases of Absolut vodka and one of Smirnoff a case of Bombay Sapphire gin, six bottles of José Quervo tequila, crate upon crate of Stella, a case of Merlot, a case of Chablis and twenty-four bottles of Bollinger, Coca-Cola, Red Bull, bottles of tonic water, ginger ale, soda water and bags and bags of ice. I knew I'd chosen the right man for the job. We nip over to Sainsbury's together and buy up all of their raspberries and everything else I need to make up a huge batch of Russian Spring Punch.

At nine-thirty the first guests arrive. A few local DJs from the Tea Rooms and their model girlfriends arrive, all Diesel jeans, D&G shirts, Paul Smith or Gucci smells; lots of air kisses, shiny lipstick, stiletto heels and then its straight to the toilets for some immediate nose powdering. It's early for people to arrive but then it *is* New Year's Eve and a rather special one at that. People want to make sure they are loaded up well before midnight. It's not like any other party where they might not turn up until eleven. They commence boshing pills straight away and start dancing in the front room to a few of Max's old warmer-uppers surrounded by snowflakes and fairy lights. Lorraine stands behind him as he puts *Leftfield* on, smiling beatifically at me as I snap her old man spinning. It will be an image of an era for me. Max spinning, that's one.

Lorraine watching, that's another. I remember as I take it that tonight is the night that Max is going to ask Lorraine to marry him. I look at them both and I have no doubt that she'll say yes. I'd better get writing that Best Man's speech sometime soon.

At half-ten Max and I are sharing a bottle of champagne outside the front of the house. We can see in through the front window: the party is really kicking off. Unbelievably, there's Nigel Dawson, the DJ from Renaissance, playing at our party.

"You still popping the question tonight?" I ask him.

"I most certainly am!" He replies with vigour, and he gets the ring out again to show me that he hasn't forgotten it. It looks huge and shiny and full of intent which is surely how it's supposed to look.

"Actually that reminds me. Can I get hold of the key out to the roof terrace? I want to do it out there. That ok?" I give him the key. What a romantic sod, I think to myself and then again, how bloody cool?

Brian who does the lights at The Cross arrives. We go back inside. I get him a Stella. Steve Lawler is here with four women, all blonde; Phil Gifford too, although he'll have to leave in time to play a 2am set at Inigo. I suppose it was a long shot to send Sasha an invite. I wonder where he's spending New Years' Eve? I ask Nigel Dawson what he wants and he takes the bottle of champagne from my hand and, placing it behind the decks, shouts,

"A line! Get us a *fucking* line!"

I grab Lulu who is walking past asking people what they want. She hands me a wrap. Nigel takes the wrap and lines up a fat, rough line with his *fingers*, on the record on his left deck – it's Blue Amazon *No Other Love*, a personal favourite of mine. He fishes a stainless steel snorting straw in the shape of a Hoover from a pocket and polishes the line clean off the record whilst its spins. He brings it in perfectly, the other tune fading out as he smiles to himself pocketing his vacuum cleaner *and* the rest of the wrap.

"Hey, you didn't pay for that!" Lulu shouts at him.

He pretends not to hear with his ears in his cans. I drag her away, giving her the £60.

I decide to have a look in the different rooms and see how they are going. In the kitchen I am taken aback to see to see Luke, Dan and

Richard flirting with each other and mock struggling over a bottle of champagne. Richard is tickling Luke trying to get him to drop the bottle as he tries to pour it. I stop looking at them when I realise how hard I am gripping the kitchen door handle. I barge through the crowd and head for the fridge to get a bottle of Stella. I shove into Richard, hard.

"Hey!" cries Richard.

"What? Get the fuck out of the way man," I say.

"What's the matter with *you*?" shrieks Luke.

"Nothing. Nothing. Just need to get to the fridge. Rich *was* in the way. That's all." I put my head in the fridge too cool it and to hide for a second.

"Ever heard of excuse me?!" I hear Richard muttering.

"Oh Fuck off Gardiner," I whisper to Stella Artois.

I get a couple of beers out, intending to offer one to Dick as some sort of peace offering, but when I turn around all three of them have gone. I look towards the door and just spot Dan's blond mullet bouncing out.

In the main room I find Flex and Lulu shouting and dancing around like a pair of idiots. I join in and we curse and toast the year just gone. We polish off a bottle of Bollinger between us and Flex opens a second. I grab Shannon and Lulu wandering past and shout at them, *"Life is much better with friends in it. Life is much better with you in it. The music sounds better with you."* Flex tells me to shut up.

Lorraine kisses Max. Shannon smiles at me again and we all hug. Star squeezes in for a squeeze. I tell Flex to go and start getting the fireworks ready but not to disturb Max and Lorraine who I see disappearing up the outside stairs with a bottle of champagne.

A little before midnight I lead the masses out onto the roof. Benevolent and surprisingly warm for December, the night welcomes us all out with low hanging clouds, bonfire smoke and the thudding sound of prematurely exploding fireworks spreading their glory all over our wonderful shared city.

One by one we make our way out onto the roof of the building. We get out via a tight, steep ladder on the 4th floor of Okeover Manor and up through the sky-light. I'm out first and when I see the two figures, their silhouettes quivering slightly against the exploding backdrop of sparks and colours, I hold my hand up and put my finger to my mouth in a 'shh!' for everyone to see. Suddenly Lorraine is pulling him up nodding, hugging and kissing. There's a round of applause. They break their clinch. Shannon rushes to them with one of the flower arrangements from the house. Star runs after her clutching a bottle of Bolli and two stems in her elegant hands. She looks so grown up tonight in her posh dress Shannon has bought her. I love her to pieces and feel a certain responsibility towards her which in my current relatively sober and drug-free state seems somewhat less paradoxical than before. Everyone is hugging, it's a beautiful moment; it may be the first truly adult moment of our funny little lives and it makes me feel happy.

"I take it she said yes then?" I say, smiling at Max holding up my glass to toast him. Lorraine has been engulfed by the crowd of females all eager to review the qualities of the rocky-ring.

Then Flex is ready with the fireworks. He's crouched over them and I wonder if he is going to get out of the way when he lights them. I wonder suddenly whether he was the right choice for the Fireworks duties; too late now. Somebody starts a loud, drunk and shambolic countdown. When most of us get to "*1 !*" Flex lets rip with the biggest rocket we have. Then he bolts over to where we are all joined arms. For a brief moment I glimpse some fleeting perfection. Shannon, Star, Max, Lorraine, Lulu, Flex, Luke, Dan, me and even Richard are standing in a circle all linking arms, kissing each other on the cheek, wishing each other a Happy New Year as the fireworks whiz and explode a thousand and one colours above our heads. It's hard to believe the moment is fleeting and yet in my heart of hearts I know that it is. I feel that I am at the end of some sort of cycle with this group of people. I am trying to change my life and although it's hard, I know I will get there. Max's life is about to change immeasurably. And even Flex won't always be…well Flex, will he?. Say it softly and don't kill any fairies but even Peter Pan eventually grows old in real life.

I get yet another bottle of champagne shoved into my hands by the manager of the 365 Bar in Clapham North. "This is a great party, mate. Quality. I'm impressed, seriously. We should do some promoting together. Here's my card. Call me." I'm enjoying getting drunk and *not* taking drugs.

I step back inside and everywhere people are kissing each other, wishing each other a Happy New Year. Shannon drags me onto the dance floor as Nigel chucks on *Silence* by Delerium, which is one of her favourites. She's holding me close and her eyes are closed as we spin round. It's intriguing looking at people when they are high and you're not. Shannon looks beautiful. I want to kiss her.

"Shh," says Shannon, surprising me. Her eyes still shut.

"What?"

"Just keep dancing," and she puts a finger on my lips.

I pull her closer and hold her as tight as I can. I really want to kiss her. Shannon opens her eyes and stares deeply into mine. She is smiling and smiling and trying to give me hope but I don't see the answer I'm hoping for. I want the deep blue of endless invitation, the reassurance that comes from seeing the answers to all of your questions reflected in the eyes of true love, the carefree abandon of total harmony, but instead I see fear. The sort of fear that is built in layers of year upon year of crushed hopes and broken dreams. The sort of fear that is born of failed hopes and so many forgotten promises, drunken arguments and dirty, filthy plain old abuse.

"Why don't you leave him?" I hear myself saying as if our thoughts had mirrored her eyes and the message they were trying to send me were as plain as day. Her eyes well up while she understands that I had seen inside those two windows into her meaning.

She runs her hand through my hair and tries to smile again. "I can't. I just can't Alex. You don't understand what it's like. It's not that easy, for me. It's easy for *you*. You're always free. You just do what you want to do. I can't. You and I, we'll…"

"Yes?"

She hides her head in the crook of my neck.

"What does he do to you?" I whisper in her ear.

"Nothing, he doesn't do anything." I think she says.

"I don't believe you."

She breathes and I feel it on my neck and the hairs on my arm stand on end.

"He," she sighs, "…it's me."

"What?"

"He…"

The tears slip silently down her cheek and she presses her head into me, so as not to be seen. I look around at the toasting and the dancing; the kissing and the highing and the flying and the flexing. The party's a success. It's a *success*! It's New Year's Eve, Millennium Eve and there's so much to look forward to, a new year, a new fucking century, but for some people I guess, it might as well be the end of the world.

I catch a quick glimpse of Richard at the bottom of the stairs, looking shifty. He shoots me a look I can't place but don't like. Then he bounds up the stairs and out of sight.

Shannon lifts her head and tells me that she wants to go to the toilet and sort herself out. Star is as always on hand and I am happy to let Shannon go if she is with Star. Star looks at Shannon and then shoots me an accusatory look. I grab her close and whisper in her ear.

"Look after her. Don't leave her, whatever you do, do *not* leave her."

She gives me another quizzical look and leads Shannon upstairs to the toilet. I grab Shannon's hand. She turns around. She moves towards me and those big blue eyes are deep lonely lakes in which she's swimming, no longer in control. Not waving, probably drowning, slowly dying. Star ushers her along as if this is woman's work and I am an outsider. And I am. A man and an outsider.

Suddenly Flex, Lulu and Max and Lorraine are all around me and we're dancing then to Garbage's *Special*, Spiller's *Groovejet* then The Chemical Brothers. Flex shoves a Russian Spring Punch in my hand and we guzzle them quickly, pausing for breath before dancing again but I want to look for Shannon, and make sure she's all right. I want to find Richard, get him in a room, interrogate him, find out what he's done, smash him up and see how he likes it.

Instead, I get dragged out to the front door by Flex, who has opened it to find the Police standing there, asking to talk to the party 'host'. Guess that'll be me then.

"Evening sir. A Happy New Year to you."

"Evening Occifer, and a Happy New Year to you two, too," I smile. We all smile at my wit, "Is there a problem?"

"We understand that it's New Year's Eve, sir. But we have had *several* complaints from local residents, and we have been asked to come and kindly request that you turn the music down."

"Not a problem Occifers," I say, because there were two of them. Lulu has appeared in the doorway and wants to flirt with the Occifers and try on their titfers They smile at her but don't say anything. Flex manages to keep her under control.

"So you'll do that, then, sir." I can see by the raised eyebrows and tone of voice that it's not really a question.

"We don't want to have to come back and come inside to take any further action. Do we?" Bobby One asks nobody in particular. Although I sense that Lulu is itching to reply.

"Of course not. Thanks for the friendly warning," I say, smiling like a clown. "Happy New Year to you two, too. Again."

Take any further action I take to mean arrest a few people, including me, which wasn't part of the pre-party agenda so I make the rounds of the various DJ booths quickly and get the sound level turned down. *Slightly.*

With that drama averted I want to be alone with my thoughts which is difficult when you're the host of a New Year's Eve party and not just any New Year's Eve party a Millennium Eve Party so I make my way outside with a beer and stand contemplating the tall oaks on the common. I haven't been stationary for one minute when Max ambles over to where I am. "Hello mate. You all right?"

"Yeah just thinking."

"About?"

"Oh you know me…"

"What? Life, the future, your *destiny*. The usual Alex rubbish?" Max gives me a dig in the ribs with his elbow as he says this.

"Yep. 'The usual Alex rubbish'. Thanks mate," I smile at him.

"That's ok. Anytime. It's a great party, this. You should think about promotion as a future career." I smile and nod.

"Yeah, maybe I will, the manager of the 365 Bar said the same, he gave me his business card. And I'm glad it went well for *you*."

"Thanks mate."

"You're welcome."

"It's funny how it's more or less the same faces are here now to those that were clubbing with us in January," he says to me. He looks like and is talking like a granddad to me. It looks like he is proud of me for not having succumbed to drug taking. He's smiling too and puts his right arm on my left shoulder and we stare out across the Common.

"And yet everything *has* changed," I say. "It's *not* the same. We *are* changing. You're changing. I've changed."

Max looks at me and smiles. It's the look of recognition and admiration I've been waiting for since that morning in Formentera.

"Where's Lorraine?"

"Gone to the ladies."

"That's a good change. As in a change that's good for *you*."

"I know. Thanks mate. I'm sure you'll find someone soon too you know."

Lorraine returns with two glasses of champagne: one for me, one for Max.

"I remember an earnest song from my misspent youth," I say, "it was a song by U2 - that band that were sent to save teenagers like me from years of angst and to provide hope that the future would be different. That people would understand us when we got older; that eventually I would be sought out for my opinion on world peace, Amnesty International and what formation England should play in Euro 2000. The thing is, that never happens. People never understand us. Well, they never understand *me*. There was this song they had, called "40", it had an immortal line: *"When I was three, I thought the world revolved around me. I was wrong."* How right he actually was that stupid numpty Bono: 'I thought the world revolved around me'.

"You still do," Max says. "And that's ok, because for us, it does."

* * *

Back inside it is hot and smoky: beautiful sweaty bodies are whooping on the dance floor. Jodie and the rest of the strippers from Ye Olde Axe are dominating the space. Most of them are in a near state of undress. Three of them; Claire, Sam and Lisa are three-waying their way through some seriously sexy moves, running their hands up and down each others' bodies and flicking their hair about. Jodie jumps up at me and gives me a sweaty hug. She bawls into my ear asking where my friend Star is and can I get them any more pills? Her breath smells of dope and champagne and her perfume is rich on her neck. I tell her I'll get Star to come and see her. Nigel Dawson puts on Iio *Rapture* and everyone goes mental. I slide past the heaving bouncing bodies as best I can which is difficult due the back-slapping and handshakes and shouted '*Great party!*'s and insistations to dance, have a line, a glass of champagne – all ignored, until eventually I make it into the kitchen. But no Shannon in here. Only a Flex. Well, the kitchen's packed, but Flex is the only person I recognise in here. He's getting his umpteenth beer from the fridge whilst a pretty but not shy young thing is grinding herself into the back of him, her hands round his waist and in his groin.

"Flexy-boy!" I shout over to him and he takes his massive head out the fridge and brushes the girl away for a second. "You seen Shannon anywhere?"

"Nah man. And I'm screwing. Everyone's asking me for pills an' I don't have that many to give away. Where's Star? She needs to sort it out, man!" The girl has got her hand back inside his waistband again so I thank Flex anyway and head back into the hallway. There's the usual collection of slumped drunks, stoned idiots and plain louts crowding up the stairs. Why do people insist on sitting on the stairs at parties? I pothole my way up to the landing. Progress is again difficult as this guy from Plastic Fantastic feels it appropriate to grab my trouser leg and shout up to me 'Great party!' 'Thanks mate,' I tell him and grab my trouser leg back. The manager who runs both The Falcon and The Sun tackles me, opening his jacket pocket to reveal the largest packet of coke I have ever seen, must be two eight-balls in one bulbous bag. I shake my head firmly and he raises his eyebrows and laughs, "What?! Alex Greene, refuse a line? I don't believe what I am witnessing! Stop the party!" He's a camp man and very loud so I brush past mumbling something about New Year's resolutions and all that.

I knock on the guest room door and there's no answer. I open the door and Jade Maclaine who works at Agent Provocateur is sliding around on the bed with two of the bar staff from SAND, one of whom is gay. One has his hand down Jade's crotch-less black lace and pink knickers which seems perverse, but then perverse seems to be the new *zeitgeist*, or maybe he just hasn't noticed they're crotch-less. His other hand is in the jeans of his fellow bar worker. Shannon and Star aren't in here. Nor Richard. Jade opens her eyes and winks at me. She frees a hand from boy 1's tousled hair and bends a finger to beckon me over to join them. I shake my head, blow her a kiss and leave, closing the door behind me. I'm getting pretty good at this resisting temptation lark. It's pretty easy when you have figured out what you want.

I try the bathroom. Locked, obviously. Then the toilet flushes and I wait. A tall blonde who I recognise, Karen, comes out looking sheepish. A younger man who I know is *not* her boyfriend follows her out a second later. Both are wiping their noses and sniffing. I must have my eyebrows raised because she says sounding defensive, "We were just doing some coke! Honestly Alex. Don't tell Stephen will you? Do you want some?" I thank her and decline and tell her that it's perfectly ok to do coke wherever she pleases and not to take too long in the toilet in the future. She kisses me and wishes me 'Happy NYE darling' and tells me to come and see the new season's things and that there are some beautiful pieces just right for me and bounces down the stairs leaving the coked-up new beau feeling not so special and clinging onto the banister. Shannon's not in the toilet either.

The spare room is full of people and is almost impenetrable. There is a fug of weed smoke that is so dense I can barely see from one side of the room to the other. The music beats slower in here than in the other rooms and it's a Café del Mar CD or a Back to Mine or something. I kneel down to look underneath the sensemilia cloud. I see nothing but a tangle of legs and arms, hands ashing and toes tapping. I'm pretty sure none of them belong to Shannon and I pull myself up on the door frame. Where the fuck could she be? She wouldn't leave without saying goodbye.

I head back outside onto the roof terrace. I must have missed her somehow on the way through. The DJ is David James, a friend of Shannon's, spinning some blinding tunes throwing in some oldies followed by some bang up to date stuff. One minute it's Schiller, *Ruhe*, then the next it's Bob Sinclar, *I Feel For You* or Fatboy Slim *Sunset* and BT, Satoshi Tomiie, and Kinesis. I want to ask him if he has seen

Shannon. But I can't get his attention. When I wave my hand in front of his face he looks up and thinks I'm asking him what he wants. He motions hovering up a line and then gives me the thumbs up and then gets back to his mix.

I spy Max and Lorraine on the far side of the terrace in a quiet spot chatting animatedly about something.

You two seen Shannon anywhere?"

"You still not found her mate?" Max asks me back. "That's weird. We haven't seen her out here. Well *I* haven't. Have you babe?"

"No I haven't either. But I saw her and Richard having a bit of an argument earlier on," says Lorraine.

"Why don't you call her?" asks Max

"No text her Alex. If they are having issues, then they might need some time to sort it out themselves," says Lorraine.

"Well, I'll just go back inside and look again."

Hello babe. Where are you? Is Star with you? Is everything OK? XX, I type out and hit send. I pocket my phone and barge back inside, tripping over the step. Cursing the step and the strewn bodies, I bound down the stairs. I kick an ashtray over and someone tells me that I'm a fucking idiot. I shout back at them that this is my house! I spot Kai the hairdresser darting up and into one of the rooms up in the attic, the one room, we had decided not to allow guests into. I follow him in through the door. I wish I hadn't though because the sight that greets me is Kai's little naked arse. He is bent over with trousers round his ankles fishing out little plastic baggies out of every nook and cranny. He turns round when he hears me enter the room. "Ah Alex. Sorry."

"What are you doing in here Kai, this is Luke's room."

A head pops up from beyond Kai on the bed. It's Luke's, followed by another and another, Richard and Dan.

I stand in front of them, hands on hips. Kai still standing mute in front me. Richard on the bed, burying his head in the pillows. They're all as high as kites. Luke smiles at me and just carries on lying there. I fold my arms and wait to hear what any of them has to say. Luke folds his arms. Dan looks around, inspecting the ceiling like he's doing a survey or something; and Richard looking pathetic in the middle, fidgeting.

"Where the fuck is Shannon?!"

Silence.

I turn and head for the door.

"She gone," says Kai.

Then I am stumbling into my room rooting around in my drawers. I can't find my keys, they are in my pocket. I am falling down the stairs again oblivious to the threatening voices accusing me of having spilled their drinks. It occurs to me dimly that I am drunk, far too drunk to drive. But drive I shall. To Shannon's.

I burst outside and get in the car.

"We don't like you. Nobody does. Apart from maybe Shannon. But that's not love. That's fear. Because you hit her. You hit her like the fucking little coward that you are. You fucking cunt. *You fucking cunt!* Does it make you feel like a man? To hit women! Does it make you feel like a MAN?! Does it?! Does it?! Does it?!" I scream at the top of my voice.

Max is banging on the window of the car. Through the windscreen I see Lorraine, beautiful lovely kind Lorraine standing in front of the car with her arms folded and shaking her head. Having seen murderous intent in me, my best friend and his wife-to-be are saving me. A crowd of people have come out of the house to see what's happening.

"Alex, don't make it any worse than it can be," Max says to me simply through the window when my racket has subsided. He gets in beside me and takes the keys from the ignition.

Max waves the keys at Lorraine but she stays standing where she is standing in front of the car. My mobile goes off with a text message to break the deafening silence in the car. It's from Shannon:

I wasn't felling well, I had to go. but Everytingsok. Star is witg me. SeE You tomnorrro. Love you. Great party! Xx

I read it out as best I can and Max says: "See, it's all right."

"It is not. She's fucked. He hits her Max, he fucking hits her. She told me. Tonight she told me!"

"Maybe mate, maybe. But you're not going to resolve it tonight. Come back inside and call her in a bit. OK?"

I am exhausted, not conscious of my drunken state anymore, blank and numb.

"There's no reason to leave the party Alex," Lorraine has come round to the window and is soothingly saying in my ear. "Everyone's ok, just sleep it off and look at it all in a different light in the morning. OK?" she kisses me on the cheek.

Back inside people are staring at me. Lulu breaks the ice by shoving a fresh glass of Bollinger into my hand. I head for the balcony and fish out my phone.

1 Missed Call. Shannon

I call Shannon and it rings out. I check my voicemails

1 New Message.

Received today at 02.42am

Her stereo is playing the Café del Mar CD in the background. **"Alex its Shannon. We're backamine. The sight of...what? Star please...I never in my worst nightmares...Fuck...I needed to feel fucked. To bend my mind away from reality a little. It's 3am, it's New Years Eve after all and I am not wasted yet!! Star, baby, why don't you go and jump inna bed if you're tired. No need to stay up."**

"Nah, nah. I'm good. Good man."

"OK why don't you roll another one up for us then? I'm jus' gonna to rack myself up a couple of lines.

They were standing there infronna me Alex! 'Well?' I shouted at Richard. And you know what he said?! 'We were just having a good time.' Whadi he think? A future where I am returning home to cook dinner, steak and chips, smoked salmon to start, and finding them humping on the bed, or in the kitchen?

Well when you're out of the way, I can put the chips in the oven. When shall I get the salmon out? Have you all come yet? I could ask them. And to think I really loved him. Really loved him. Swept me off my feet he did. Drinks at The Atlantic, Dinner at The Ivy, got a room at the Dorchester, all on our first date, bought me a ring after a month, holiday in Miami after a year. He even bought me a beautiful car that I managed to write off.

I've got a lossa drugs over here. Maybe you want to come over? Come over here. Think about all those lovely warm fuzzy cuddly feelings the pills would give us. I'm going to my room now. I'm looking through my clothes. My favourite dress. You love this one. I was wearing it when i met him. That black three-quarter-length lace one. We had a party at our house and I wore the dress with just a tiny black thong underneath. No bra. We were rock solid. I loved him. The last time I wore this was on Richard's birthday. I waited until three-thirty in the morning for him to come home. When he eventually did he was blind drunk. He ripped the thing off. He started fucking me and he was so drunk he couldn't come. When I told him it didn't matter he thought I was patronising him and started shouting, slapped me all over my body shouting that it was my fault that I couldn't make him come....

I hear a loud snort.

I've just slipped on the gorgeous D&G belt you bought me for my Birthday last year. Now that Star's asleep I can really get going. But where to? Where shall I go Alex? I wish you were here. But I know you need to entertain everyone. I'm looking at the mantelpiece. There's all our photos, all of us. You, Flex, Luke, Max, Lulu, him and me. The TimeOut photographer took it at Renaissance, sometime last summer, do you remember? I should probably do my make-up in case anyone pops over. What a fucking cunt! How could he do that to me? On New Year's Eve? I loved him.

Another snort.

Ok, better go now. I'm slightly fucked but it is New Year's Eve, so I should be. Fuck it. I'm just going to do another pill. What about another half? Fuck it. The halves aren't touching the sides now though. A whole. I need a vodka and tonic now though. This is going to be a mission. S'let's have a nice fat line or two first, to get my spirits up.

Another snort.

See you tomorrow Gorgeous Boy, my Special Boy. Everything will be all right in the morning. Sleep tight and see you in the morning. Well done on holding the best party ever! The Millennium Eve party!"

No More Messages

* * *

There's not a word that properly describes how I'm feeling as I leap up the stairs of Shannon's apartment block. There really isn't. I'm there not through supernatural premonition but because at **07:01** this morning my mobile shook with violence and pleading urgency. It was as if the ringing contained all the horror that it needed to convey and I sat bolt upright and I only had to listen to the muffled wobbling and straining of Star's voice on the other end of the phone before I jumped straight into my car and drove, high blood-alcohol levels or not. The streets were deserted and I drove from Clapham Common to Kennington in seven minutes.

Shannon is lying star-fished behind the sofa in the middle of the floor. She is naked apart from a tiny black g-string. Her skin is yellow. Not yellow as in bright yellow like a Smiley but yellow as in pale yellow, as in pus. Her hair is straggled and plastered in thick condensed strands to her face and fanned out around her on the floor. Around her waist and in between her legs is a large puddle of light coloured liquid. Around her mouth is all crusted and bubbled. It hangs open and inside her mouth is white and there are more creamy bubbles. Down her left cheek is a light brown stain of dried liquid, maybe bile, maybe blood, leading to a bigger round stain of the same coloured stuff on a pillow she is clutching in her left arm. It smells like vomit. Acidic, chemical vomit. Next to her on the far side of her body, there is a piece of paper with writing on. Star is sitting nearby, hunched up in a little ball rocking back and forth, her mobile at her feet. Next to her I recognise the D&G belt I got Shannon for her birthday last year.

In my pocket my mobile goes off with a text. It says:

Alex, sorry for disappearing to my room last night. I am with Richard and Dan. We're all heading down to Dan's in Brighton. Back in a few days. Happy Millenium. Love, your brother Luke. x

DEEP DOWN

Shannon was pronounced dead when the ambulance got there.
A separate car comes and takes Star and me to Max's. Lorraine comes in and consoles and cuddles Star. Lorraine hugs me and tells me that it's not our fault and that we are lovely. Max calls Linda, Shannon's Mum.

Both exhausted, Star and I sleep together all day in the same bed in the spare room, curled up, until Lorraine comes in and wakes us up gently with some cups of sweet tea and bowls of soup, at around 7pm. Star starts sobbing straight away, and I get up so that Lorraine can sit on the bed and put her arm around her. She persuades Star to drink her tea and eventually her soup. I find Max in the front room watching a black and white film on TV. I recognise Rome in the background.

"Here mate," he says passing me a whiskey. "Drink that and sit down and watch this. *La Dolce Vita*. It's great; one of my favourite films of all time. It's beautiful."

I sit down on the single-seater across from Max and cradle the tumbler gratefully in my palms. Lorraine comes back in and sits down very close to Max. Star's dropping off to sleep again

"I think she'll sleep right through. I gave her two Nytol to calm her down," says Lorraine.

I sleep until to the morning and I only wake because my mobile is ringing. I'm confused and disorientated. My brain is telling me that the phone is ringing but I am looking for an alarm clock. I can't understand this though because I don't have an alarm clock; I always use the Alarm function on my phone. Eventually I pick up the phone but I am still trying to turn the alarm clock off rather than answer the call. I see Star lying next to me. I feel gut wrenchingly sick. I look for a bin. Then I realise what I am supposed to do and I take the phone out of the room so as not to wake Star before looking at the screen. It's ten past ten.

Linda <<calling>>

Oh Christ.

"Hello Linda" I answer.

"Yes it *is*. How did you know?" She asks genuinely surprised. She sounds calm; sanguine even.

"It comes up on the phone Linda. Your name comes up when you call." There's not one thing around me at the moment that doesn't feel utterly surreal.

"I just spoke to my friend Bill," says Linda.

"Bill?"

"Oh Bill, he's my *friend* – he's an undertaker."

"Oh. OK."

She starts crying. Then I do. Lorraine passes me a tissue. I feel sick rising in my belly again but I have to keep it down. "Oh Alex, how did it happen? What were you all doing?"

"I don't know. I, we…we were just…I…" I can't carry on.

Linda sobs. "That's it. They're all gone now."

I stand up to try and clear my head and concentrate on what Linda is saying and begin pacing up and down the room. But what *is* there to say to that? Between sobs she manages to say: "Alex, I don't blame you for what happened to Shannon. She always was a real wild-child and no one could control her. She always ran her own life."

"Thank you Linda."

I sit down on Max's sofa. He comes in from the kitchen and offers me a cup of tea. He pours a shot of brandy into his coffee and offers me the same. I decline. Lorraine comes in and puts her arm around my shoulder, which doesn't help a bit. It just makes me feel even weaker and more helpless. Large teardrops bowl down both my cheeks. I rest my head against her full belly and wipe my eyes.

I look outside and see that the sky is a dull grey and that it is raining and that London looks ugly. I look up at Lorraine and Max who are standing above me. Max has his arm round Lorraine's shoulder. He is frowning and has deep creases in his forehead.

I start crying uncontrollably. Tears flood my eyes and salty water burns my skin as it runs down my face. I could never understand people who'd say *it hasn't really sunk in yet*. I know exactly what it means; that we will never ever see Shannon ever again. She is gone. Final. No more. She is dead for fuck's sake. Full stop. Lorraine is kneeling in front of me and puts her hand on my knee and then hauls herself up; she kisses me on the forehead and stands next to me, stroking my hair. I rest my head against her again.

* * *

On Wednesday morning at 9.30am I am almost ready, I just need to find my only plain black tie. We're getting the 10.32 to Norwich. The funeral is at 3pm. I head out and run across the Common in the mist and jump onto the tube to King's Cross. They're all waiting for me at the top of the platform when I sprint across the concourse: Lulu, Star, Flex, Max and Lorraine. I look around at my friends. Star looks older. She seems paler but still beautiful. Her hair is cut like Shannon's.

Flex goes to the bar to get a couple of beers and a few sandwiches for himself. I give him £50 and he goes and gets enough booze in for everyone.

We get to Norwich at 2pm. The cemetery looms out of the mist and the grass is still frosty and crunches under our shoes as we make our way over to Linda. She smiles when she sees us. She is sat in her wheelchair wearing a huge black shawl over her shoulders. Her hair looks whiter than I remember in the freezing January air. She beckons me over to her and introduces me to Bill, her friend who is looking after her, a tall and kind-looking man. There's no sign of Richard, Luke or Dan.

Linda reaches out to me; I lean in close to her and she holds me there. "Oh Alex," she sobs in my ear. I can't think of anything to say in return. I extricate myself and go and inspect the flowers Richard sent. In truth you couldn't miss them. Typical Richard. He's sent a huge bunch of pink roses, there's maybe forty? They are wrapped in a huge gold bow.

I stare into the blackness of the coffin as it is lowered. Bill rolls Linda over to us after and a girl who I think looks familiar and who was standing next to Linda during the reading is a couple of feet behind him.

We are allowed five minutes alone to say private prayers, before the internment. I decide to start writing. I want to say something to Shannon, to put something in there with her. In the rush to leave the house this morning I hadn't had the time to think of anything. I am struggling with this fucking posh pen that that Dad got me for Christmas that was in my jacket and this shitty little piece of paper. I write, "People need like minded souls. Life's too hard on one's own. And life's too short not to connect. I will never, ever lose sight of you. You will always be just there. I know." I don't know what it means or where it came from, I just write it and throw it onto the coffin. I turn and head for the main reception. I want to get out of there right now. I want to be on that train back to London.

Inside I walk to the window and look back at the hole in the ground and press my forehead against the window because I am overheating and I hope that the glass will cool me. I leave the sweaty imprint of my forehead on the window.

On the train my mobile starts vibrating in my breast pocket. I can't be bothered to move for a second, my feelings numbed by the events of the afternoon and the four pints of Stella; I am tempted to let it ring off. Two more rings...

"Alex, answer your fucking phone!" Flex shouts at me, drunk too.

Dad <<calling>>

Star leans over to me and nudges me. I look at her. Her eyes are puffy and red. She wipes them and she tilts the screen so she can see it. "Take the call," she whispers to me, "it could be important."

"I don't want to. I never want to."

"You don't mean that."

"I do."

"You don't, you're just upset. They love you, and deep down you love them too." She takes the phone, presses green and presses the phone to my ear.

"Alex, this is your father. Your Mum has had a fall. We had to go to hospital. She's ok, but would like to see you. And I could do with a hand around the house. You should come home now, for a bit, if you can? Can you? You and Luke?…"

"Yes, I'll come, Dad. I'll get Luke and we'll come home soon; sometime soon."

THE NEAR FUTURE

In January I stay in and paint; my father's plea tugging at me. I know I should go but I don't feel ready yet. Star calls daily and tells me I should go, that I will regret it if I don't.

I paint prolifically, I've bought some canvases. My paintings have become dark, but that's understandable I suppose. They are still good. And I am happy with them. I am going to give Max and Lorraine the first one I ever did for their wedding present, the one that Max said reminded him of Renaissance. I have branched out into portraits. Not classical style portraits, but close-up slightly abstracted ones, usually using artificial colours, not flesh-tones. Black and blue faces seem natural to me.

The weather is awful and no one else is off work, so I spend my daytimes alone. Days come and go without me leaving the house. Rain falls, it's January, time passes. Sometimes several days pass without any other human interaction at all. I am glad in a way that it's like this and I cry for my friend. Dazed, I sit and stare at the pristine white walls of my front room for hours on end. I see us all together. Clubbing, laughing, dancing round this room, chatting, everything. All the crazy moments of the year are projected onto the walls like the slide shows my Dad always used to show us when we were younger. There always seemed to be one of me in the garden standing in front of the camera with my tiny penis in my hand pissing on Mum's geraniums, laughing and laughing and laughing. To say I'm not that child anymore seems fatuous, but I'm not. I'm really not.

Max comes over sometimes after work and talks about records; compliments me on my paintings; tells me about artists I should investigate, and galleries I should go to. We drink tea with milk and infusions without; green tea with Jasmine tastes like bubble-gum to me. Then eventually he has to go to get home for Lorraine. She has moved in now and is six months pregnant. It's going to be a girl.

The faces around me change slowly: life is moving but keeps repeating itself as if it's giving me chance after chance to do better. Or are they opportunities to make the same mistakes twice? It really doesn't matter which. Names and places and even people come and go, and what do I learn? I make a decision and then go back on it, change direction and contradict myself every day. There has to be more to life than keeping your head above water. And I do know now that there is. I know that I love my life, even if I don't quite know how to live it yet. That's no crime is it? I believe in love, beauty and belonging. I believe in romance. I believe in trust, honesty and understanding. I believe that the future will be good. I see my future in these paintings, in the clouds and swirls of senseless random colour I paint. Somewhere in there is my future.

* * *

On a rare sunny Saturday morning, still early in the month, I am painting a portrait of Star who, peacefully bathed in the watery fragile January sunlight, is sitting with eager yet patient poise when something in her smile makes me stop.

"You all right?" I ask her

"Yeah, I was just thinking of Shannon."

"You're smiling."

"I know."

"That's good."

"I know. I remember this one time we were here, me and you and Shannon shared a few spliffs and laughed together. We watched that film, *Less than Zero*. One of those old ones you two insisted on watching with Robert Downey Jr. in it. Shannon and you rolled around the floor in hysterics the whole film. I loved how she laughed, every time Robert Downey Jr.'s character did some coke, you *both* laughed. I watched as Shannon chopped out two lines of cocaine. "Always two, you see Star? Always two." I remembered that. Then I watched as you and then Shannon *hoovered* up the lines. You were always slow and silent and with a deep breath. Shannon crouched right down and then a quick snort, much quicker than you. Did you notice that difference? Then the two white lines were gone. Then you and Shannon kissed, as if you had forgotten that I was there, sat on the sofa opposite you! I didn't know where to look. I was so embarrassed, man. But I looked at Shannon. I wished my lips were where yours were, touching Shannon's."

"Did you?"

"Yeah man!"

"You minx!"

She smiles.

"Don't worry silly, I know you liked her."

"Did you?"

"Yeah of course. It was lovely. She liked you too."

"Wow…"

"Don't…carry on."

"And she opened her eyes whilst she was kissing you and looked at me, looked into me. Then you offered me some coke as usual, but I knew it was just a test and I refused. She was just *so* beautiful, Alex."

"I know, *so* beautiful."

"She told me that time. "You're gorgeous." She told *me* that! That *I* was gorgeous! Can you believe it? And she *smelt* lovely too. One day I asked you to find out what perfume Shannon wore, do you remember? 'Coz I wanted to smell the same. I didn't tell you that bit. Did you know?"

"No, how would I?" I lie.

"Anyway, the next time I went round to yours to deliver some stuff, you gave me a yellow plastic bag, with Selfridges written on it in that posh black lettering. I looked inside and saw a shiny bright red box. I looked up at you but were busy counting the money."

"I don't remember that."

"You wouldn't, you were high. I wanted to kiss you but I just said thanks."

"I don't remember that, I don't remember that at all."

"That's a shame. It's a shame you don't remember more. I wish you remembered these things, like I do." A tear rolls from her left eye. "Maybe now you'll be better Alex. Maybe now you'll remember more." And another tear.

I turn back to my painting, the huge portrait of Star, really close up on her beautiful face and abstracted slightly. I smile at Star's stories. It's true I don't remember the details and that *is* a shame, but I do remember the feelings and *those* memories make me smile. I wipe my eyes and take up my brush again, my new weapon now and paint with fast confident strokes. The canvas is large and forgives me for my still-developing technique like a patient mentor would. I move the paint around and Star's features begin to form in front of me. Her wide inquisitive eyes stare back at me and her high cheekbones emerge exaggerated in blues and reds. I give her huge eyelashes and start to work on her smile.

I think of my Mum and the photos my Dad used to show us in the slide shows when we were younger. She looks like my Mum did then when she was younger and beautiful.

I look up at Star and she is still smiling and staring back at me. I feel at ease and calm. Looking up at her smiling back at me I see limitless possibilities and new priorities. In her eyes my future is swimming in front of me. In fact I am crying. A huge tear rolls out of each one of my eyes and I well up. I wipe my eyes and I look and there are tears rolling silently down the cheeks of Star's face. But she's not sobbing, she's smiling, and nodding as if she's agreeing with me. I look at my phone and I look back at Star. She looks at my phone and nods again. There is something I finally feel ready to do. I reach over for my mobile and with paint-covered fingers I scroll down looking for 'Home'.

THE END

ABOUT THE AUTHOR

Oliver Merlin is a witty and concise writer of observational fiction. Clapham High Way is his dazzling debut novel. It *is* the new Human Traffic.

Oliver spent 15 years working in the City as a consultant and then reluctant executive. He escaped the rat race in 2013 to write books and paint. He now lives between Ibiza and London with his partner Sarah, his son Jean-Jacques and two French bulldogs. He is hard at work on his second novel and several paintings.

To follow the author on twitter please go to:
    https://twitter.com/artitude38

Made in the USA
Monee, IL
11 March 2020